LEGENDS OF THE ANCIENT SPRING: THROUGH THE DARK

Charity Nichole Brandsma

Cover Design: Sara Oliver Designs
Publisher: Charity Nichole Brandsma
Map Illustrator: Rudolf Van Schalkwyk
Publish date: 2020
Publishing city: Raleigh

LOVE MUSIC?

I wrote an album of songs just for this book! Each song was written to give you a more intimiate understanding of characters or events in Through the Dark, transforming the way you read. I can't wait for you to hear them!

Follow me on Instagram at charity_brandsma, or keep an eye out on Spotify and itunes to learn more!

Dear Ursula Le Guin,

thank you for showing me how to marry together

the hard questions in life with a good story.

TABLE OF CONTENTS

PRONUNCIATION

Michale'thia: Mee-cal-ay-thee-uh

Michale: Mee-cal-ay

Syra: Sigh-ruh

Dagen: Day-gen

Luik: Loo-ick

Enith: Ee-nith

Kallaren: Kuh-lar-ren

Aleth: Ah-leth

Broyane: Bro-aen

Lohan: Loe-hon

Jyren: Jai-ren

Jyres: Jai-ers

Syllrics: Sill- rics

Anaratha: Ann-uh-rath-uh

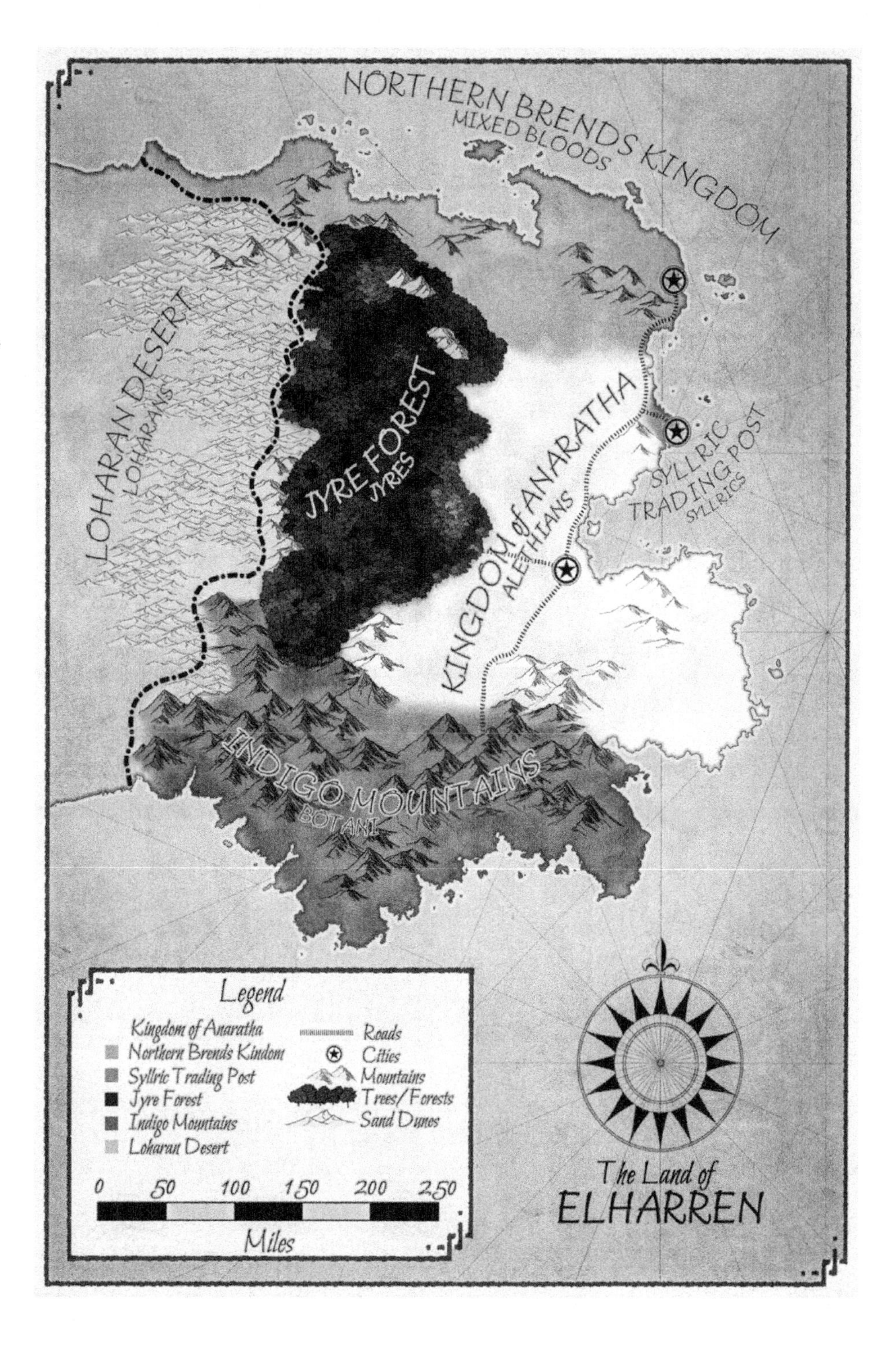
NORTHERN BRENDS KINGDOM
MIXED BLOODS
LOHARAN DESERT
LOHARANS
JYRE FOREST
JYRES
KINGDOM of ANARATHA
ALETHIANS
SYLLRIC TRADING POST
SYLLRICS
INDIGO MOUNTAINS
BOTANI
Legend
Kingdom of Anaratha
Northern Brends Kindom
Syllric Trading Post
Jyre Forest
Indigo Mountains
Loharan Desert
Roads
Cities
Mountains
Trees/Forests
Sand Dunes
0 50 100 150 200 250
Miles
The Land of
ELHARREN

PROLOGUE

In the Age of Creation, the Ancient Magic bore seven sons into an empty world. With only grey fog and dry land, the Ancient Magic beckoned each son to come and touch Its spring, where the Ancient Magic gave vision, knowledge, and artistry to finish Its world.

Of the sons were: Drendar, with his fiery hair and pale skin, who brought up vegetation of every kind for beauty and for food, bringing delight to the eyes of his brothers as they tasted for the first time something and knew the richness or tang of fruit.

Brendar, whose light brown skin matched his eyes, created a new substance that was slick to the touch, running through one's fingers, which could quench a thirsty mouth and rise up in great masses he would someday name "waves".

Broyane, often called the most beautiful with his deep brown skin and black hair, created tall forms of land that rose up to the galaxies and pointed to their glory; these mountains, he would call them, were to be a refuge.

Lohan, whose eyes shape was tilted and saw what was behind the world, created languages where simple impressions used to be, delighting in the building together of words and phrases into poems and stories- all pointing toward Truths about the land around them.

Then there was Syllric, with dark hair and light skin, who created stones of every kind, from dull to shining, those that mirrored the galaxies and those plain which could someday be used for dwellings.

Aleth, with deep auburn hair and light brown freckles across his tan nose and cheeks, created people. New people taking after the brothers, with differences in every way, all celebrated and loved deeply.

Jyren, known for his incredible beauty amongst his brothers, created the grandest thing of all: brightness, to ward off the dark. A light in the sky, great and mighty, which brought new color to all other creations, and new beauty to the world, giving warmth and joy alike.

It was in joy and love that the land of Elharren bore up nations who lived in perfection under the care of the seven brothers.

By the 200th year of the land, the brothers began to hear whispers of Jyren changing and perverting the good the Ancient Magic had instilled in him to do. Jyren's laws slowly changed as he took on more wives, took for himself slaves, and began experimenting on live animals and humans. It was then the beautiful brother proclaimed his intent to find the Ancient Spring again and drink of it so could gain more power and rule all the lands.

Drendar attached himself to Jyren's cause, seeking to gain from his power, and Syllric and Brendar, not to be left weakest, followed closely to also partake if Jyren found the spring. After years of war, Jyren found the spring, murdering Drendar in an attempt to keep the location secret, which was later found by the Syllric and Brendar.

In desperation, Aleth, Broyane and Lohan made a pact to drink of the spring only to stop the darkness their brother was creating. Not knowing if their plan would work, Lohan set out to find the Ancient Magic, who had long since distanced Itself. He never returned.

Aleth and Broayne gathered their nations to wage war against Jyren's powerful army. For years the brothers fought, staking claim to lands and losing them. Broayne, seeing the evil and greed the war had become, withdrew his people to the Botani mountains and left the war, swearing to never again be lost to the inner darkness of humanity.

In the midst of war, the brothers mysteriously vanished and the people were left to pick up the pieces of their nations alone. The Anarathan Kingdom flourished on the coast, comfortably becoming the greatest in the land. The Syllric people built for themselves a trading system, pledging themselves to the art of creation as they sought new ways to ease their lives with gold. The Jyre people retreated into the Dark Forest, where they would continue on Jyren's wicked path in secret, and the Loharan people retreated into the desert to await Lohan's return. The Botani warriors remained on their mountain, quiet and separate from the world.

It was not until the 500th year of the world that a peaceful "normal" settled in and the Age of the Prophets arose, declaring hope to come. New rulers and religions were formed and new marriages and cities sprang up, each fighting to find their own source of joy and peace again. Each oblivious to the consequence yet to come.

Kingdom walls arched high and proud over the golden city. A bright light shone just above peaks in the distance, bringing life to the steam of the sweetbreads baked every morning for the swarms of children who, too antsy to stay in bed, made it their joyful duty to pad out of the house long before anyone else woke and fill their baskets with fresh rolls and pastries for the day.

Their soft chattering of shy wonder woke the kingdom from a peaceful slumber, whereupon each would enjoy their families and relish their freely chosen way of contributing to the kingdom.

The school system incorporated tender care for the elderly, alongside rigorous study and innovative inventions, which propelled bountiful crops and a wistful ease of life for the kingdom's citizens.

As evening came to a close, older children were excused to the streets where lively discussions and dramatic exhibitions of theater, music, or painting ensued. The adults would gather together with family and friends, or tuck in as still love-struck couples, ready to laugh the night away. There was no kingdom in the land like this one, perfect in every way.

Today, as on every first day of the new year for what seemed like an eternity, each citizen would shuffle down into the city's deepest caverns with trepidation and face the reason for their utopia. It was their yearly reminder of what their joy cost: the girl ceaselessly tortured in the cage.

Children younger than five were spared the tradition, but for all else, the law declared each must pass by and lay their eyes on the girl whose own treacherous life propelled their perfect lives on.

When they trudged in, their eyes would meet a skeleton of a creature instead of a girl, held up only by chains, face contorted in eternal agony, hair matted from sweat and dirt, and eyes pleading for an end. For a moment, the younger ones would turn away and sob, thinking there must be another way, but soon after the realization of all they would lose if the girl were set free would settle in, and they would look away in shame before fleeing in both grief and relief.

Some would return, but only for a few moments. In the end, this was the price every citizen agreed to for their own beautiful lives. This condemned, rotting girl fueled their kingdom. She was their savior. Whether she wanted to be or not.

***

CHAPTER 1
MICHALE'THIA

Kingdom of Aranatha

Year 1250

The shy ticking of a clock lost somewhere in between bookshelves whispered throughout the lonely room. Some corners of the grand library were washed with light, pouring through the large arching windows, while others, usually right next to those exposed areas, were cloaked with night, which too often seemed to disguise itself as shadows.

Michale'thia was not the only young royal to make their way to the library; no, every so often, she would hear footsteps and see glimpses of an ambitious royal student, hoping to gather books for an exam or project, but none ever stayed long.

It was rumored that these library halls were haunted with spirits from the past, crying out the secrets of the kingdom. Michale smiled to herself and tapped her pencil on her book page.

Wouldn't that be nice? To simply waltz into a library and meet a ghost willing to tell her exactly what she wanted to know.

Her fingertips slid along the book pages, stroking them tenderly as if they were lost treasure rather than old texts. She sighed. Someday, she would explore every corner of these books, finding beauty and darkness in each one and *finally* understanding the questions she had yet to find answers to. Someday.

Michale'thia tapped her pencil again, shaking her head as she remembered what she was doing.

Ti kilna sho

Li amehe Oen

Oenna li'sana amiahe li nolhe

So children wait,

for the Perfect One

Who will lead the pure into the sun

Tap, tap, tap.

Michale'thia pulled an even older history book from the stack and flipped through it, stopping at a page she had marked earlier.

After the war, the Ancient Brothers disappeared, leaving the nations alone in the land of Elharren. Prophecies began to arise, filling the world with both doom and hope as they spoke of the curse the land and people would endure until the Perfect Heir appeared, leading them into perfection again.

She leaned back in her chair with furrowed brows. Was this referring to multiple people speaking the same prophecy, or numerous prophecies? The question had never occurred to her before and unleashed a thousand more questions into her mind.

Michale'thia scrambled to write down her notes in her journal before gently closing the texts in front of her and moving back to study the prophecy again. She had read and reread the ancient tongue and modern translation many times.

Il shanahe
Il shanahe
efortemine
Tana Elharenhe il
Oounelhe tsieri
Li kehe il'line
Tsainihe tsainale
Achhe bruot
Rissoe wal li hoom
Elharrenhe bruot
San geasharhe
Almaharesoom
Ti kilna sho
Li amehe Oen
Oenna li'sana amiahe li nolhe
kilna sho
kilna sho
kilna sho

From the ashes
From the ashes
One Perfect will rule
Free the land from
the Ancient curses
To the days before
The Twisted twisted
And the brother slain
The blood cried out for justice
The land dies
until the spring
replenished
So children wait,
for the Perfect One
Who will lead the pure into the sun
Children wait,
children wait,
children wait.

Michale'thia closed her eyes for a moment, wishing the prophecy said more. When she was younger, the bard songs about the Perfect One to come had captivated her, as it had every child in the kingdom. They all dreamed of growing up and proving to be the beloved Perfect Heir. But while it was just a game for the mix-bloods, their lives largely unaffected by the prophecy, Michale'thia was an Alethian, one of the four families directly descended from the Ancient brother Aleth. Which meant *she*, or any other child from the Alethian Royals, could be the one the prophecy spoke of. A Perfect

Heir, born of perfect blood. She couldn't simply live in full transparency as the mix-bloods did, allowing herself to show anger when the world made her angry, or talk back when a condescending word was spoken. Instead, for the sake of her people, she smiled and moved on. Every time.

Since the young age of ten, the Alethian Royals were watched carefully for *any* moral failing. A lie, a single disobedience to a parent, a failure to attend prayer times—any single act would disqualify them from the running. And Michale'thia, at 19, had yet to fall.

She stood quietly to find another text, searching for one as far back as she could. *Maybe* all the scholars had missed something. Something that would tell her *how* she was supposed to lead her kingdom into the Age of Perfect if she passed her Testing Day. Finding nothing, she sat down at the table again, staring at the prophecy as if new words might magically appear.

She rested her chin on her hand, feeling her mood darkening. Her Testing Day was just a few short weeks away. The kingdom seemed to be holding its breath, waiting to see if their beloved princess would pass her Testing Day, but she was the one who felt like she was suffocating. Michale'thia sighed, feeling as if her bones were one hundred years old. If she passed her Testing Day, would this be her fate for eternity? Endless striving and controlling every small movement for the sake of her people? And if she didn't pass, would she end up like her mother? She shivered at the thought.

The clock struck the sixth hour of the day, making Michale jump. A stray wisp of hair escaped her loose bun as if trying to lead the rebellion of waves to freedom. At least *they* could rebel without consequence.

As Michale'thia gathered her books, a clang rang through the room, startling her yet again. Bending down, she gingerly picked up her crown, inspecting it for cracks and grimacing at the thought of breaking the heirloom. She traced its smooth, heavy metal, knowing she could have just left it in her room, but it was a symbol for her. A weight she could not leave behind, even if she wanted to.

Michale'thia returned to the work of hiding her books under a nearby stuffed chair for easy access the next day, then gathered up her crown and her notes before walking softly out of the library in hopes of slipping past the bookkeepers without notice.

"Miss Digarrio. I presume you placed everything back the way it ought to be today?"

Michale looked up into the shallow cheeks of Thalem Ornto, one of the leading palace bookkeepers. Dark shadows under his eyes only made his face look gaunter, which in turn only made him more frightening.

"I placed them in a safe place for tomorrow, where I will pick up again. You know how I love this place, and I don't want to waste any time in my studies tomorrow!"

She smiled at him, tucking the stray curl behind her ear. His hair was dark for an Alethian, who usually boasted auburn locks, and his freckles were paler, altogether different but superior, according to him.

His glower darkened, "Princess Michale'thia, this library is not your personal playground. You are not, nor will you ever be, a scholar of our ranks, and you ought to not continue traipsing through our halls! If you have a question about our history, we are happy to answer it from our *lifetime* of study."

Michale'thia bowed her head, breathing softly out of her mouth to control her expression. The bookkeepers were a strange group, rarely seen and often studying, priding themselves on being who the kingdom went to for knowledge. Even from a young age, she had seemed to frustrate them with her questions, and as soon as she had been able, she had begun searching for answers on her own, to their chagrin. She had a right to search for answers, and they had no right to stop her.

Michale looked up at Thalem and nodded, "I understand, Sir. Please accept my apology."

He eyed her through slits and gave a curt nod, leaving her alone in the doorway of the grand library. Michale'thia waited until he had walked away before clenching her jaw and turning around to begin the long walk through the palace back to her room.

***

Michale'thia slipped back into her room and quietly shut the door, thankful she had a half-hour to nap before needing to *actually* be up for the day. It had been like this every morning for the past few months. Somewhere around the fifth hour, just as dawn was creeping in, she would wake to anxious dreams of her grand crowning as the Heir of the Prophecies, where every eye in the kingdom was watching her, waiting for her to do *something*. And each time, she ran. She would wake in a hopeless sweat and, desperate to find out more about the Perfect Heir so many thought she would prove to be, she would throw on a simple dress and sneak through the halls to the library. After an hour of research, she would make her way back for a nap before her maid would wake her for the day.

She smiled at the thought of her maid. She had learned a lot about her kingdom's waking hours in this past quarter of a year. Especially about her maid.

Michale melted into her bed, quieted her racing mind, and found a more peaceful sleep.

***

Gentle shaking woke Michale, and even before opening her eyes she could feel something was off. The hands on her shoulder were not the small, petite hands of her maid, but the strong, powerful kind she could easily peg to be her mother. She squinted her eyes open to confirm, groaning inwardly and nearly rolling over before catching herself and smoothing her face, still not wanting to deal with whatever matter would bring her mother all the way across the palace and into her room in the southeastern corner. But she knew her place, and that meant meekly opening her eyes and bowing her head in respect to the queen.

"Mother, what brings you here this morning? Is everything alright?"

Her mother was beautiful. Perhaps one of the most beautiful queens in the history of the kingdom, but there was a sharpness to her eyes that showed beauty would never be enough.

Elana Digarrio stood up from Michale'thias bed and contemplated her child for a moment, her eyes piercing and scrutinizing as if cataloging Michale's every flaw. Did she know about the dropped crown? Of course she did. She probably knew the moment it fell.

"We have made a decision, Michale'thia, and you will not like it." The queen's large skirts swished around her as she moved regally about the room, peering at every item on Michale's dresser and desk, stopping to inspect her large closet full of dresses, and sniffing in disdain as she turned back toward her daughter.

Michale waited patiently, trying not to let her hands fidget as she waited for her mother to get to whatever she came to say.

"Michale, your wardrobe needs to be updated. New styles began to surface weeks ago, and if you are to be a *queen* someday, you must lead in *every* respect." She shot a glare at her daughter and raised an eyebrow.

"*I do* have standards for my replacement on the throne, and will make sure you rise to those if there is even the smallest chance you will be the Heir of the Prophecies."

Michale gave a small nod of assent as she waited silently, refusing to give in and beg her mother to hurry up with her real news. By this point in her life, she knew her mother well enough to know the queen enjoyed dangling things in front of people, like a cat enjoying the chase of a mouse, not quite eating it until she was finished batting it about.

Her mother pierced her with another look, and for the briefest of moments, her features softened into something close to regret and maybe even love. Michale's eyes followed her mother's fidgeting hand, to where she rubbed the dark circle on her wrist—the sign that she had failed her own Testing Day so many years ago. Her mother caught her stare, and all softness was quickly replaced by the condescending scrutiny Michale'thia had learned to live under.

"Michale'thia Digarrio. It is time for you to choose a husband. And you must choose before your Testing Day in two weeks. You may not be the heir to the kingdom as an unmarried woman, as tradition holds, so you will make a decision in no more than a week's time." Her mother's auburn braid cascaded down her back as she looked out the window and squinted, reaching over her daughter to shut the window drapes.

Michale's sat perfectly still, taking in the news with inward panic but outward acceptance, a painting of perfect, gentle submission. She knew her mother hated it, even if it did mean she may pass the test.

Her mother turned abruptly and strode from the room, pausing to turn and fire her last shot, "And Michale'thia, your first suitor arrives today after classes. Be ready to host him in your receiving room."

***

"...and of the seven Ancient Sons, only Aleth stayed true as he drank the forbidden spring, making our line the sole pure one, untainted by darkness and mixed-blood." The boy at the front of the room sneered as he said the last words, his nose rising in the air.

Michale'thia glanced over at the servants standing by the far wall, quietly looking above the students' heads as if they didn't hear the hatred in the young man's recitation of Anarathan history. But Michale could see it, the set jaws and tight skin around the eyes. They heard it all, and they were only working in the palace because they knew how to let it go.

"After Jyren let loose his dark creations on the land, beginning the Hundred Year War, the Ancient Brothers all disappeared, the Jyres retreated to the forest, and the Age of the Prophets began. The prophecy was our kingdom's only in those days, and our beloved Aranatha successfully came together to interpret the words so many prophets had exclaimed. Then, lead by the Alethian royals, who never stooped to intermarriage but kept their bloodline pure, producing beautiful heirs like myself," Kallaren winked at the ladies in the room, causing ripples of laughter from his classmates as Michale'thia contained an eye roll, "...our nation rose higher and greater than the rest, living to extinguish moral failings in the name of the Ancient Magic."

Kallaren's eyes met her from the front of the classroom, and Michale's heart raced as he seemed to sense her annoyance, his own eyes hardening slightly.

All the royals in the room were descendants of Aleth with the purest bloodline, flaunting auburn hair, naturally tan skin, and light freckles, mingling exclusively with other royals who could be their husband or wife someday. She had grown up with Kallaren and seen him work tirelessly to be approved for a Test Day, as rare as the privilege was.

The day she was placed two years ahead of her peers into Kallaren's class, she had stood in awe of him, smitten like many women in the room. But when his Testing Day came two years ago, he had come back with the dark mark on his arm, signaling his failure, and he had never been quite the same since. Recently, he began to direct unwanted charm in her direction, becoming more and more watchful as her own Testing Day approached.

"We obey the Ancient Magic's will, waiting for the royal heir who will live a perfect life as Aleth did, never stumbling or committing wrong. To test this, worthy royals at the age of 19 will walk through the dark Jyre Forest, where every dark desire is brought to life." Kallaren swallowed, his beads of sweat forming on his temple as a distant memory returned to haunt him for the moment.

Shaking his head, he returned to the present and continued on, a mischievous smile on his lips as he spoke of his own failure almost as a private joke between him and the classroom. "None have withstood temptation and passed, though I think I did get the furthest.

Michale'thia kept her eyes down, feeling Kallaren's gaze land on her face again.

"So, in two weeks, we send in our beloved princess with the *greatest* hope that she may be the long-awaited Heir of Perfection, and pass through the forest untouched by darkness. Michale'thia, the beautiful, intelligent, and so far perfect, you are the end of our history class this semester."

The class clapped, the girls in the room more loudly than necessary, and Michale'thia smiled at her classmates, giving a slight nod in their direction before returning her gaze to her desk, breathing out quietly and wishing with each recital of their history that she could melt into the ground..

On the final day of classes, each royal student was made to get up and recite a summary of the entire half-year in a one-hour speech. There were ten students in her class, and it was agonizing to even the brightest of them. She secretly believed her professor did it on purpose just to spite anyone who didn't listen during his lectures during the half-year.

"Well done, you have successfully recited the major historical events leading up to Aranatha's success." Professor Leal's high voice echoed across the lavishly furnished room. His eccentric eyes widened and his auburn mustache twitched.

"But you did fail to recite the Ancient Magic's demands for justice! The Ancient Brothers stole from the Ancient Magic, all except for Aleth, stealing the of the Spring meant to keep Elharren alive. The curse of this land is twofold, class." Their professor looked each student in the eye. "First, the natural consequence of the Springwater being drunk without the Ancient Magics permission means Elharren will die too soon. The land is now cursed and dying as we speak. When will it finally end? We don't know. Second, is the relational consequence: the Ancient Brothers were *sons* of the Ancient Magic, and when Jyren first stole from the Ancient Spring, he tried to *become* the Ancient Magic in a sense, leading his brothers to do the same. And now the Ancient Magic is gone. We are cursed, no longer getting to live in the utopia the Magic intended us for. We are refugees at best."

Michale'thia leaned forward in her chair, the stirring in her chest building with each word her professor spoke. She felt the brokenness of her land keenly and ached inside for a change. Maybe that was why she tried so hard to be the Heir of the Prophecy.

Glancing around the room at the bored expressions, she kept her eyes down and stopped the question in her mouth from coming out: So how would the Perfect Heir change anything?

Mila's name was called next, and Michale smiled. She didn't talk with the girl often, or really any other royals for that matter, but she knew Mila to have a beautiful voice and a love for storytelling. She could bring anything to life. Michale'thia closed her eyes to picture the lulling tale of Elharren's history.

"In the beginning, the Ancient Magic created seven brothers on the empty land of Elharren: Aleth, Lohan, Broyane, Brendar, Drendar, Syllric, and Jyren. The Ancient Magic gave each a drink of Its Spring, empowering the Brothers to create, as It had created. Broyane rose up mountains as a refuge for the lost, and Lohan languages to bring poetry to what was once grunts. Brendar created waters that rose and fell. Drendar created creatures of every kind for food and aid. Syllric created stones of beauty and use. Jyren created a great light in the sky to bring new color and warmth to the lands. And our dear, beloved Aleth created people of every kind. Nations grew as the lands lived in perfection, and the Brothers created new things for the good of all. But when Jyren began to desire more power, he went in search of the Ancient Spring again. Drendar made a tragic alliance with him, and Brendar and Syllric followed closely behind so they were not left the weakest. Only Aleth, Broyane, and Lohan sought out the Spring with pure intentions, making a pact to drink the Ancient Spring only to stop Jyren and his evil. Thus started the first wars in the land. Eventually, Lohan set out to find the then-distant Ancient Magic again to gain wisdom, and Broyane retreated with his people to the Indigo Mountains, where they live to this day, though no one has seen them for decades..."

Two hours later, the bells began to ring, signaling the hour lunch break, and the class sighed with relief as students sprang up from the elegant couches and desks to gather their books and leave for the day.

***

Michale headed back to her room to prepare for her first suitor. She had spent the past two hours working through every angle of it and still wasn't sure how to feel about the whole situation. She knew she had to wed... but it still seemed to have snuck up on her. She tucked a piece of hair behind her ear absentmindedly, carrying her books in one hand and her pen in another, as if ready to write at any moment.

Turning the corner, Michale suddenly collided with what felt like a wall and nearly fell backward if not for the steady hand around her waist.

Slightly disoriented from both collision and the man presuming to touch her, she stepped back and found her bearings, slowly looking up and cringing as her eyes registered the broad shoulders and large pin with the Melvor estate emblem on it. Kallaren.

He stood smirking down at her as if he had just proved something to himself and picked up the ribbon tied around her waist to rub the material between his fingers.

"Michale'thia, always running off somewhere."

A thousand choice words popped into her mind for the man in front of her, but Michale'thia swallowed them down, stepping back and gently removing his hands from her dress.

Kallaren was too sure he would marry her, and unfortunately, she wasn't too unsure of that herself. She had few options to choose from, and she knew most of them already, beside the very few who lived in the border estates and rarely made it to the palace.

Kallaren was the perfect age and had the perfect ties. And he knew that.

Michale'thia attempted to sidestep his large frame and continue on her way but found herself face to face with him again as he shifted to block her path.

He kept his voice casual, giving her a strained smile as he persisted in trying to get her to meet his eyes, "I heard you have quite the few weeks ahead of you. Can I walk you somewhere? The library?"

Michale hid a scowl and relaxed her features. She couldn't let the kingdom down over one small incident with another pretentious royal.

She looked up at him and widened her eyes, painting a smile on her face and tilting her head to the side.

"Kallaren. Unfortunately, I am not going to the library, I have a suitor to entertain today and need to go prepare. You know how it is, the joys of being a royal." She looked down and moved her body slightly away, trying to nonverbally end the conversation. Michale really did need to get back to her room to prepare.

Kallaren's hand encircled her wrist and gently pulled her back facing him, his defined jaw tight and rigid.

"Oh, I do know how it is, Michale'thia." His smile took on a wolf-like thirst.

"I know that while every other student in the class goes out with friends or finds their lover, you quietly slip away to the library, taking notes and marking page numbers. I know that when you are afraid or unsure, you pucker your lips just like you're doing now to control what you show lest you be condemned as a moral failure like the rest of us." He lifted her hand and placed it directly on his own wrist, where the small dark circle marked him, staring at it before looking up at her with a smile again, tempering the bitterness seething right beneath the surface.

Michale's mind raced, feeling the danger of the situation as the last of the student's rounded the far corner, leaving them alone. Both indignation and fear threatened to choke her as she worked through scenario after scenario of actions she could take and their possible consequences. If she lifted a finger against him, it could be seen as a moral failing, especially as a woman. Could she make the case, if necessary, that self-defense was not an evil? How could a perfect person hold on to her own life if she cannot even fight back? She couldn't slap him, as much as her hands itched to, or raise her voice, or threaten to have her all-too-willing guards reshape his chiseled face or—

"I know you, Michale. I *was* you. And with me, you don't ever have to pretend. It won't be long before your own Testing Day, and we both know I am the best candidate for this kingdom in marriage. And if you fail, at least you would be married to someone who understands you. You would never have to pretend when we are alone."

She jerked her hand away on impulse, stepping back and calming her nerves as she breathed out and tempered her voice, barely able to manage a smile.

"Kallaren, you forget yourself. I will choose who I choose for marriage, and my hope is to meet with every eligible man so I can make the wisest choice possible." She stood her ground, needing to walk in the direction he was blocking, but refusing to move any closer within his reach.

Anger flared in his own eyes, and she wondered how long he had been planning this entire thing. “Do not fight me on this Michale’thia. I will not be manipulated by you. Meet with your suitors, but remember this—none of them have lived the lives *we* have. None of them will see past your facade and know there is a different you inside, always chained down for fear of the world seeing. I am the only one who will ever give you freedom in marriage, so choose wisely.”

Michale’thia clenched her jaw, her own anger rising then falling as the truth settled in. He was right. And she hated him for it.

She understood now, and she could barely blame him. She was the only one at the castle that could know what he had gone through his entire life, and until she admitted to the struggle between her inward and outward self, he was alone, a failure and a fraud. Well, she wouldn’t deny him that at least. She took a shaky breath in as tears sprang to her eyes, allowing him to see what his words had sparked.

“Kallaren, I have much to do today. Please.”

He stood still for a moment longer, eyes searching her face desperately for any sign of falsity. Then he slowly moved to the side so she could pass. She could feel him watching her walk away, eventually hearing him slide down the wall and sit alone with his memories.

***

Michale's eyes remained closed as her maid continued the precise artwork on her face, adding a shimmer on her high cheekbones and a delicate touch of rose to her lips. The two women sat on the bed across from each other, as they had done since they were both children, allowing Michale to gaze out the window as Syra used the natural light to catch every detail, constantly searching for any mistake she could have made, her large green eyes stark against her white hair... She took every task more seriously than anyone she knew.

Syra was shorter than her, but had an unassuming intensity that could only be born from the adversity of her youth. As princess and maid, they had grown together out of the dangly confusion of adolescence and into womanhood, and Michale'thia had fought waves of jealousy over Syra's impossibly full lips and angelic face, unnaturally beautiful because of her half Jyre blood. It didn't take long to realize what Syra's beauty brought and witness the pain her mixed Jyre-Alethian blood caused her every single day. The averted eye, the twisted lip, or the sudden need to speak about "dirty mix-bloods who ought to stay in their slums"—it all reminded both women of Syra's sinister, Jyre roots. One could forget the physical differences, but society would never allow them to forget their bloodlines.

Syra’s mixed-blood made her inferior in every way, an abomination, some may even say. Her Alethian freckles did not outweigh her Jyre white hair, and that was that. With the tension rising between mix-bloods and pure-bloods, Michale’thia had long learned to keep her eyes and ears open, watchful for days when Syra needed to be kept busy inside her room instead risking a walk through the halls.

Michale’thia watched Syra as she worked. There in her eyes was something truer than any royal she had ever met. She lacked the broken bitterness of those who had failed their Testing Day, and the haughty, power-hungry smile of those hoping to marry up. She was just good, and Michahle'thia wished she could be as kind as this person the world had named a wretch.

“Alright, spit it out.” Michale swatted Syra’s hand away from her eyes, playfully rolling them while she was at it.

Syra smiled wryly, shrugging off any facade of ignorance.

“You waited longer than I thought you would to ask. At least you are ready.” She glanced at Michale from the corner of her eyes while packing up kohl and powders. She heard Michale’s telltale tapping and laughed, setting the bag aside and settling in with her legs crossed on the bed, white hair flowing over her shoulders.

She lowered her voice in secrecy, raising her brows, “He arrived early this morning. His name is Shelby Din Freys, and he is not the worst looking man, according to the other maids.”

Michale couldn’t hide her smile anymore and leaned forward in excitement.

“And? Is he tall? Short? Round? Thin? What does he like to do? Is he arrogant?...Of course he’s arrogant, he’s Anarathan.” She huffed, turning her playful frustration on her friend. “Syra! You *must* know more, I’ve trained you to be at least a moderate spy. There has to be more than that.”

Syra chuckled and continued, rubbing a corner of the sheets together as she spoke.

"I heard he is not tall, but not short, and he loves to hunt. He is ten years your elder and is to inherit a large estate. And, according to him, he came very close to being considered for a Testing Day. The only downside to him though... it sounds like he doesn't...read much."

Michale gasped in mock horror. "Oh no, whatever will we talk about?" She giggled and then sobered for a moment, realizing how much she was actually put off by that last piece of information.

“But really, it would be nice to talk about subjects other than balls and horses and estates with whomever I marry. Even if I am queen someday. It would be nice to enjoy the people around me, rather than simply tolerate them. Can’t you just find me a few more people as kind as you? And then that’s it”, she pretended to wash her hands, “we can live peacefully and joyfully no matter what happens.”

Syra smiled sadly at her, knowing there was nothing she could say to make life in the palace better for Michale. It was a kingdom of piety, which meant that no one from the inside would ever be real.

A knock on the door made both girls start, and Syra jumped to her feet just as the door opened to a guard announcing the arrival of Shelby Din Freys.

Michale’thia took a deep breath and nodded to her guard, making her way to her receiving room.

Lord Freys was waiting by the table which had been set with tea and a light lunch, dressed in a fine coat and a layer of sweat already shining on his forehead.

When she arrived, he bowed so low his head almost touched the floor, and Michale folded her hands in front of her until he was finished, thankful she had chosen to wear her green dress instead of her favorite after all.

Lord Freys had all the normal Alethian freckles and auburn hair, which were set upon a uniquely round face that looked like it belonged to a babe more than a man. Was he really ten years her elder?

As she had decided earlier, her first test for each man would begin with her refusing to be the first to speak. The first words of someone meeting another in a higher position were important. Her history books had shown General Whilston's first words upon being captured by the Jyre King in the Dark War were, "You will not win." It was said that the statement rattled and angered the king so greatly that he killed the General in a fit of fury, instead of torturing him for information or twisting his body into an unnatural form, as Jyren had been known to do to other captives. This first sentence would bleed information, and Michale needed that.

She kept the table between them, holding a curious but intense gaze as she silently urged the man in front of her to speak. His soft cheeks began to glisten, and he wrung his hands in front of him, looking around the room and letting out a nervous laugh, as if wondering when the punchline was coming.

Michale didn't let her polite silence falter, refusing to give in on this and ignoring Syra's own battle not to laugh at the situation.

He chuckled and wiped his face with a handkerchief, still looking around as if a practical joke was being played on him. Finally realizing Michale's stare wouldn't budge and the guard would not re-enter the room to help the awkward situation, he scratched his neck and held out his damp hand.

"Right, uh, Miss Digarrio, uh... I suppose you weren't expecting me? Right, well, shall we sit?" He motioned to *her* sitting area, causing her to raise an eyebrow before she could catch herself. Out of all the things he could have said...

She sighed and gave him her most charming smile, grasping his hand in her own and watching some of the tension in his body dissipate.

“Hello Lord Freys, thank you for coming. I am delighted to have you here. Let us sit.”

He sat with clear relief and began piling food onto his plate with a jolly bounce to every movement. Once he had built something akin to a mountain of food, he wiped greasy fingers on his pants and finally looked up at Michalethia’s concerned face, mumbling an apology.

“Dear Lord Freys, let us be honest.” She gave him a level look as Syra moved to pour them both tea.

"I presume you do not want to marry me, and these first horribly awkward moments only solidified that." His eyes widened in fear, and he glanced about the room, searching for an escape route.

“And I do not want to marry you either.” His startled eyes met hers in a near panic he stuttered, trying to find something to respond with.

Michale laughed and continued, "Lord Freys, this is a good thing! Please, drink some tea with me and let us relax as friends." She gestured to the teacup in front of him, and smiled when visibly relaxed, taking a sip.

“Please understand, we do not have to marry each other to support each other. I want nothing more than to support the people of this kingdom, whether or not I am married to them.”

He gave her a sheepish look then, confirming her theory.

“And my bet is you have a hoard of women back home falling over you and a father who wants to know you tried your best to win me over so I might show favor to your estate. We can both agree you did an incredible job, and though we do not desire marriage, you have managed to charm me into ensuring I will forever look kindly upon your family.” Michale’thia flashed a dazzling smile at him.

“Problem solved. You may go tell all your relatives that you succeeded in winning my favor, and I will gush about you to mine, growing your respect here in the palace walls.” Michale lifted her fork to her mouth and took a bite, glancing up at him to find jaw hanging open in disbelief.

Then all at once, he sat back and laughed, placing his hands on his stomach in relief.

“Miss Digarrio, you have just saved me.” He seemed to realize the implied insult he just made and stuttered again.

"N-n-not that it would be bad to marry you!" She waved him off, and he sighed again, continuing with more ease.

"I just... I like my estate and uh… we do not seem the most compatible. And I uh… well… to be quite honest, I do have a lady friend who I would not trade for the entire kingdom, and a father to make proud." He looked at her and shrugged, suddenly quite uncomfortable in his chair.

She stilled at that, taking him seriously for the first time, thankful he had something worth saying no for.

“You will make a great ally, Lord Freys, and I should like to meet your lady friend, if ever given the chance.” She looked up at

Lord Freys with a wink, "And if you ever decide to propose, I should like to throw her the grandest party."

Lord Freys blushed so hard she thought his ears may fall off, but smiled and nodded, obviously pleased at the outcome of this visit.

The rest of the meal was eaten alongside shared stories of home, the latest news on his estate, and tales of the woman he planned to marry. By the time the clock struck, signaling the late noon hour, and they parted ways, both were happier than when they arrived.

Syra shut the door behind him and smiled, "Well done."

***

CHAPTER 2
SYRA

Dark, cracking claws encircled her as his harsh voice rasped, "You are mine, child, and you can ever escape that. Your purpose is far greater than you can ever imagine. Come back to me."

The familiar face flooded into view as he stood far above her own height, mouth flicked into a smile below his narrowed eyes. He was possibly the most beautiful person she had ever seen, and the most heinous. His beauty only seemed to magnify the danger emanating from every movement.

"Ah. I see. The Magic is awakening inside of you. How does it feel?"

A tear escaped her eye as she struggled to both break loose of the dark tree's roots covering her body and crushing her lungs.

He grinned at her anxious attempts to flee and kneeled down in front of her.

"I will tell you how it feels for me. Like fire, scorching every inch of your body from the inside while giving it the sweetest drug you could ever imagine" He chuckled darkly.

"How agonizing it must feel to keep it all hidden inside of you. Where are you, my little bird? Come back to me, and together we will set it free. Father and daughter."

Syra felt bile rise to her throat at the thought, and her own blood began to pound in her ears, drowning out all other noises. Through now blurry eyes, she could see him frowning at her as he spoke again, but the sudden rushing sound in her ears drowned his words out.

For the first time in her life, she saw panic in her father's eyes as he began to yell something she couldn't hear. And then a towering wave of white light crushed them both.

Syra gasped and bolted upright from her pad on the floor. She scrambled up and to the small washroom bucket where she heaved her stomach's contents.

This was the third dream this week he had stepped into, but she had never seen *that* happen. Whatever it was, it had stopped him, and that was enough for her.

She scooped some water into her hands and sank her face into it, refreshing her soul alongside her body.

As she reached for a rag, a glimmer caught her eye, and her breath caught as she looked at the strange, white, almost luminous marking on the inside of her arm, just above her wrist. It was nothing more than a circle, but upon closer inspection, it seemed as though it were a part of her skin. She dunked her hand into the water and scrubbed desperately. When that didn't work, she jumped up and threw on her trousers, covering her hair with a scarf so as not to draw attention to herself, and made her way out of the palace. It was long before sunrise, and she still had an hour before she needed to get to work, so today she would train early and harder than before. He was getting close and too powerful; if she was going to have any chance of stopping him, she had to be ready.

Her boots crunched the gravel beneath her as she made her way quietly out the palace and toward the southern gate of the city. She set off in a fast run, determined to train her body to move quickly when the time called for it. The guards were used to her leaving by now. For the first few months, they had followed her to keep tabs, but when they realized she was training, they shrugged it off as a weird "Jyre thing." Some were kinder and even offered to help her train with the sword, which she always eagerly obliged.

Syra rounded the corner of the city walls and descended onto the beach. Without any hesitation, she ran straight into the frigid water and dove, sucking in as much air as possible before the water covered her completely.

Minutes ticked by, and Syra continued to swim beneath the surface, moving her arms as swiftly and precisely as possible until her lungs could no longer take it and, she burst out of the ocean for air, coughing and fighting the urge to hyperventilate.

She squinted as she looked back toward the beach to gauge how far she had gotten this time. Two hundred yards farther than her old record, she guessed. She smiled and relished the soft roll of the water beneath her.

When she was younger, she never saw the sun. She saw shadows and dark puddles of water when it rained, but she never knew real color, much less the blue ocean. It was a reality lost to her people.

Syra stared at the sky, losing herself to memories and allowing herself to be gently lifted by the swells of the water around her, rocking her body gently like a mother lulling a child to sleep. She vaguely heard running in the distance, and then a heaving of something heavy, but didn't take notice until the small contraption was nearly upon her.

There, on what seemed to be a mix between a sailboat and a flat board, was a young man in loose trousers and only a strap across his bare chest holding a small bag to his back. His arm hooked around a rope attached to the mast, and he reached down to skim the surface of the water as the wind propelled him swiftly toward Syra.

When he drew near, he pulled a rope to his left and moved the small sail sideways, stopping his boat-board near her.

"Are you alright? I saw you go under, and then you just disappeared!" He looked back at the shore and then back to her, squinting as if the sun was hurting his eyes.

"Springs, I'm thankful I had taken this thing out yesterday and already had it ready to go, here, hop on board, I'll get you back to shore."

His light brown skin shimmered with water, and he pushed his hair out of his face. Syra blushed and frowned, realizing she was staring, causing him to light up and smile, two dimples forming on his cheeks as he laughed.

"I see I'm not the great savior I had hoped I'd be. Please forgive me for intruding on your..." He raised his brows in question.

His eyes still held mirth, and Syra suddenly felt foolish in front of this stranger, unsure of how to respond without making herself look even more odd.

"Training. My training. I run, and then swim as far as I can."

She tread water awkwardly, wondering when his smile would turn to disdain. He must have noticed her hair-

Syra's hand flew to her headscarf, realizing she had forgotten to take it off. He had no idea he was talking to a Jyre mix-blood.

"Well, I am not sure what you are preparing for, but I'd be happy to give you a ride back to shore if you'd like?"

About to say no, she looked up at the sun's position in the sky and realized she had spent too long daydreaming to be back in the palace in time. Of all days, today she could not be late.

"Yes, thank you, I will ride. But, that is all. Just a ride to shore." Her cheeks burned at her own insinuation, but his lighthearted laugh put her back at ease. This man did not take the world as seriously as most here in Anaratha, and there was something refreshing about him.

"You have my word. Climb up and grab hold of this rope. It is going to feel counterintuitive, but find your balance and lean back a little, then just try to hold it. I'll navigate around you."

She climbed on the board and wobbled as it tilted below her, eventually finding steady footing as the man turned the sail, and they caught wind, moving quickly back to shore. The rippling water beside her flew by, and she smiled in delight. She was riding the ocean.

***

Syra barely heard the man's goodbye as she raced back to the palace, knowing she was dangerously late. Not that Michale'thia would punish her, but her mistress needed to be awake for her next suitor, and if she did not have her ready in time it would reflect badly upon the princess. She made her way through the back servants' door and up to her room, throwing on dry clothing and braiding her hair as quickly as she could.

Hurrying down the busy halls, she made her way to the kitchen to make sure the morning's breakfast was ready and grabbed some fruit to eat on the way to Michale's room.

Picking up a large stack of clean towels, she made her way to Michale's room, walking swiftly as she thought through all that needed to be done before her next suitor arrived that morning.

In her hurry, Syra nearly collided with three royals she knew to be in Michale's classes as final year students. She halted before coming into contact with them, dropping the load of towels in the process.

Eyes lowered, she bowed and apologized, bending to pick everything up and move out of their way.

The first two girls, likely sisters, had more freckles than most Alethians, and their hair was a shade oranger than was considered pure, while the other girl, with a calculating look in her eyes, boasted perfect light freckles and hair, with full cheeks and a plumper body.

"This is disgusting." The girl nodded toward Syra, crossing her arms across her chest.

"I know, I still can't believe they let her keep this little rat. I just don't feel safe in these halls with her sort around."

Syra kept her focus on her task of retrieving the towels, knowing better than to interact with the royals, and grabbed the last fallen apple before moving to walk around them.

The leader of the small group waited casually as she neared, only lifting her hand to the wall seconds before Syra would try to slip through the only open space. With eyes still lowered, Syra walked directly into the girl's arm, and havoc erupted.

“She touched me!” the girl shrieked, cradling her arm as if it was broken.

“Jeneane! She didn’t! That rat!”

“Are you okay? She probably tainted your blood!”

Wide-eyed and sensing the growing danger of the situation, Syra stepped back and tried to move around the girls on the opposite side of the hall, but it was too late.

The girl named Jeneane howled for guards, and a few royal boys, flanking an older one Syra came running to the girls’ rescue, taking in their distressed story with narrowed eyes and clenched fists. The older boy she knew as Malroy sneered with anger, ordering the boys to hold her. Puffing out their chests, they each grabbed her by an arm and held her still, sending the towels and fruit rolling all over again.

She struggled against her captors, but Malroy yanked her long hair back.

"Stay still, or I promise I will be the one to teach you a lesson, Jyre rat."

Syra stilled, angry tears rising in her eyes. Between her training in the Jyre Forest and her training outside of the Jyre Forest, she was more able to get out of this situation, but if she raised a hand against a royal, she would likely be executed that same day.

Panic began to swell inside of her and, she continued apologizing desperately, trying not to meet their eyes and provoke them more, yet not wanting to be taken by surprise.

Jeanne murmured something to the girls beside her before walking toward Syra, stopping directly in front of her.

“Learn your place, Jyre.”

Before Syra could see it coming, a slap rang out in the hall, sending the world spinning. She barely had a moment to register Jeanne's dark delight before the next strike came.

The metallic taste of blood seethed onto her tongue, and Syra squeezed her eyes shut in resignation.

"You are to never touch a royal." Another blow came hard across her face, this time harder than the rest. Her ears rang, and the world spun again, making her ironically thankful for the boys holding her up behind her.

“And you are never to look...” Syra waited for the next assault, still disoriented, and struggling to hear.

“...better to do…”

"....don't you know… overrun the palace…"

“Here is what I do know.” A man’s voice came into focus, each word clear and precise.

“You will not slap her again, because believe me when I say the Thorn estate will cut all trade with your family if you so much as touch her, Jeneane. She isn't some hollowed-out girl, she is human, with blood, spirit, and soul just like you, and I'll not stand by while you lord your hair color over her in such a disgusting way."

Shuffling was heard, and the two boys holding her darted off, leaving Syra in a heap on the floor. She looked up to the girls walking away quickly, with noses in the air, and Malroy standing nose to nose with the tall stranger.

The man had perfect auburn hair, but it was lighter somehow, as if the sun had lifted some of the dark shades out, something she had often seen in those who worked outside for long periods. His skin confirmed the theory, obviously slightly darker than the royal in front of him. This man was likely a stable boy or some kind of outside servant, soaking up the sun from morning to night. How did he dare speak to a group of royals this way?

His voice was brittle as he held Malroy's gaze.

"Walk away, Malroy."

Malroy studied him back, breathing heavily as he weighed his next move. Syra watched his hands clench into fists and open back up over and over again for what felt like an eternity. Until finally, he stepped back and laughed, straightening his shirt and patting the man on the chest.

"You always were a goody boy," he grinned and sauntered down the hall, disappearing with a final laugh.

Syra closed her eyes as Malroy's footsteps faded away, and she allowed her tears to fall, covering her face for a moment as a sob escaped. She was safer in this castle than she had ever been in her life, but her spirit still ached from these moments. She was more tired than she could ever express, weary of continually watching every movement and policing her own presence for fear of the royals.

Wiping her cheeks impatiently, she began thinking through what she would tell Michale as she stood to pick up the now-bruised fruit and disgruntled towels from the floor.

The sound of a throat clearing reminded her she was not alone, and she braced herself for the anger or pity she knew would be in the eyes of her rescuer. She avoided looking at him as long as she could, busying herself with the fallen towels until he picked up the one she was reaching for. To her surprise, he folded the towel and added it to her pile alongside the last few pieces of fruit.

"You dropped these. Well, they dropped these." His eyes held unusual compassion, and Syra nearly started crying all over again.

She nodded to him, her dry voice coming out cracked, "Thank you." She cringed hearing the lilt of her Jyre accent peek out.

Her shame rising, she quickly averted her eyes and gave another respectful nod before grabbing the towels and hurrying down the hall, eager to put this behind her and prepare Michale'thia for her next suitor.

Syra heard him sigh and jog up beside her, surprised when he took half the towels back and kept pace.

“Does that happen often?”

She frowned to cover up the tears that sprang to life again, wishing the man would just go away.

“Sometimes. I must be used to such things. My blood marks me.”

He continued walking beside her, somber in the wake of such hate.

"Prejudices will never end until, for the sake of those beside them, people stop fighting for their own rights and their own gain." He paused, lost in thought, "But it's hard."

Syra started at the implications behind his words. It was both so simple, yet felt impossible.

"And the Princess, does she treat you the same as these royals?"

Syra stopped in her tracks and faced him with full indignation.

"Princess Michale'thia would tear the kingdom apart if she heard of such things happening. She does not share the disdain others do." Thinking about her friend made her soften. She had been given a true gift in Michale. Any other royal and her life may be very different.

"I see." He rubbed his rouged chin in thought, still keeping his tone casual. "And why is she so different?"

Syra frowned at him, frustrated by his nonchalant accusations against her friend.

"Maybe because she cares about real people and doesn't spend all of her time trying to climb to the top of this kingdom, yes?" Syra realized her mistake too late and clamped her mouth shut, afraid of what would come next. In all the emotions of the past few moments, she had allowed herself to insult almost every royal in the kingdom. If that was heard, she could be imprisoned. And from his earlier threat, this man obviously had close ties to the royals he worked for.

He laughed then, turning to her and raising his brows with an impressed smile.

"You certainly seem to understand this kingdom more than most."

Syra wasn't sure what to make of all this, or how to get him to leave, and opted instead for a more blunt approach.

"Well, I must get to my mistress's room now. We have a busy morning… so thank you, and goodbye."

She sped up her pace only to find, to her chagrin, that the man hadn't understood the message.

"Funny, I was heading that way too." He smiled to himself, obviously amused by the situation as he continued to walk beside her.

Syra raised a brow, "What takes you to the southeast side of the palace?"

"I wanted to give the princess a visit."

"You cannot just go to the princess's chambers any time you like, she has a schedule and much to do. Who are you?" She stopped, planting her feet in a refusal to lead him any further without knowing who she was dealing with.

He paused and shot her a wry smile. "Right, I guess I should have led with that. I'm Lord Dagen Thorn. I'm supposed to be having breakfast with the princess this morning. Something about marriage? I don't know." He winked at her, as if punctuating his own private joke and continued his stroll down the hall.

***

CHAPTER 3
MICHALE'THIA

Michale woke to the sun assaulting her face through the open window and knew by its position something must be off. She sat up and looked at her clock, realizing it was an hour later than she normally woke. Sitting up, she realized with a smile that plans must have changed for Syra to have let her sleep in, and she decided to use the free morning to go over her latest findings in the library.

After a quick rinse of her face, she threw on a lightweight dress and pulled her hair back into her standard loose bun, allowing the few escaped curls to frame her face.

After a week of royal suitors from all over the kingdom having breakfasts and dinners with her, she wanted to weep with relief over this one glorious morning of quiet. Michale stared at the distant mountains for a moment. She really wasn't opposed to marrying, and she didn't consider her standards unreasonable. Still, so far, all of the men she met had been either too naive or too arrogant, and she would not tie herself to someone lightly.

Light flooded through the large, oversized window by her bed and touched everything, providing the perfect ambiance for study. She smiled at the thought and moved to her small desk, rereading through where she had last left off.

A gentle sea breeze floated across her marbled floors and brushed a few of her loose notes across the room. She moved to pick up the closest one when she heard Syra outside, speaking rapidly to someone before opening the door with a pleading looking on her face.

The minute she came in Michale could see bruising on her swollen cheeks, and a cold rage filled her.

“Princess, I am sorry but—”

"Who did this?" Michale struggled to keep her voice calm. She tried to remind herself that she had a kingdom to uphold and that every action determined where she stood, but the anger threatened to choke her.

Syra hung her head and wouldn't meet her gaze. Michale could see everything. The hurt, shame, embarrassment, anger. All of it in those large, green eyes her maid chained to the palace floor too often. Tears sprang to her own, and she crossed the room, wrapping her arms around Syra, giving both of them permission to cry.

She stepped back and looked at her dear friend.

“Syra, you *have* to tell me who did this, I will make sure they are punished, if not for harming a person, for daring to abuse *my* maid. I don't care how I have to word it, but they will be dealt with, and I will make sure they never so much as look at you wrong again."

Syra only shook her head, stubbornly unwilling to let Michale'thia start this war on her behalf. The image of her rescuer floated before her, and she gasped, remembering who was with her.

"Princess, your suitor this morning! I haven't even had time to do your hair or makeup!"

And with that, a man stepped into the room from behind Syra. He picked up a page of Michale's notes that had been blown by the doorway and studied it for a moment while Syra explained her tardiness and introduced Lord Thorn, who seemed to be engrossed in the page he was holding.

Michale froze in surprise. She was certainly not dressed to impress anyone, and furthermore, was not used to being ignored. Thinking fast, she folded her hands patiently in front of her, as she had with every suitor, and waited for him to say the first word. Time ticked by, and she watched as his eyes flicked back and forth across her notes, reading with open eagerness. Michale's own curiosity grew as his brows furrowed and raised, seeming to stumble upon something she had missed.

When Dagen, as Syra had called him, finally looked up, he pointed to the word she had circled and tilted the page he was reading so she could see.

"This phrase didn't even come about until at least the year 950. You'll want to search the archives for something around the year 700 if you want to know the origin. That's about when medical research advanced to let us know we had those organs." Michale's own mind began to reel as she snatched the paper back from him, reading through it and smiling widely at his discovery, forgetting Dagen was a suitor at all.

"So they wouldn't have meant 'heart'? Of course! That's why I haven't been able to match translations—they couldn't be word-for-word if the term hadn't come about yet!" She hurried to her desk with the paper and began writing down notes, giddy with excitement.

She kept scribbling furiously, suddenly understanding the other translations more clearly.

"Syra, can you have one of the other maids bring me a cup of kauf? And with the sweetened cream this time. We are celebrating."

Michale could barely keep her thoughts at bay as new questions surfaced. This could be the lead she was looking for!

Syra looked back and forth between Michale's distracted scribbling and Dagen's amused expression, unsure whether to actually obey or remind Michale that her suitor was still in the room. Thankfully he took it in stride.

"Actually, make that two. Or three—do you drink it too?" Syra rolled her eyes and decided they'd be just fine, slipping out to give a passing maid their orders.

Michale managed to shake herself out of her own thoughts and set down her papers, remembering with embarrassment that Dagen was still in the room.

"Lord Thorn, forgive me, I am proving to be a horrible host so far. Let us move into the receiving room and we can talk there. I will continue my research later."

She pulled out a chair in the receiving room to sit, only to find that Dagen had brought in her notes, a few extra pages, and the books she had on her desk. He moved the food aside and settled in to read some more.

She stared at him, taking in the handsome stubble on his chin, and his sea-blue eyes, feeling a few waves crash in her stomach.

"What is this for, anyway? I've rarely seen anyone read even one of these texts, let alone all of them." His words startled her out of her thoughts and she felt her cheeks redden, looking down in an attempt to hide them.

"It's actually a project I've been working on for a while. We don't have much in the way of original manuscripts of the prophecy, and if I am the Heir of Perfection, I would want to know everything I possibly can about them. The archive keepers and teachers all agree that the translations don't allow for much clarity, so I've decided to keep studying and see if there might be a better translation of the last few lines." She tucked a curl behind her ear, suddenly self-conscious.

She remembered then what he had said earlier and realized he must be quite the scholar himself. "How do *you* know so much about Anaratha's history? You can't have grown up in the palace, I would recognize you."

The corner of Dagen's mouth lifted in a smile, but he didn't offer an answer right away. He hesitantly smelled his cup of kauf, then took a drink and coughed, grimacing as he sputtered, "What is this?"

Michale laughed and poured sweet cream into his cup. "It helps my mind work. Try it this way, it's much better."

He took another sip and seemed to accept the milder flavoring, picking up a sweet croissant from the chair where he'd moved the pastry platter.

"I grew up in my father's estate on the southern border. We grow most of the fruit this kingdom eats, but my father cared greatly for his books too and made sure even the farmer's children were able to read. Schooling under him meant I was fluent in the ancient languages from an early age, and I took an interest in ancient history, from before Anaratha's time." He shrugged as if it were an ordinary life he described, which she supposed, to him it was.

“What kept you from coming to the Royal Academy? You could have had access to all the archives and learned under some of the most prestigious tutors.” The fall breeze played with her curls before settling down again, and Dagen folded his arms, looking up at the ceiling as he sat back in his chair again.

"My father wanted a different life for me, I guess. One where I played with the mix-blood farmer children and sweated the days away picking apples just as they did. It's a different life there. A different world."

Michale sat quietly, caught in between agreeing with him and feeling the sting to her pride at the implication that a place could be better than her home. But he was different. Easy somehow, with his simple white shirt and rolled-up sleeves, ready to work. He caught her looking at him and winked, causing a deep blush to cover her cheeks.

“And here I am, on a first date with a beautiful woman over a study desk. It’s so fitting.” He smiled as he took a drink of kauf.

Michale’thia laughed. It *had* been quite the morning for him.

"Yes, well, I suppose this is a date, isn't it?" She looked around, at a loss as to what they should do next with this table full of notes and books.

Dagen grinned, looking like a child, and picked up a few of her notes, opening a book next.

"Well, at least it can be a date we will both enjoy. I haven't studied this deeply into the ancient language in years. Tell me more about where you were going with this."

She nodded, her mind switching gears back into scholarship, and she picked up the deep blue history book.

"We know from this text, which has been pieced together by scholars from fragmented scrolls in the ancient tongue, that after Jyren betrayed the Ancient Magic and stole the Springwater for himself, the Dark War ensued. But sometime after that the brothers just... disappeared, and it would seem like Ancient Magic began to gift certain people with the power to see the future."

She tucked a hair behind her ear as she bent over the book, opening it to a page with pictures of the prophets.

"What I don't understand is why the Ancient Magic would gift people with just enough information to know to wait for the Perfect Heir, and not enough to show them what to do when the Heir of Perfection comes. According to history, every single person who has been given knowledge by the Ancient Magic was born with that Magic from birth. So either the Ancient Magic had to have provided more prophecies for the heir to follow, or the heir would have to be born with the knowledge of *how* to lead the people back to the Age of Perfection."

Dagen's brows furrowed as he thought through what she was saying, no longer interested in his croissant. He looked at her carefully, studying her for a moment.

"So, what you are saying is, either we are missing prophecies with information the Heir would need to rule, or the Heir would *have* to have been born with magic, like those who had first spoken the prophecy."

Michale swallowed, realizing she had just given a stranger some of her greatest fears.

"When you say it that way, it sounds much worse than I thought," she murmured softly, holding her cup of kauf in front of her as a shield.

Dagen let out a long breath, folding his arms across his chest as he thought. Michale'thia watched his brow unfurrow as he seemed to realize something, straightening in his chair and giving her a sideways grin.

"Let's keep researching then."

The morning was nothing like it should have been, with her beautifully put together before he walked in, giving the first test confidently and leading him to the breakfast table to eat over light conversation. Instead, they sat for an hour and a half with papers strewn about and multiple cups of kauf nearly gone. Syra had done all she could to busy herself elsewhere around the princess's quarters and had finally given in to sitting at the table with them, listening as they talked through different findings and theories.

They only stopped when they realized they would need more books to find the answers they were looking for. Michale'thia sighed, knowing time would not last forever, and they still needed to discuss the reason he had come.

Michale glanced at Dagen and smiled. “As much as I have enjoyed this more than I can say, we do have some important things to figure out about each other. Would you care to move to the sitting area?” Michale glanced at Syra, suddenly not wanting to be the only one in this conversation.

"And Syra, come on, join us, it would be fun to have you in the discussion. You can ask him all the hard questions." Michale threw a smile over her shoulder at her friend, who couldn't help but chuckle, thankful for a restful moment on a hard day.

The three sat down on the plush couches, the women moving aside the heavy, golden throw blankets and colorful pillows as they settled in across from Dagen. Syra must have motioned to the maids outside, as they came in with fresh tea, blinking for a moment when Michale motioned for them to also serve Syra.

Feeling in charge again, Michale decided to jump right in.

“So, Lord Thorn—”

“Dagen.”

Michale paused, slightly put off by the interruption and wondering if calling him by his first name would violate the rules her parents had set for proper conduct.

“*Lord Thorn*, tell me why we should marry.” She had gotten into this part of the conversation with only three other men, and found the results astounding, ranging from finances to looks, but more than anything, to their future children.

Dagen laughed at that and swirled his tea around in his cup, looking from Syra to Michale before lifting his brows and whistling.

“What a question. I’m sure that’s tripped up many of your suitors.” He smiled knowingly, earning a hard glare from Michale and a knowing chuckle from Syra. He saw through her games too easily for her comfort.

"I don't know. I barely know you. My father asked me to come give this a shot, and you are perhaps one of the few royals I have ever met who... shares my love for people—all people, from what I have seen. So I guess… why not keep getting to know you?"

Syra couldn’t keep the disbelief from her face, looking at Michale to gauge where she was in this whole ordeal.

Michale'thia struggled to keep her frustration from showing. This man obviously had no regard for her station or the possibility that she could be the future queen. He should be falling over her and begging to marry her, but here he was, saying, "why not?" She fumed inside, seriously considering if splashing her tea in his face would be worth letting her kingdom down.

“I see.” She murmured flatly, keeping her eyes disinterested as she tried to hide the hurt behind them. And to think, she had wondered if she may actually *like* this man.

“If that is all, we can be done here.” She rose, signaling his time to leave, but he stayed sitting, refusing to take the cue.

Syra watched differing emotions play across his face before speaking up.

“Lord Thorn,” Syra glanced at Michale before turning her full attention to their visitor. “No one is forcing you to be here. If you did not care to come, then why did you? Surely you or your father must have a greater reason than sheer curiosity.”

Again, he stayed quiet, his hands steepled in front of him until he stood.

"I came out of obligation if I'm being honest." He sighed, and Michale couldn't help but notice the muscle accentuated on his arms as he ran a hand over his face. But he wasn't the first handsome man to come along, and he certainly wouldn't be the last.

"Princess Michale'thia, I love my home. I love the people, and I love the freedom I have. But I also want to do something with my life, something worthy of my time. Living here in the palace terrifies me, and dealing with politics makes me want to find a rock and make a home right under it. But I guess I didn't expect the perfect princess of Anaratha to be so fun to be around, or intelligent, or genuine. And you can sort out the mess of thoughts there, but really it comes down to this: you seem like a friend I would like to have. I think you're beautiful, but that shouldn't surprise you, no man alive could think differently. I don't know if I want to marry you. There is a lot to think about when it comes to marriage. But I do know I would like a little more time to see if we are a good fit, or if we could love each other. And, if I did marry you, I'd want to whisk you and Syra away to my estate, not dress up in a tight suit and heavy crown."

He ran a hand over his blue eyes again and groaned. “I’m messing this all up, aren’t I? I’ll go.”

He bowed and walked toward the door without another word, stopping to look at her just before he had entirely left.

“Just give me time to think, and maybe to go on a few walks together. Michale’thia, would you be willing to do that?”

Michale looked over at Syra in surprise, unsure of what this all meant and how she felt about him, but nodding nonetheless.

She found herself deeply relieved he hadn't just left. She couldn't blame his reservations, but they may very well disqualify him for her. If she passed her Testing Day, she would be queen, and she had to marry someone ready for that. For the kingdom's sake.

CHAPTER 4
LUIK

Ice water woke Luik from his drunken sleep like a ton of bricks, shocking his system awake and simultaneously freezing his lungs mid breadth. A hand clapped on his shoulder as an obnoxiously loud voicc called right beside his ear.

“Rise and shine, princess! You wouldn’t want to make the Anarathans believe mix-bloods are drunken slobs, would you?”

Luik grasped for the sheets, a blanket, anything that could possibly make him warm again as he attempted to pry his eyes open, only squeezing them shut again when the sun’s rays proved too bright.

“Mmmm… Dagen, it’s too early. Have you no bloody heart? I am the Prince of the Brends here on a diplomatic visit,” he said into his pillow, his words muffled. “You should be making me a hot bath and sweet breads." He lazily rolled over in his lavish bed, a sleepy smile on his face, "I was having a wonderful dream where at least five beautiful women—"

"Ah—" His friend held up a hand to stop him. "I don't want to hear it. Keep your twisted thoughts to yourself and get up. It's three hours past the noon sun. If you'd agree to wake when normal humans do, I would be happy to have the maids bring in breakfast for you. But as it is, you are the laziest, most drunken fool I know, and I am *trying* to keep you from destroying any dignity you still have."

Dagen picked up a crumpled shirt from the floor and grimaced before finding a clean one and throwing it at Luik.

"Come on, Dagen! Quick, get up and dress. An envoy from your father arrived not long ago, and he will be here any minute."

Luik started at the mention of his father, twisting abruptly to attention. He sat up, pulling the shirt over his head and then with fumbling hands put on some trousers.

"What? Why? My father would never drag himself off his bed to send an envoy." Luik raked his hand through his dark hair and splashed his face with water, suddenly awake and ready for battle if need be.

Luik watched Dagen rush around the room to restore some sort of order to the furniture, grinning at how good of a friend he had. They may not see each other often, but he could count on Dagen nonetheless.

Luik had just finished buttoning his jacket when a knock rattled the door. The two men jumped over to the sitting area. Luik opened a book, and Dagen sat with his ankle resting on his knee, poised with a pen as if he had been writing in his notebook all morning.

The envoy opened the door and stood at attention, waiting for permission to enter the room. Luik lazily looked up from his book to feign annoyance when he realized the envoy before him was none other than Fain, captain of the Royal Guard and one of his close friends back home. Fain may be shorter than most, but he was faster with a blade than anyone Luik knew. He wasn't a man to underestimate.

His face taught, he took one look at Luik and rolled his eyes.

"Don't even try to convince me you were actually reading, Lu. Plus, the books upsidedown."

"Fain! Sweet springs, it's good to see you. How did you get out of palace duties?" Luik tossed the book on the floor and stretched out on the couch, grinning like a schoolboy.

Dagen, sat upright and leaned forward, shushing Luik.

"What brings you here?"

Fain nodded a curt thanks over to Dagen and pulled a tightly rolled, small scroll from his belt.

"Read this." He unfurled the scroll on a large table in the corner of the room.

Luik sighed and walked over. "Alright, what's wrong?" he smirked. "Did fine lady Liana reject your proposal?"

He sobered at Fain's unwavering stare and picked up the scroll, quickly muttering the contents to himself. His gaze sharpened and he looked up, anger and terror darkening his features.

"Springs, this is bloody madness." His voice was hushed, not wanting anyone outside this room to know what his father had done. "If this continues, it will be the ruin of our entire kingdom."

He stared at Fain. A knowing look passing between them as he let Dagen take the scroll from his hands.

Fain leaned into the table, "That's just it. We can't tell if the king is mad, or if someone is pulling strings behind him."

Dagen spoke up then, tossing the paper back on the table and running a hand over his face, his eyes wide in open shock.

"And who is *we*, exactly?"

Luik and Fain glanced at each other for a moment, an unspoken conversation happening. Luik finally nodded, and a decision seemed to be reached.

"It's about my father's...health. We have been monitoring him this past year, since my mother's death. He's changed. And some of his laws have become… more than questionable. I was approached by royal after royal, until I finally began to organize us into a… well, a group. There's a number of royals and countrymen now who are loyal to me."

Luik kept his eyes averted.

Seconds ticked by.

When Dagen spoke, his voice was quietly piercing. "So. You created a group ready to mutiny at your command."

"Springs, Dagen! Don't look at me like I am the villain here. If we don't do something, my kingdom will bloody burn!"

The three sat in silence again, unable to stand from the weight of the situation.

Fain spoke then, knowing what needed to be done.

"Luik, our kingdom, the refuge for mix-bloods and mix-morals alike, the place where no one feels ashamed, has gotten out of hand. For as long as I remember we straddled this line between championing every walk of life and keeping order, but the day your mother died marked the day chaos began to break loose. Springs, Luik, I know you have heard the stories." Luik averted his eyes, the pressure in his chest growing as he realized he was going to have to face one of the realities he had tried so hard to party away.

Fain turned his attention to Dagen, one hand on the table as he spoke with a fire in his eyes.

"Last week, a man was raped to death by half a city block. And this isn't the first time, nor is it the only problem of that level we have been seeing come from our king's lax position on justice. But Springs, Lu," he slammed his hand down, "if your father *publicly* announces the monarchy's abolishment, chaos will erupt. The kingdom will destroy itself, and we will have nothing left but the echo of the parties we once enjoyed. Now is the time. Before we no longer have the *privilege* of letting our moral convictions stop us."

Luik could feel the burning in his chest, threatening to burst. Anger at the injustices his people have done against each other, at his father's sleeping away each day as if his bed were his throne, and at his own reluctance to sacrifice for his people. Why couldn't they just be like bloody Anaratha? He might be living in the slums for his mixed-blood, but at least he wouldn't have to worry about needing to kill his own father.

Dagen looked up at the ceiling, contemplating the situation.

Luik had met Dagen four years ago, during a country exploration his father had let him go on only because it had been a wish of his mother's. He had stayed at Dagen's father's large estate, and the two had struck up a friendship immediately, continuing to visit each other as the years passed. One thing Luik knew, was Dagen had the wisdom of a hundred-year-old man, and, as much as he hated to admit it, he valued that wisdom more than anyone else's. Bloody Anarathan.

Dagen sighed a deep, heavy breath, and Luik could see his soul was already aching from the pain this would bring.

“Luik, I don’t have a better answer. I don’t know a better way. I just know that this will kill you inside. You can’t be the one to kill him.”

Fain rounded on Dagen, “You know what must happen! Luik must be prepared to take the throne exactly when his father dies, or we’ll find ourselves in a new war of clan leaders competing for that power.”

Silence screamed and the stillness in the room suddenly felt like an executioner.

“Fine.” Dagen’s sad eyes met Luik’s. “But I’m coming with you. I’ll write to my father immediately.”

Dagen rose and left the room, leaving Luik with only Fain and the grim task before him.

***

The next morning, Luik took Dagen's advice and woke at a reasonable hour. There was too much to do, and he had little time. Dreading the conversation he was about to have, he bounded down the hallway through the castle toward the southeastern quarters.

He knocked on the large door and ran a hand through his hair as he waited for a response. When the door finally opened, he came face to face with Dagen, looking as surprised as he was.

His friend recovered quickly. "Luik! I didn't think I'd see you here, especially at this hour. I was just having a word with Michale'thia." Dagen nodded a goodbye and left without explanation, closing the door behind him. Luik squinted in suspicion, wondering what Michale could possibly want with his friend. Dagen was too noble to talk freely, so he would have to get it out of Michale.

Still bewildered, he began to knock on the now-shut door again, unperturbed by the fact that the palace guards refused to acknowledge him. This time when it opened, his heart nearly stopped.

Before him stood the woman from the beach, except with long, white hair flowing down her back, framing her deep green eyes.

He hadn't noticed she was part Jyre, and it only made her more beautiful.

She cleared her throat, causing him to jump. Had she noticed him staring? He looked at her sheepishly, ready for the fiery gaze he was sure to receive from anyone remotely associated with Michale'thia. But instead, there in her large eyes was something more profound than sympathy, a look that made him want to squirm as if she saw him and still did not condemn. It was the kind of look that reminds a man of all his awful habits and all the reasons he could never be good enough, while still drawing him forward helplessly.

"Can I help you, sir?"

The lilt in her voice only made her more attractive, and Luik struggled for a moment to remember his own name.

"I… uh… It's…" He turned around and ran a hand through his hair, unsettled by this woman before him.

"Sweet springs, do you always do this to men?" he huffed, frustrated at being caught so openly flustered.

A wry smile twisted her lips, and her eyes twinkled. "Just you, my ocean friend."

Luik smiled at her and laughed. At least there was no need to be ashamed around her.

"Well, I am Luik, I'm here to speak to Michale if she's around."

The maid's brows rose at his familiar use of her nickname, and she turned around, seeming to see all the confirmation she needed before turning back and smiling.

"I'm sorry, she's not here."

Luik laughed. He deserved that. He raised his voice and stood on his tiptoes, trying to peer around the maid.

"Michale! Let me in, I'll pick your maid up and move her if I have to! This is serious."

Syra folded her arms across her chest, one brow arched as she widened her stance slightly.

"You can certainly try, but I guarantee you will not make it past this door."

Luik knew he could easily move the maid over if need be, but the subtle position of her feet showed she had enough training to make it difficult. He was contemplating his next move when the door swung open wider. Michale'thia stood there, eyes ablaze. Springs protect him.

"First of all, Luik, don't underestimate Syra, she could probably knock you out sooner than you can blink." Michale's affirmation seemed to shock Syra, as she shot a quick glance at her mistress. Michale'thia, however, stood with her arms folded, staring adamantly at Luik.

"Second, you do not get to force yourself upon my time schedule. I am sure in the Brends they don't have an ounce of respect for royalty, and I am more than sure you get your way all too often with women, but believe me when I say I am not afraid to have you thrown into the street. Prince or not."

At the word "prince," Syra glanced back at Luik, and her eyes widened. Neither had recognized the other, then, when they first met in the ocean. How did they not know? He guessed it had been a good ten years since he had visited, though, to his credit, he had *tried* to write when he was younger, but Michalethia's tight-lipped moral perfection ended any real conversation between them soon after. He had gained more freedom as he grew, and she less.

Luik sighed. She must hear the rumors about him from other women in the court. He did like to travel and often visited Anaratha's estates when he came south. There was always a ball or two to attend during these visits, and he went for more than the dancing.

Suddenly a thought came to him, and it was all he could do to not grin, knowing he had won.

"Anemone."

Michale's glare only intensified.

"You can't just—"

"Anemone. You promised."

"Luik it's been nine years-"

Luik folded his own arms across his chest, unwilling to waver, ignoring the echo of pain from their long lost friendship. No, *paused friendship.* It may have died out years ago, but he wouldn't let this go. Too much was at stake.

"A promise is a promise no matter how old, Michale."

Michale'thia brought her hands to her hair and breathed, realizing the importance of the situation if he was willing to come to her quarters *and* invoke their historic promise.

"Come in."

Luik nearly danced in victory, but instead followed her into the room. He noticed the maid's questioning look—she was clearly at a loss as to what just happened—and beamed as he settled onto the couch to explain.

"She wouldn't tell anyone now, but we used to be *best* friends." He glanced at Michale with a cheeky smile, only slightly disheartened when she didn't roll her eyes or shove his shoulder like she would have when they were children.

"Really, we were. And one day, we had claimed a tree as our own for the climbing, establishing our own kingdom there in the branches, and Michale decided that we absolutely must have our own code word for any time we needed to discuss things of the kingdom privately. An emergency word, if you will. She chose 'Anemone, because those were the wildflower seeds that are carried off to distant kingdoms by the wind. So we made a pact that day to always be there if one of us said the code word. And she can't lie *and* be Miss Perfect Savior, so here I am!"

Michale groaned, leaning her head back in the chair, waving her hand at him to quiet his story.

"Can you just get on with why you're here?"

"Sure. But first, what was Dagen doing in here? Don't go enslaving him in these court games you Anarathans like so well."

A look flitted across Michale's face, and Luik knew he was suddenly treading in very dangerous waters. Her features softened, and she lifted a side of her mouth sadly, her voice coming out as the gentle, wistful little girl he remembered.

"He asked me to marry him."

Luik nearly choked on the water Syra had offered him, leaning forward as he struggled to breathe again. Bloody traitor! Dagen? His level-headed, countryside friend?

"What? How could he have asked you—But we are leaving in the morning!"

Michale sighed, rubbing her temples for a moment, working through something in her own mind.

"I know you leave tomorrow. He told me, Luik." She turned to face him square on. "I don't think I have any other choice, to be honest." She held up a hand to stave off the retort obviously coming and continued.

"Meaning, I must marry, and I have *two weeks* until my Testing Day, which means I not only need to pick a husband by then, but I need to also wed by then. I may be the Heir of the Prophecies, but I am a woman and am not permitted to rule without a man at my side. In the past week, I have hosted a great number of men in hopes of finding someone both compatible with me, and a good leader for the kingdom. None of them have even come close…but Dagen… In one sitting, he became a friend to me and a champion to Syra. And he's wise, I can see that; he isn't some royal we used to make fun of, or a pompous jerk following power. I cannot imagine there being someone better than him in the entire kingdom for this, and I would happily say yes to someone I know I can enjoy and trust. Luik, I could fall for this man all too easily, *and* he acts like a just king. I couldn't have found a better person." She ended her speech with a pleading stare, and Luik couldn't help but steal a glance at her maid to see what she thought.

If Luik was honest, he didn't think there was a man in the kingdom more worthy of sharing Michale's rule. With the Princess's Testing Day coming up quickly, it was very possible this wedding would put Dagen on the throne even before Luik could hope to secure his own.

Politically, this was a perfect move. It would guarantee him strong allies when the time came. But personally, it felt like he was about to lose one of his new best friends to his old best friend. And it smarted.

Sweet springs, he was acting like a girl. Luik ran a hand through his hair and huffed, unsure of whom he was more annoyed at, Michale or himself.

"Well, we are leaving in the morning, so your little wedding will have to wait." He folded his arms and glared at her, daring her to argue. His kingdom was more important than some outdated court tradition.

"I would need a week, Lu. That's it. Dagen has explained the situation, and I understand, but by Anarathan law my husband-to-be must be at my wedding. My Testing Day is in two weeks, so the timeline is decided whether or not either of us like it."

"Michale, you can't seriously be asking me to wait a week. My kingdom would be in ruins by then, by my own bloody father's hand!" He could feel his own anger rising, knowing it wasn't fair to blame Michale for any of this, but cracking under the weight of yet another decision he couldn't control.

Syra, feeling the tension, set down her drink and cleared her throat softly, reminding the two royals of her presence.

"Luik, would it be possible to send Dagen home in a week, in time for the wedding? Surely you would have accomplished what you need by that point."

Michale shot her maid a frown, but stayed quiet, waiting to see what Luik would say.

How could he tell them what he was about to do? About to face? He needed loyal friends near him in these coming months. Not just to remove his father, but to ring out as clear voices of good amid a kingdom sinking in corruption. They couldn't possibly understand, having lived here in their perfect, closed off utopia.

People lived free here. They had peace. Waking up in the palace guest rooms these past few mornings, he was sure even the sun shone more clearly in Anaratha. Even if they were all too bloody rigid for his taste, at least he didn't have to see... everything he saw in his kingdom.

Luik shook his head, defeat threatening to crush him.

"I can do that. But Michale, I need your word. If you pass your Testing Day, you *have* to send me aid should I ever need it. I need an ally in Anaratha, not a complacent bystander."

"You have it then. Anaratha will stand by you."

Anger rose to the surface then, kindled by years of bitter resentment toward the king of Anaratha, who time and time again refused to send even the smallest group of soldiers to help.

"Are you bloody sure about that? Are you sure you won't be bloody swayed by all your new advisors to stay far away from the Brends for fear their mixed-blood may soil your kingdom's perfect life, just like you all stay far away from the mix-bloods in your own kingdom, letting them live in starvation and filth in the furthest corners of your slums?" To his own surprise, he felt a hot stinging in his eyes.

Springs, this was all too much. He knew his anger at her was uncalled for, and he could feel the hurt in Michale's. But it was all true.

Syra laid a hand on his arm as if sending the stored up sun in her tan skin straight into his own. But it wasn't just comfort she wanted to give, piercing him with a stare that had neither condescending sympathy nor indifference.

"There has not been an Anarathan royal in this entire kingdom who would dare touch me, a Jyre. My people are worse than yours in every way you can imagine, and I am hated here more deeply than you can know. Yet Michale'thia has counted me as her friend, and I have never before known a love like she has shown me. You can trust that she will not be her parents. She will be much greater."

Syra's stare had gone hazy while saying that last line and Luik swore her eyes turned a slightly grayer shade of green, as if she saw something far away, echoing in the distance.

And then the moment was over. Silence overtook the small group.

Michale spoke hesitantly, her voice coming out in a small whisper as her eyes stayed glued to the floor, afraid to be heard by anyone else.

"Lu, I've been studying our ancient scrolls. Something... isn't right here. The way we do things, it doesn't make sense. It doesn't fit with how the people closest to the Ancient Magic lived. I don't know what it is, but there are holes in our history, and somehow… somehow I think we may have gotten something terribly wrong." Her indigo eyes bore into his then, and it was as if he was being transported back to their eight-year-old selves, right before she proved him wrong about girls not being able to climb trees.

"And I intend to fix it. Whatever it takes."

CHAPTER 5
MICHALE'THIA

Three days. She would be wed in three days. Michale'thia stared at the high ceiling above her bed, intricately patterned with golds and blues to mimic the night sky. It had been a present from her brother, who knew more than others of her desire to sleep under the stars. She smiled at the thought of seeing him today, even if it would be in the War Room.

After failing his Testing Day, her brother, Enith, sought out a position in the army despite her parents' disapproval and seemed to have been away these past three years more than he was here. He had a brilliant mind, excelling in everything he did, and he used to have a depth of love for the people of Anaratha that was unfathomable to her. She loved her kingdom, of course, but Enith used to sit and watch the people all day from his window overlooking the town square and never tire of it. He had yearned to judge fairly and to find new ways to champion those under his future rule.

Then his Testing Day came, and he was never quite the same. The forest changed him somehow, and he withdrew. From his people. From his family. And from his kingdom.

Michale sat up when she saw the time, eager to move away from any thoughts about her upcoming Testing Day. Syra opened the door softly and smirked when she saw her study books untouched.

Michale rolled her eyes, "There was no chance of me doing anything productive anyway. Plus, I memorized the content three weeks ago so I would finish before my Testing Week."

Syra didn't even glance up at her as she rummaged through her closet and picked out a dark gray dress. They had long ago learned that to be taken seriously in the War Room, Michale needed to stay far away from anything bright or colorful, even if the men could use those colors.

"So, what were you doing this entire past hour then? Daydreaming about your future husband?" A smile lit Syra's face and Michale's own cheeks heated.

"I was taking a much-needed break from the large number of fittings I have suddenly had to partake in." She arched a brow at Syra, feeling completely justified in her hour-long break. The past four days had been filled from sunrise to well after dark, meeting with advisors about the legal implications of marriage, drawing up contracts, picking flower colors, foods, bridal parties, and having at least 20 new dresses made for her new life as a married woman. Not to mention the wedding gown itself. She deserved an hour.

Syra smiled and quickly wound Michale's hair in a tight bun at the top of her head, allowing a few curls to escape but otherwise keeping all frills tucked away.

"Thank you. I hope this isn't bad news."

"Why would it be bad news?" Syra's brow lowered as she looked Michale over, adjusting a sleeve.

"My brother returned and called this meeting. If he had his way, he would never have to talk to any of my father's advisors, so there must be something pressing."

Syra nodded thoughtfully, now wondering the same thing herself, as she followed Michale out the door.

They crossed the palace quickly, trying to avoid people as much as possible for fear of being made late to the meeting because she had to settle an argument about which flower petals to throw at her wedding.

They made it to the door, and Michale'thia gave Syra a thankful smile, opening the dense wood and leading them both inside. Syra disappeared to the back wall, keeping her eyes down and posture still, doing her best to blend in with the stone.

Michale searched the group until she finally found her stoic older brother's tall form in the back corner of the room, arms folded and nodding at what General Martes was telling him.

When she caught his eye, she could see his shoulders visibly relax. He said something to General Martes and came toward her, scooping her up in a huge hug with obvious disregard for propriety.

"Michale'thia, it is better to see you than you know." He held her at arms' length, not ready to let her go yet.

She smiled up at him, happy to hear that he missed her as much as she missed him.

"Six months is too long, Enith. And what's going on?" Michale lowered her voice and took him by the arm, leading him away from others coming into the War Room. "You *hate* war meetings, what happened while you were out there?"

Enith's face darkened for a moment, and she could see something close to fear behind his eyes.

"We were riding in the northern part of the kingdom-"

"Gentlemen, let us proceed." Her father's booming voice ended all conversation and any chance she had of learning the reason for this meeting before it started.

Enith took a seat on the king's left and she sat across from him on the right, eager to begin.

Quiet settled over the group, maps and large wax candles grouped in the center of the table. This room was the darkest because it lay in the center of the palace, with doubly thick walls to block all sound from escaping.

"Today the prince returned with grave news. I'll let him explain." The king sat back in his chair and stroked his beard, turning to Enith.

Enith nodded to his father and then looked around the room for a moment, either not noticing or not caring that the silence was eating away at most people around the table. Except Lord Thilan, who simply watched Enith, expressionless.

"The past six months my squadron was called to investigate rumors in the northern hills of deaths no one could account for. When we arrived, we found villages terrified. Most of the farmers had stopped farming, and no children played outside. We continued to hear fables of monsters and wolves, but didn't find the truth until three months ago, when we were attacked—by a *delvior*."

Gasps and nervous fidgeting could be heard throughout the room, most now listening with frozen expressions of horror.

"The creatures were larger than we had been taught. Somehow, the wolves were not just twisted in nature, they were misshapen. Larger."

Michale felt her own heart racing, as Enith suddenly seemed lost in some past trauma, struggling to continue.

"We found... bodies. Children. Women. Mangled and strewn about. We had been battling the delviors for three months and only to realize there were just two of them. We refused to leave until they were slain. I have returned now with only half of my squad. Two of these creatures killed 15 of my men and countless villagers, and now we have heard rumors of deaths even farther north."

Enith said the last line grimly, looking into the eyes of the men around the table, turning them all into soldiers before him. Michale wanted to sob, and not just for the implications, but for her brother, who seemed to be growing farther and farther away from the lighthearted jokester she once knew.

Lord Thilan slammed his hand on the table, startling her out of her woes.

"Well, let them stay to the north then! Our walls are strong enough to keep any dark creatures out, and our armies will destroy any who come near!"

His passionate response garnered agreement from a few men, while others seemed encouraged by his idea to voice their own.

"We should draft more men-"

"There is no need for a greater army, the prophecy says we will not be touched if we honor the Ancient Magic!"

"And the Princess is soon to have her Testing Day. When she passes, we will enter into our eternal peace with the Ancient Magic. Why waste lives now with hope coming so soon?"

"At least expand our patrols!"

"What about the farmers in the hill country?"

Michale could barely believe what she was hearing. Looking across at her brother's dark face, she suspected he didn't believe it either. Her father, on the other hand, seemed to be listening and genuinely taking their suggestions to heart.

Her head was spinning. Leave the northern lands to these dark creatures? No one knew if she would even pass her Testing Day, how could they possibly plan their entire future around the hope that she would be the Heir the prophecy spoke of?

The arguing continued, and Michale pondered the situation, trying to drown out the voices around her.

Her skirt moved slightly, and Michale could see from where her brother's eyes were locked that Syra had just been behind her. She reached down to the ground beneath her skirt and picked up a small piece of paper, the method of communicating in these meetings they had created years ago.

She opened it as subtly as possible, casting her eyes down slightly to not draw attention.

Jyres never do anything by accident.

Michale pushed the paper down in the fold of her dress and sat for a moment, dazed at the realization Syra had brought. Her mouth was still parted in surprise when her brother's voice cut through the squabbling at the table.

"I believe Princess Michale'thia may have some wisdom for us."

The table was silent as all eyes turned to her. She nodded to her brother in thanks before looking around the room, still deciding what to correct and what to let go.

"We cannot forget where these creatures come from. The Jyres in the Dark Forest corrupt and twist and work with a shrewdness like none other. If they have let out a few of their creatures, it is because they are making more and testing their limits." Her gaze hardened as it fell on Lord Thilan, whose face was now hard as stone.

"And we must not think we can shirk this problem, leaving others to die while we survive. What my brother has found is proof we cannot deny. Gentlemen, we are about to have another Dark War on our hands."

Men around the room slumped back in chairs with stricken looks as the news sunk in, undeniable now that it was spoken.

Michale jumped as her father's loud laugh filled the room, his head thrown back, and his hands resting on his large stomach. Around the table, the tension eased and the men all began to join in, some unsure why they were laughing.

"My daughter, you have a gifted foresight, but in this case, I think our problem is only an unfinished past. These are just remnants from the *Dark War* hundreds of years ago. It would make sense that some delviors would survive the war, and now they have resurfaced in one last push for glory. The Ancient Magic needed to create them now is gone, and we need not worry ourselves over fictional problems. Let us honor those who were fallen and let the Brends fight their own battles. They can deal with the last delviors on their own. Maybe it will knock some dignity into them."

The advisors chuckled in agreement, relaxing visibly at the king's words.

Michale looked around the room in astonishment, then back at her father. This must be a joke. They couldn't possibly believe this was *nothing*, or leave the northern lands to the creatures. She clenched her hands in her lap, schooling her face to a look of submission. She could not allow herself even a single slip up—for the sake of her kingdom.

Looking across the table, Michale locked eyes with Enith, taking in his locked jaw. She nodded slightly at him, hoping he would see her warning as she flicked her eyes toward their father, who now sat chatting amiably with those around the table.

Enith looked at his father and the advisors once again before standing, knocking his chair back in the process, and leaving the room.

The rest of the meeting was a blur, but one thing was clear: the kingdom was too sure she would pass this test. And if she failed, more would be lost than hope.

***

After the meeting ended, Michale excused herself quickly with apologies of wedding planning still to be done, bringing a chuckle from every man in the room, and strode down the hall back to her room, using every bit of self-control to not sprint there as fast as she could.

She slipped inside and sat down at her desk, pulling loose paper and grabbing her quill to scribble an urgent note.

Luik,

Trouble at your doorstep. Delviors are back. I will send help when I can. Until then, be on your guard, and bring those in the farmlands within your walls.

MD

She folded the note, stamped it with her seal, and handed it to Syra.

"Send it by bird. They need to know immediately."

Syra nodded and then was off, leaving Michale'thia alone to struggle through her raging emotions in the stillness of her bedroom.

Her wedding was in three days, her Testing Day in ten, and now it was apparent the Jyres planned to unleash their twisted creatures on the world again soon. The last time they did that, during the Dark War, it nearly destroyed the world. If not for the Ancient Brothers, every soul would have been extinguished. Now they had no Ancient Brothers to save them.

Michale felt a sob choke in her throat as she shakily sat down on the ground, with her back leaning on her bed.

And in all this, she must carry the weight of moral perfection, a burden so heavy she could barely open her eyes some mornings. She could neither lash out in anger nor fight against her parents. She was to be everything on the outside this kingdom needs. Strong. Meek. Controlled. Intelligent. Charming. Pure.

She rested her head on her knees and allowed the sobs to come silently, on and on, grieving the loss of herself to this life.

***

A firm knock sounded at her bedroom door, and Michaleth'ia stilled, hoping whoever it was would leave. But the knock pounded on the door again, and she stood, trying to brush out any wrinkles from her dress and wipe her eyes before croaking for the person to enter.

Her brother stepped in, eyes ablaze in anger, clearly ready to vent his frustrations, but when his eyes took her in, the fire was snuffed out and he crossed the room to hold her for a moment. His embrace brought more quiet sobs, but healing was in those tears at the same time.

Enith understood all too well the pressure of being the most promising royal. It wasn't too long ago that he was in this same position. Perfect, morally unflawed, ready to be the savior the kingdom needed.

They finally pulled away and Michale returned to her seat on the floor, Enith following suit and kicking off his shoes.

She rolled her head to the side to look at him, attempting to glare.

"You can't just fling your shoes about. Look at the mess they've made."

He grinned and stretched, clearly unperturbed.

"I thought they made the place look a little better." He winked at her, earning a shove in return.

She could almost see the old Enith beneath all his stubble and anger.

"I sent a letter to the Brends Kingdom," she said. "They will be ready."

His anger returned and he folded his arms, tilting his head back to stare blankly at the ceiling.

"And will that be enough? It's like Father is purposefully blind to the world around him. And those idiots around his table do nothing to advise at all. What are we going to do when more appear?"

Michale laid a hand on his arm, "If I pass my Testing Day, Father won't be able to do anything about it. I will. I've already told Luik we won't abandon him, and Syra knows her people better than any. We'll figure this out."

He looked thoughtful for a moment, hesitant to say what was on his mind.

"You may actually pass, Michale. You may actually be who the Ancient Magic sent for our kingdom. How... do you feel about that?"

He kept his eyes forward, buttoning and unbuttoning his knife case.

She sighed, unsure of how she felt herself. She wanted to rule and take part in righting the kingdom, *but* she also ached to live a life free of others' expectations. And then...

The small fear she had pushed back, far back, into her mind threatened to come out again. The sense that they had missed something in all their translations and desires to understand the Ancient Magic.

"Enith... what do you think the Ancient Magic meant by 'perfection'? Would it mean that you knew everything? Wouldn't a perfect ruler not lack in any knowledge?" She could see he was taken back and hurried to continue.

"I've been doing research, trying to figure out what we are missing. I can't seem to find *anything* more about the Perfect Heir, except that one exists. It's like we are missing a huge chunk of information we were supposed to have. I can't help but think *something* is off."

He sat there, quiet for a moment, and she could see by his eyes he was thinking through this all for the first time, piecing together the puzzle in his own mind. He finally shook his head, keeping his eyes down.

"I don't know. All I know is we aren't as good as we think, here in Anaratha."

CHAPTER 6
MICHALE'THIA

The next three days flew by faster than Michale could have imagined, full of exhausting direction given to countless servants and balancing both her mother's wishes and her brother's anger. It had all come together in time, and while others still rushed about outside of her bedroom door, frantically working to ready every last detail for the ceremony, today she rested and wed.

It had been a sleepless night, with too much tossing and turning brought on by her nervous mind, but when she awoke to sunlight pouring through the window and a warm bath ready for her, filled with fragrances of every kind, all anxiety melted away. Today, she would marry a man she saw fit to rule both the kingdom and her heart.

Syra was already bringing in a tray of fruits, rolls, and tea, followed by a battalion of maids to perform her wedding day preparations which would span the next six hours. She would be lathered, pampered, and coddled today more than any, and she couldn't say she was disappointed at that. Michale smiled at Syra and rubbed her eyes, climbing out of bed and picking up a piece of fruit as she spun about the room, smiling.

The maids laughed and stretched out a screen so she could bath in private while they busied themselves with other preparations. Her day would first consist of the traditional Women's Brunch, in two hours, where she would be spoken to of the most sacred and intimate realities of marriage. Then she would go to a lunch with her family and Dagen's family, which he would not be at, having his own time with both families at an early breakfast. And then, just a few hours later, the wedding would begin outside in the palace courtyard.

She soaked in her warm bath, enjoying the smells and tranquility of the moment, while being careful not to get her hair wet.

She climbed out when her skin couldn't get any more prune-like and slipped on her underclothes. The moment the divider was taken away, at least six different maids began working on her. She was put into a new dress, childlike and simple in cut but with a thousand small details sewn in, signifying her innocence to the older ladies. It was mint green and made from a soft material that felt sweet to the skin, covering her arms all the way to the wrists and trailing behind her in a small train.

Her hair was left mostly down except for a few pieces in the front being pinned back with flowers, and her face was left clean, purposefully unpainted, just as a young girl would be. To be honest, it was not much different than her usual face routine.

This was the first of three times the maids would dress her today.

When she was ready, Syra gave her an approving look-over and then lead her down the hall toward the women's banquet room, stopping in front of the doors and checking a clock on the wall before knocking.

Michale could hear hushes and quickened steps behind the closed doors. She wondered what this event would bring. No unmarried woman was allowed to know what happened during these brunches, and it became a sort of game in their palace for the older women to keep their lips tight about the subject.

When the large doors opened, and she stepped through, thirty royal women stood before her, dressed in golds and silvers, with hair done up to greater lengths than she had ever seen taken for balls. In the middle of them all, outshining every single one, was her mother.

The doors shut, and the queen stood with hands folded behind her body and a tight smile painted across her face as she waited for the gentle hum of conversations to subside.

Michale stood before all the adorned women waiting, only slightly apprehensive of what was to come.

"Michale'thia Aleth Digarrio, today you join together with a man, tying yourself as one for all eternity. And in your honor this late morning," the queen gestured to the tables, filled with food, "you may enjoy every kind of your favorite delicacies.

"Because after this, Michale'thia, your body will be devoted to creating an heir, should you not pass your Testing Day. For those of us who have failed, the Ancient Magic gives us the task of bearing children of the purest blood, in hopes that one shall be the savior of the kingdom."

The women shook their heads solemnly, looking at each other with an understanding she couldn't yet comprehend.

Her mother lifted her hands slightly, and all murmuring ceased. She began a slow walk around Michale'thia, appraising her as if she were a cow about to be bought.

"Being a wife means staying loyal and obedient, even in the most trying times. When you want to scream, you smile; when you want to run, you stand firm." She stopped, and her eyes hardened so slightly Michale was sure she was the only one who could have noticed.

"But then, if you truly are the Heir of the kingdom, you won't have to worry about any impure actions like those," she added.

"To prepare you for the task ahead, you must learn to deny your body what it thinks it needs in order to stay true to your commitment. Each wedding, the task looks different. This one has been made specifically for you. Follow me."

There was a glint in her mother's eye that scared Michale'thia, just as it did when she was younger, witnessing the cruelty of her mother's sharp hand upon a servant. The more she drank, the worse it got, and she only drank too much in front of her family.

The ladies parted to follow her mother, revealing in the back of the room the women's bathing pool, a small area usually kept warm by heated coals in a cavern beneath it. Now, the small pool was surrounded by floor cushions and couches, as if the women planned to be there without getting in. Flowers floated on the water and candles lit the sides of the pool. It was beautiful.

The group gathered around the pool, quietly waiting again for her mother to explain.

"You shall enter this pool and go under the water. Your lungs will burn, and you will believe you need to rise. Your task is to deny your body what it thinks it needs and stay under until you are bidden to come up."

Michale'thia stared at her mother blankly, waiting for the caveat she knew was coming. When her mother simply stared back, she sighed and began moving toward the pool.

As she lifted her dress to step in, her mother's sharp voice halted her.

"No. Take off your dress. It must be only you, pure and unhindered by worldly things."

The women began to murmur to each other, looking around uncomfortably but eventually quieting down.

Michale stood there grimly, looking around at the women, waiting for any of them to speak to the unnecessary humiliation of this request.

Through hooded eyes now, she studied her mother, not pleading or asking anything, but seeing a side of her for the first time. Something in her wanted Michale to suffer.

But she wouldn't be cowed. And she wouldn't give up.

Determination spurred her on as she removed her clothing slowly, resisting the urge to cover her body with her arms and instead standing as tall and regal as she could in the moment.

Her mother smiled sweetly at her and beckoned her forward into the water.

That the water was freezing cold almost didn't surprise her at this point, even if it did steal the breath from her lungs. She guessed none of the other women knew the water had been mixed with ice and the coals removed from under the bath.

Michale bit the inside of her cheek, breathing out slowly and trying to turn off every emotion and feeling in her body, sinking into a dark place in her mind she created long ago for times like these. She wouldn't let her mother see a thing.

She walked in slowly, nearly crippled by the cold. She struggled not to halt or run away. When the water was finally up to her chest, shivers began wracking her body involuntarily, and the women began to whisper around the room.

"Is it…"

"... so cold… Were you told of this?"

"... see them turning blue…"

"...poor child…"

Her mother's quick glance stopped all whispers, and she held up the sand timer on the table next to her, nodding to Michale'thia. Michale'thia held her breath, dreading what was to come, and began her descent backwards into the water, watching her mother turn over the sand timer.

She could do this.

Submerging her head was the final straw. Her limbs began to numb, and her heart raced. She began to count the seconds, trying to turn off everything in her mind and ignore all the warning bells from her body.

.. 15...16...17…

It was an art really, to die inside just to survive. She could turn off everything in her body-every raging anger over injustice or heartache from lost love, but the result was a hollowed-out version of herself, one that more closely represented the perfectly unfeeling heir the kingdom wanted than who she was. The only feeling she couldn't shake while in this state was the whisper of a fear that this empty version of her would be what killed her in the end.

...42...43...44…

But it was in this dark hole that she found strength. Strength to be the savior her people needed her to be. Strength to take every single insult thrown at her and never respond back in kind.

... 54...55...56

Strength to not care if her own mother hated her, or brother left her. The strength to simply keep being this person the world needed her to be even when it was crushing her soul.

Was it strength, though? Or escape?

... 61... or 63… She was losing count.

In some distant reality, she felt her lungs burning, just as she felt the dull race of her heart.

..92...93...94…

But she couldn't leave, not until…

Until what?

Michale shook her head, trying to shake off the black mist covering her eyes.

***

All at once, the peaceful corner of her mind slammed her out, and she could feel every sting of her screaming lungs again.

She had to get up for air.

She pushed out of the water, gasping-

And a hand pushed her back under, holding her firmly on the chest as she sputtered and fought, choking on the water she inhaled on the way down.

The world swirled around her in waves of ice. She couldn't fight the hand any longer, her limbs numbing with each second spent in the pool. The darkness intensified, and tears spilled from her eyes, unnoticed and unseen.

She heard muted shouts somewhere above her as the world faded, and then everything went black.

***

Michale could faintly feel herself being lifted from the water, faintly registering her own stomach retching as her lungs violently fought to rid themselves of liquid.

Slowly, she began to feel her limbs again and attempted to open her eyes. The spinning world around her disappeared as she closed her eyes again, longing to drift back into the sweet black sleep, and only held back by a gentle hand shaking her, urging her awake.

".... Come, princess… don't sleep…"

A strong fragrance was thrust under her nose, forcing everything back into focus as her lungs spasmed under the scent.

Michale opened her eyes, squinting against the abrasive lights. She sucked in a haggard breath, realizing there was a blanket around her now.

"There you are. Sit up a little more and cough as much as you need." The elderly woman gently rubbed her back and tucked the blanket around her, making sure no one could see her bare frame anymore.

Michale searched the room for her mother, but she was nowhere to be seen, and the other royal women now had drifted a cautious distance away from the pool, none meeting her eyes.

The older woman followed her gaze and shook her head, cupping Michale'thia's chin in her hands, almost as her own grandmother would have done, had she still been alive.

Michale'thia took in the women's too-few freckles and paler skin, realizing she was a servant. The wrinkled woman was risking her job by touching Michale, and her life by undermining the queen. Her voice was low and powerful, breathing courage into Michale'thia as she spoke.

"Child, don't let them see you break."

Michale looked numbly at the royal woman watching her. These women with power and position in the kingdom, who had little to lose by stopping her mother, and yet they did not step in as she was almost drowned. Then here, this mix-blood servant, who could lose everything and had little say in any area of Anaratha, did.

She held the woman's crinkled eyes for a moment longer, letting her alone see the broken pieces of her soul, before nodding and taking a breath.

"Thank you, auntie."

Michale heard a few gasps in the room as the royal women registered the term of honor and endearment given to the servant, indignation spreading like wildfire through their whispers.

Tears filled her eyes at the injustice of it all: they should be so outraged at honor given to someone society considered lower in every respect- ignoring the greater wrong they just committed in their own silence.

Lowering her voice, Michale kept her eyes on the woman, taking her hand.

"My mother won't forgive you for this. Pack your things quickly and move to the servant's quarter in my wing. I will make sure you are protected and given a position of honor."

Her soft wrinkles lifted into a sad smile, and she squeezed Michale's hand for a moment before letting go and walking quietly out of the room.

Michale shifted and faced the royal woman silently from the floor, still shivering beneath the blanket and wincing at her bruised lungs with every breath. She waited for an apology. An explanation. Congratulations. But all she was met with were turned heads and averted eyes.

She slowly forced her arms to move and her legs to stand. Her gaze stayed on each woman for an uncomfortable amount of time, demanding they feel some weight of what they had done.

Then, standing taller than she ever had before, she let the blanket fall to the ground and walked slowly over to her clothes, donning her undergarments carefully as she worked to stop her body from shaking. When some of the women finally moved to help her, she stopped them with a glare, continuing to clothe herself.

When she finished, she looked at them one last time before walking out the door, it's thud shaking them all to the core.

It was possible that in all the history of the kingdom, silence had never said so much.

Each woman went home without a word, the breakfast feast untouched on the table.

***

The maids were shooed from the room, and Michale didn't have the heart to tell Syra what had happened behind the closed doors. Instead, she slipped into her bed and lay, facing the ocean and the Indigo mountains in the distance, allowing the tears to stream down her face.

***

An hour had passed, maybe more, when her door slammed open, and her brother strode into the room, eyes blazing with fury. Startled, she turned her swollen eyes toward him before turning back toward the window again.

Enith stood in the middle of the room. She could hear him throw his gloves and kick over a chair, yelling in rage.

Then he fell to his knees and sobbed with his head in his hands. His cries brought Michale'thia another wave of tears, and the two royal heirs were together in quiet, sobbing at the brokenness of life.

When they had both stopped and their hearts had found solace in another grieving soul, she sat up with her legs crossed, moving so he could join her on the bed.

"I think she would have killed me," she said.

"I know," he replied.

Enith's hands clenched until they were white, and she could see his jaw tensing.

"And they all just stood and watched."

"I know." He looked at his hands then, palms open, as if in surrender.

"The beautiful Kingdom of Anaratha. Where we send our most perfect children to the dark, and strive to keep our hands clean from the filth and needs of all other people in the land." He scoffed and looked up.

Michale just watched him say all the things she felt but couldn't speak. Every movement counted toward her ability to satisfy the Ancient Magic. Even in private.

When Enith spoke again, his bitterness seemed to have faded into sadness. "I told Father we were canceling lunch. Instead, Dagen's father asked to have a quiet meal with you in the gardens."

A rush of gratitude overtook Michale and she let out a breath of relief as she laid her head back against the wall.

Enith looked over at her with a small smile, "You know, we haven't even talked about this lover you're marrying."

Michale'thia gasped in shock, laughing at his pointed choice of words, and threw a pillow at him. Inside, she was thankful he had finally brought up Dagen.

"He isn't my lover! In fact, I think we are both marrying in the same mindset. We aren't in love, but we could be friends." She shrugged, then smiled to herself, thinking of Dagen's kind eyes and handsome face.

"But, you know, he certainly wouldn't be bad to look at for the rest of my life." Michale threw a smile at her brother, who began a dramatic show of gagging.

"Gross, Michale... never talk about that again. Brothers aren't meant to hear these things." His face spasmed in grimaces again and he acted as if he were barely holding down his stomach, giving her a wink at the end of his dramatics.

"In all seriousness though, I've met Dagen." Michale's brows shot up in surprise, though she wasn't sure why. Dagen and Enith were the same age, so they were bound to have met.

Enith laughed at her reaction and continued, "Yeah, it was a year or two ago, riding out to our southern borders. I believe I mistook him for a farmer since he was surrounded by a hoard of little mix-bloods, playing a foot ball game in the dirt. Once I realized who he was, I'm embarrassed to say I didn't speak to him in the kindest way at the time. I also met his father while there. Very impressive, those two. I wouldn't mind having men like them in my ranks, even if just for the good spirits they'd bring. It's strange though, if I remember right he was offered a Testing Day but refused it. I guess he and his father claimed he had already morally failed many times over and didn't need to be tested. Must be how he kept…"

He trailed off, looking down at his hands. Michale'thia watched emotions flit across his face, a mix of confusion and anger, punctuated with a mutter that sounded close to language she wouldn't expect from him.

"Well, I'm glad to have your approval. He will go back to Luik tomorrow, but that shouldn't matter. We'll have plenty of time for married life later. Right now, Luik needs good allies."

"I heard about that all." Enith shook his head in disgust. "What was King Jarr thinking? There must be something else going on." He grimaced, remembering the War Room meeting. "With all the kings these days."

Enith refused to leave until Syra came in with five bustling maids once more. Syra bowed to him briefly, as his rank required, but Enith kept his eyes averted and quietly took his leave.

As they grew out of childhood, Enith had slowly accepted Syra as Michalethia's friend, and the two had begun to grow close in friendship too. During their later teenage years, Michale was sure the two had fallen in love. But then Enith's Testing Day came and afterward, he couldn't seem to meet Syra's eyes again, and Michale didn't know why. If she tried to bring up the dark day with him, his entire mood would change, and he would shut himself off from her.

The maids began getting out the new dress, made just for the meeting with Dagen's father and her parents, but Michale'thia stopped them, needing to explain.

"A moment, all of you."

The maids stilled, surprised to be addressed and slowly turning to look at her, questions filling their eyes. Each had standard Alethian features—freckles, or a dark auburn tint to their hair, tanner skin—yet also yielded telltale signs of impurity somewhere within their bloodline, whether it be brown eyes instead of blue or a lack of red tint to their brown hair. One girl, younger than the rest, even had skin closer to the brown she had seen in the Brends Kingdom.

"How many of you already know of the incident in the women's quarters?" Michale'thia stood before them, watching each one carefully.

None raised their hand, but she could see their quick glances to each other said differently.

"Come, I am not my mother. I will never raise a cruel hand against you, I promise you that." Michale's voice softened, and she decided to let them see the realities of her life.

"I'm not sure if my mother hates me or if she is jealous of my potential to take the throne. Or even if she is just… cruel for reasons I can't understand, but I know I don't want to—I *can't* see her right now. My brother has graciously canceled lunch, and instead, we will be meeting my future father-in-law in the garden of the east wing this afternoon. I just want a simple dress and simple face paint. And I just want…" She didn't expect the tears to spring up, and she turned toward the window to gather her emotions back under control.

"I would like a quiet meeting." Michale turned back to the maids, surprised to see tears welling in many of their eyes.

She continued, "And please know this: I will be a refuge from my mother. You may spread that to the other maids. If she harms you, you may come here. I cannot do much, but I can offer a place to recover and get bandaging. And if I pass my Testing Day, I promise you, she will be given a comfortable room somewhere in the palace with its own kitchen where she will have no need for maids to help her do anything. And believe me, she *will* learn. If I fail...forgive me. I wish I could do more."

She looked around and found Syra in the back, surprised to see a piercing stare that made Michale feel almost *too* seen.

"You will pass, princess. I am sure of it."

The maids appeared to gain courage from Syra's confidence and nodded in equal assurance, each thanking Michale quietly and giving shy smiles before beginning to ready her for the lunch again.

At the end of their careful preparations, Michale'thia looked in the mirror and smiled. They had dressed her in a simple, light blue dress that covered half her arms and gathered simply at her waist by a darker blue ribbon. Her hair was done in her favorite fashion, comfortably gathered in a low bun, which upon closer inspection was actually made up of a myriad of braids and twists, resulting in a beautiful yet subtle intricacy. Her makeup was simple and light, with a brush of gold shine on her cheekbones. These women had made her beautiful in her own self.

It was hard not to contrast the two groups of women, the royals and the servants. How was it that these mixed-blood maids could be so tender under such prejudice when her own people seemed so calloused in their lack of want or care for anything?

Syra touched her arm and smiled, "It is time to go."

Michale'thia turned around to look at the maids, now lined against the wall for her departure and stopped to thank each one, holding each of their hand as she did so. She needed them to know that their blood didn't make them untouchable.

***

Enith walked Michale and Syra to the eastern garden, where a small table for two had been set up in the middle of the lush garden, steaming dishes and aged wine awaiting her.

Lord Thorn rose when he saw her, waiting with an easy smile on his face with tight wrinkles surrounding it. He looked to be older, a man in his sixtieth or seventieth year, but had a muscular build that spoke to his continued work on his estate, likely right beside his farmers.

As she neared, he pulled out her chair and took her hand in his, giving a small bow.

"Princess Michale'thia, you have made a father very happy."

She smiled at him, genuinely pleased to find such an agreeable man in front of her. Up close, she could see where Dagen got his eyes and strong jawline.

"Lord Thorn, I am thankful already to have such kindness greet me. Shall we sit down?"

Servants rushed forward to pour their drinks but were waved off by Lord Thorn, who chuckled.

"Why don't you all go take a break? We can pour our wine just fine. The guards are still here. Go on. The beach is that way." He motioned to his left, where the beach was only a short walk away. The servants stood frozen with slightly panicked expressions, looking from Michale to Lord Thorn.

Michale was surprised, not that they would have to serve themselves, but that Lord Thorn would take charge of palace employees. There was something in his manner though, that spoke of kindness, not a power struggle or a chess game.

"I think that's a fine idea. In celebration of my wedding, take an hour at the beach. We will have a bell rung when you are needed again." Michale smiled at them, laughing at their looks of excitement as they trotted down to the beach on their unexpected break.

Michale looked back over at Lord Thorn's thoughtful gaze, as if reading something in her own eyes. He gave a nod of approval and smiled, filling their cups.

She seemed to have passed whatever test Lord Thorn had concocted, and Michale suddenly found herself fighting indignation at the thought of being tested for worthiness by yet another person. Was Dagen's whole family this way? With standards for humanity, she obviously had to prove herself against? She swallowed her irritation and accepted the wine.

Michale glanced up at Lord Thorn to gauge his mood, and was met only with a kind, knowing look.

"My dear, I am not trying to test you. I have heard enough from my son to know your character, and I wouldn't have taken such liberties if I hadn't already known your own caring heart."

He set down the fork he was holding, putting his own meal on hold.

"Before Dagen went to Luik's kingdom, he came home and we took a walk through our orchards. He told me about a young woman he met while away, and do you know what he told me?"

Michale shook her head, not wanting to say a word and make him slow down his story.

"He said, 'Papa, I met a woman that I think I can love. And I think I can love dearly. And I think it will be hard sometimes, but I think she's worth it.'" Lord Thorn raised a bushy brow at her.

"Then he looked at me quite seriously and said, 'What would you do, Papa? Oh, I bellowed a laugh then. Of all the things I've taught my son, how could he not know the answer?

I saw in his eyes something I haven't seen before. My young Dagen, who is so strong, and has so much of his late mother's peace about him, didn't understand that for love of a good woman, a man ought to fight the world. I saw in him longing, and he's never had that. He has had a good life, and loved everything about it, but *you* made him long for more."

Lord Thorn took a sip of wine, smiling around the rim as she tried to suppress her joy. There had been a fear inside that Dagen felt nothing at all for her, that he had proposed out of political ambition, or even honorable intentions to serve the kingdom. But could it be that he was growing to love her too? Of course, it was asking a lot of a marriage arranged in a week—they didn't even know each other, so how could they truly feel anything? But still. She wanted to be wanted, not settled for.

Lord Thorn continued, "You aren't the only girl to like him, you know. He has had hordes of women chase him, for money or for looks I don't know, and he has never batted an eye. Then here he goes, humoring his old man's request to be a suitor for this princess, and he comes back ready to give everything for her. You must be special indeed, Michale'thia."

Michale let out a breath she didn't know she had been holding, so thankful to hear not only acceptance from her future father-in-law but something akin to love.

"I can't even explain how much that means to me, Lord. I don't know Dagen very well, but it didn't take long to see that he was... quite different than any royal I have ever met. If I should pass this Testing Day, he will make one of the greatest kings our kingdom has ever seen."

She couldn't be sure, but she thought she saw a tear in the older man's eye, which blinked away quickly.

"Well, let's eat! I have kept you from food too long, you must be about to swoon with hunger."

They filled their plates with savory foods and ate in amiable silcnce, enjoying the soft breeze and gentle sun.

"Tell me, Michale'thia, what do you like to do for fun?"

Michale smiled, knowing from what Dagen had said about his father's large library that this could be a fun conversation indeed.

"Well, don't tell anyone, but I wake early, before all the servants are awake, and sneak to the library to study. I love the ancient languages and I love to learn."

His eyebrows shot up, clearly excited by the turn of conversation. "And what do you read about in these secret study sessions?"

Michale'thia didn't need any more encouragement to launch in, excited to talk with someone who knew more history than she likely did.

The two talked more than they ate, their hearts finding better food in discourse than they would in the delectables before them, and before they knew it their hour had long since passed and Syra was jogging out to gather Michale'thia for ceremony preparations. They rang the bell, bringing back a laughing group of servants, all sunburnt, tired, and happy.

"Thank you, sir. I have not had such easy company in a long time. You have certainly made this day brighter."

Lord Thorn grinned at her, looking very much like Dagen. With a fatherly look, he opened his arms, giving her a hug and somehow transferring strength and healing in a gesture that may feel useless to the elder, but was filled with everything needed for the younger. He gave her a light kiss on the cheek and whispered as he did, "She ought not have done that, and they ought not have let her." When he pulled away, his face was kind, but the grin was gone.

Michale didn't know how he knew, other than from the servants who all looked to him with admiration, but his words were a balm. One royal had acknowledged it. And at least a few would have stopped it.

Michale was then pulled away by Syra, who typically wasn't so forward, but this time all but dragged her back to her room, explaining they had lost a precious hour of preparation.

***

They had two hours before the wedding, and Michale was bathed again, oiled with fragrance, and hair redone with precision. All too soon, she found herself stepping into one of the most breathtaking dresses she had ever seen.

White surrounded her body, gold touches delicately laid on the bodice and a skirt that defied the traditional round, rose-like shape, and instead hung simply to the floor, more akin to a wildflower trailing in the wind. She hadn't realized until this very day how well her staff knew her. Michale'thia hadn't given much thought or direction to the dress, almost spurning the tradition in her desire to keep far away from her mother and any other royals in the castle, yet the dress was more beautiful than she could have ever imagined.

Turning from the mirror, she stood to face Syra, grasping her hands as they held each other's eyes, speaking more clearly through their steady gaze than their choked up words could have ever expressed.

This was it. After today she would be tethered to another, for good or for bad. After today she would find out if Dagen was the same man after the wedding as he was before it. After today she would either pass her Testing Day and rule beside her husband or fail and begin trying to birth the next Heir of the Prophecy. How could a wedding be so beautiful and so grievous at the same time?

Michale'thia walked through the echoing halls, followed by a line of ten attending maids. Servants lined the walls, different complexions, hair colors, face shapes, freckle counts, and eyes gazed at her in awe as she passed, each disturbing a thousand butterflies in her stomach. The old woman who had saved her from her own mother was in the line, looking at her with tender understanding and nodding once, a reminder to stand tall in the face of fear.

These are my people, and someday I will set them free.

The thought came unbidden, and Michale'thia stopped mid-step as it came, realizing a new passion had slowly been unfolding as she stared into the eyes of each servant. Beautiful. Unique. Worthy of dignity and honor.

Her words echoed softly in the halls, then.

"You are my people."

The minute she said those four words, she realized the danger they brought. Any of the king's counsel could accuse her of speaking out against the Ancient Magic's will for purity of blood. The implications of giving mix-bloods equal standing in her eyes could be catastrophic…

But then she watched as shoulders straightened, chins rose, and tears welled in the eyes of those hearing her words. They were a balm to weary hearts, a small sliver of hope for those who had been born to nothing in Anaratha. And they were a promise of change.

Michale'thia swallowed as she walked on toward the courtyard, hoping she could live up to her promise.

When she arrived, she was hidden behind the doors, waiting for the cue from the wedding master to enter. She could see the large crowd through the cracks, sitting in their new dresses and sharp suits, but what surprised her most were the common people. She had been to plenty of weddings and never seen an attendance like this.

On every building top, and every high place, even lining the walls to the courtyard, were people of every variation of freckles and hair color, standing and eager to watch.

A quiet melody of bells drew her from her awe, and Michale'thia was given the cue as the large oak doors opened and her father stood ready with his arm.

Then, slowly, they began to walk.

The soft music actually came from a stringed instrument, played in a way that gave a light, airy sound from the lone musician, but with every step toward her husband-to-be the music grew and new musicians joined in, weaving together melodies so beautifully she believed the sound could have been played at the beginning of time when the Ancient Magic first created.

And there at the end of the long, lace-laid walk, was Dagen. His dark blue suit fit his frame, and he was looking at her with a look she couldn't place but knew held admiration and apprehension mixed together.

When she reached him, he held out his hand, and for a moment, her stomach dropped.

This was it. A beginning and an end. The greatest risk she had taken so far in her entire life, and yet the bigger test of living their lives together was still ahead. As she looked into Dagen's eyes, remembering their first encounter's laughter and lively discussion, his kindness toward her closest friend, his wisdom and willingness to sacrifice for the sake of others, she knew that at very least she could trust him with her life. And her heart.

She gave him her hand and let out a soft giggle at his own schoolboy smile, his nerves only showing through as he wiped his spare palm on his pants.

"Michale'thia Aleth Digarrio, today Anaratha has come to witness their beloved Princess pledge herself in marriage..."

The ceremony sped by as Michale'thia struggled to listen, not make a mistake, and also look happy and at ease the entire time. At one exceedingly long speech on the topic of symbolism within traditional weddings, Dagen looked at her with a private smile of exaggerated boredom, and it was all she could do to keep her anxiety from overflowing into obnoxious laughter. By the time the ceremony was coming to a close, her cheeks were aching from maintaining her polite smile.

"Michale'thia Digarrio, do you willingly bind yourself in all things to Dagen Thorn?" Michale'thia looked at the man in front of her and smiled genuinely then.

"By the Ancient Magic's Spring, I do," she said, meaning it.

"And Dagen Thorn, do you willingly accept this binding, as one who will lead a family toward a future Heir?"

"By the Ancient Magic's Spring, I choose to accept."

The wedding master standing over them gave an approving nod.

"You may go forward."

Michale'thia's hand in his, Dagen walked with her toward a stone arch wide enough for two to pass through, decorated in flowers and vines, and they walked under it to the cheers of the crowd.

"As you have passed under the arch, so we will all soon pass through to the Age of Perfection, hopefully through you both. I declare this union true and right. Congratulations, Michale'thia Aleth Thorn and Dagen Aleth Thorn. You are now bound, until death's parting, in marriage."

Cheers and cries exploded throughout the courtyard as Dagen took her hand and they walked back through the crowd toward the oak doors, wildflower petals floating from the sky as those on the walls joyously scattered what they could afford, and music struck up into a dance-worthy song. She passed her parents, barely registering her mother's tears, and was wrapped into Enith's arms before he turned to put a brotherly hand on Dagen's shoulder. The crowd continued to cheer, and the celebration had begun. Dancing lined the street, and hours' worth of food was presented. The night sped by as they turned to fulfill their first duty as a married couple, thanking hundreds of people for attending and dancing with every man or woman who asked.

It was with sore feet and happy hearts that Dagen and Michale found themselves being signaled by the wedding master and given leave to retire.

Michale's heels echoed against the torch-lit hall, and Dagen's own shoes made equal noise, though deeper. Michale realized she hadn't been told where they would stay and hadn't even thought about what may happen this evening. Fear crippled her, knowing the expectations and realizing from this point on for her, the moral right was to submit in all things to her husband. If she was the Heir, that would look slightly different when giving ruling commands, but... She breathed out slowly, trying to find that place inside to escape the suffocating fear building within her. Eventually, they came to a halt, and Michale realized with surprise they were just down the hall from her own bedroom. In fact, they were just south of it. Before the doors opened, the servant gave her a note, which she opened immediately.

A wedding present. I couldn't let them take your beloved view.

- E.

The servant opened the doors, and Michale was met with one of the largest rooms she had seen in the palace. It was three times the size of her own, with her desk moved in, across the room from another desk, and a wall filled with books. Directly in front of her were large windows flanking two glass doors which opened onto a balcony overlooking the sea. The Indigo Mountains were only dark, looming figures in the night, but she could already see in her mind the sun glowing off their peaks come morning.

"This must be the corner suite," Dagen mused, more in awe than she was. It was beautiful.

With a bow, the servant shut the door, and they were alone. Candles had been lit everywhere. The pair stood in silence for a moment, Michale barely breathing as she waited, unsure what to do with the stranger before her.

Finally, Dagen cleared his throat, wiping his hands on his pants and looking nervous himself.

"Look, Michale'thia, I don't want to do... uh... anything tonight. Or tomorrow. I mean-" He growled in frustration, running a hand over his face and turning to her.

"You are my wife. But we are also strangers. Tomorrow I leave back to Luik, as we spoke of, and then hopefully in a week will return. After that, I want more than anything to grow our friendship and marriage, but for now, I just... I want to be your friend. And your husband, but in all intimacy, your friend. That is until we are no longer strangers and can look at each other without fear or hesitation."

He looked up at her nervously and relief settled in when he found an unsuppressed smile on her face instead. She was a lucky woman indeed.

They sat out on the balcony, exhausted but happy in each other's presence. Dagen eventually gathered blankets and pillows from inside and laid them out in the open air. The new bride and groom fell asleep after hours of comfortable conversation under the stars, and they sleep until the sun rose in the morning, bringing with it a new day.

CHAPTER 7
MICHALE'THIA

Michale'thia strolled down the steps and through the front gates, not giving a second glance at the sputtering guards flipping through papers to confirm her escort. They'd catch up.

Going to the annual Trade Market was a tradition for her, one started long ago as a way to buy thoughtful presents for those she loved, but to this day she secretly went just to get outside the palace walls. She could just as easily send maids to buy everything she needed, but today she wanted a firsthand say in what she bought, and the privacy to do it.

The city courtyard was just a few blocks away, but she took the longer route, making her way toward the northern dwellings first. Something Luik had mentioned in the heat of their discussion had made her realize how infrequently she purposed to visit the more poverty-stricken areas of Anaratha's capital. In fact, for most of her life, she hadn't even known there *were* poverty-stricken areas. As she continued her walk north, now hearing the familiar footsteps of guards following her, she could see the subtle changes become more blatant. The walls lacked shine at first, and paint seemed worn. The children in the street played happily, but with the occasional hole in their shirts.

Now, however, roofs had holes in them and dirt littered the street. Women with creased faces from years of hard labor sat outside scrubbing worn laundry as their children kicked pieces of trash around in a game. They were living, and she was sure it could be worse, but it could also be much, much better.

"Michale, wait up!" Michale turned in surprise to see her brother jogging up the stone alleyway toward her, dressed in his 'casual' wear, which consisted of his older military suit rather than his newer versions.

He came to a stop beside her, frowning as he looked suspiciously around at every open door and window in view, but he stayed quiet, seeming to understand her need to take it all in.

"It's different, out here." He spoke quietly.

Michale'thia looked up at him with concern etched across her face, unsure "different" described it very well.

"Why do they live like this?"

Enith shrugged then, either not knowing or not wanting to talk about it. Michale sent him a hard glare before making up her mind. She would get answers.

She walked up to two women washing dirty rags in a bucket, both stopping with wide eyes as she approached, standing to bow to her.

"No, I am not here for that." She smiled reassuringly at them, realizing they had less on their bodies right now than the clothes she slept in.

One of the women spoke up, awe filling her bright brown eyes and full cheeks. "Swit Springs, you're the princess. I'know, I saw you gett'n married." Michale'thia saw it then. They had no freckles, no auburn in their hair, and perhaps a hint of the tanner coloring she had, but hardly any at all. The one with brown eyes had the slightest red in her hair, but her tight curls could only be seen as brown, and the other woman's black hair and blue eyes marked her as some mix of Syllric, but gave no sign of Alethian blood at all. They were mix-bloods, descended from mix-bloods who had married mix-bloods and likely generations later bore children here in Anaratha.

Enith spoke up for his sister, covering for her dazed silence.

"You did! She was beautiful, wasn't she?"

Both women blushed and giggled at his attention and Michale shook herself out of her thoughts.

"What are your names?" She smiled at them and reached out a hand in greeting.

They just stared at it though, fear looming in their eyes.

It was a little boy, no more than five years old, who ran over and spoke up with hands on his hips and a know-it-all look on his young face.

"That's my ma," he pointed and Michale could immediately see her brown eyes on his small face.

He pointed to her black haired friend next, "and that's Mis' Tereasa. And, uh... missus... they can't be goin' n' shakin' your hand. They'd get mix-blood on you. And you can't scrub mix-blood off, that's whu my momma says!"

The brown-eyed women rushed to hush her son, scooting him back into a doorway quickly and coming back to stand before Michale with fidgeting hands and frightened apologies.

Michale brushed the woman's fears aside, determined to press on as she began to make connections in her mind.

"Please, don't worry. I'm glad he explained to me, I didn't mean to offend. Can you tell me, what jobs are you able to get in the kingdom?"

Both women kept their eyes glued to crooked alleyway stones, and Michale'thia could see the shame in their frames. But there was something else too. Anger.

It was Tereasa who finally spoke.

"We're mix-bloods who weren't blessed with the right looks. They say our blood's too mixed to have any soul left in us. We wash clothes of the mixed-bloods who've got more Alethian looks, 'n our men go outta the kingdom to mine, 'cause their blood's more expendable."

Her words were chilling, yet they lit a fire inside Michale'thia's chest. She shot a look at Enith, confirming all she needed by his own guilty expression. No souls? These were *humans. Her people.* Springs, she was going to throw up.

Michale turned and walked away for a moment, breathing slowly as she fought back sobs. What had her father done? Or her grandparents? Or whoever stood by while an entire generation of people were taught they were expendable? What had *she* done ignoring it all?

"We're sorry, miss, we didn't mean t' upset you," the brown-eyed woman added gently from behind Michale.

Michale'thia took another breath and turned to face the women, digging out her coin purse and taking out one of the twenty gold coins, which what these women likely only made in three months. She tucked the coin into the fold of her dress and drew the coin purse closed before walking to face the women and closing Tereasa's calloused fingers around it.

Her eyes widened and the women both stilled as if moving would cause Michale to snatch it back.

"You deserve more than this." She began to walk away, thankful she could do one small act to help, when she realized Enith had continued talking with them.

He spoke quietly, counting on his fingers for a moment before, to her dismay, accepting everything back from them except one gold coin each. They thanked him profusely and hugged each other, tears streaming down their faces as they left their wash buckets and hurried inside.

Michale'thia could rarely say she felt rage, but it was she could feel then. White, hot rage as she watched her own brother take from the most helpless in the kingdom. Had the Dark Forest twisted him this much?

He walked toward her, reading her anger and putting his hands in the air in surrender as he pleaded with her to listen, but she would have none of it.

"You *dare* to take what I have lawfully and rightfully given for yourself? How *could you!* Are you so far gone that you would act like Mother, dangling things in front of people only to snatch them away?" Michale was barely in control then, feeling herself slipping. The existence of this part of the kingdom meant she had been lied to. Red, rose-colored lies for the sake of Anaratha's image of perfection and prestige. And that is not even what disgusted her the most—it was the deep understanding that had Syra not shown up years ago and been so human in her own mixed-blood, Michale would probably be happily preaching the very ideals that destroyed the women before her. She would *believe* they were not worthy of life.

Tears streamed from her face and Enith stood several feet away, understanding evident in his own blue eyes.

"Michale, I am not keeping the money. I am sorry, I should have explained first." He moved a step closer, freezing when she stepped back away.

He spoke slowly, seeming to understand how fragile her current state was. She knew it too. One wrong move or word and she was disqualified from her Testing Day.

"Right now, those women have yet to learn a skill that would allow them to invest what you gave them. With the money you gave, they could last about five years without working if they kept the money for themselves, but they wouldn't. They would share the money with the entire block, saving their husbands and loved ones from the mines for just one year, and then after that, they would be forced to go back to their old lives, sick, hungry, and tired.

I told them I would keep it for them and use a small sum to pay for a tutor to come and teach them and the women on their block to sew. This money will pay for their lessons, their startup tools and resources, and even rent on a small shop they can employ someone with more Alethian features to manage if they wanted to. This could give them a lifetime of income if they learn how to use it well. I want to give them that."

Enith looked at her with such pleading for understanding, and Michale knew she had just been a fool. All those years he would stare out his own window at the people below, or disappear into the kingdom streets to play with the common children... he had been learning. And he still loved them.

She closed the distance and threw her arms around her brother, pride and shame bursting from her now, as she realized the depths of her own naivete. She couldn't even *help* right.

Michale let go and looked up at her brother, seeing him in a new light.

"Where did you learn to think like that?"

He smiled, accepting the compliment.

"From watching and listening. It's the same thought process for war plans but used for people. I used to draft up ways to change these parts of the cities. Father never took them seriously though, he'd just mutter something about the Ancient Prophecies and move on."

Michale frowned, truly confused. She had studied the prophecies too often to believe one could *really* read them and think they were clear enough to force this kind of life upon people.

Enith smiled, holding his arm out to her.

"Well, little sister, I do believe you have one more coin to spend and I fully expect to receive the best gift this year." He gave her a stern look, the sparkle in his eye betraying him.

Michale laughed, shaking her head at how quickly he could move on.

"Unfortunately, this coin is reserved for some fabrics I need. But I'm sure I can figure something out for you too."

***

Michale sighed as she lifted her fabric onto her bed. This would do. A clang of bells reminded her of the time, and she moved swiftly to retrieve her notebook and writing pencils before heading to the library. She had an hour before she was to meet with councilmen Salis to review her Testing Day schedule and wanted to spend it well.

The walls soared high in the southern hallways, lined with lanterns and pictures of royals past. She wondered what she would be known for someday. So far, she was only renowned for being the most promising royal to be given a Testing Day, and that renown would either fade away in light of her being the heir, or fade away in light of her not.

Michale looked up at the ceiling, lost in thought as she strolled through the halls alone.

What if she didn't want to be the Heir of the Prophecy? And what actually defined perfection?

The thoughts came unbidden and she looked around, afraid someone nearby would hear her quiet doubts.

This was silly. She would be what her kingdom needed.

As she rounded a corner, she caught sight of a particular window with curtains drawn back and a picture of an old battle scene of the Dark War. Grotesque images of giant wolves, their mouths twisted and their skin gnarled as they ripped apart the flesh of men, suddenly held her attention more than they had in the past. She had nearly forgotten the news her brother had returned home to deliver, and the scene before her now brought a new heaviness to it.

Michale eventually made it to the library but felt too keenly the ticking clock counting down the seconds until her Testing Day. She had too little time to figure out what she would do if she was to pass and be crowned the Heir of Perfection.

***

After hours of sleepless thoughts, Michale woke at her normal early time to the sudden realization that she had not yet studied the *histories* in their ancient language. As much as she loved the kingdom's scholars and librarians, recent experiences had taught her that she may disagree with how they have interpreted certain events. She rushed to put on a proper dress and get to the library.

This had been a discussion she and Dagen had on their first night of marriage while overlooking the sea. How often do scholars try to read the prophecy in the ancient language, only to interpret it through their contemporary bias? A question Dagen posed, which she had never heard any students of the ancient language ask, was, 'what was the *writer* of the prophecy intending this to mean?

Michale stared at the thousands of books before her, thinking through the question again. Much of what they knew about the past was through old documents telling of the wars and first days, all of which would have been written by people with a specific culture and time much different than their own. Is it possible they had read things *into* the ancient histories that weren't there?

All her questions came down to this: what would it look like to study all she had been taught, from the first sources and with an unbiased mind?

She set to work, piling up every book she could with the original languages copied from the fragile scrolls, working through them meticulously as she compared the modern translation to the ancient tongue.

After hours of work, the only discrepancy she could find of value was a single marking.

In their history classes, royals were taught that there was *one* single prophecy proclaimed by many prophets, which validated the credibility of the prophecy. But what she was finding, was the ancient tongue used the term "prophesies," in the plural form. Michale sat back in her chair, exhausted but on the brink of something and unwilling to quit.

She had discovered a crack where there might be a door. Was it possible that scholars had interpreted the word incorrectly because they didn't *know* of any more prophecies when in reality, they didn't have the entire thing?

Her heart began to speed up as she straightened, tapping her pencil on the table. If she looked at the text alone, forgetting what she had been taught from history classes and modern translations, there was *no way* she would ever believe the ancient text spoke of just one prophecy. *This* was what Dagen was talking about!

Michale couldn't keep the smile from her face as she raced to jot down all her notes in her small notebook, carefully rewriting the ancient tongue and her own interpretation of the word.

She paused then. This meant there was other information out there. Possibly information she *needed* if she were to bring the kingdom into the Age of Perfection.

Michale'thia finally closed the books in front of her, her head pounding from lack of sleep. By this lunch hour, the library was empty and the only things moving were the clock hands ticking somewhere in the looming shelves. Michale closed her eyes, too tired to continue, but too close to her Testing Day to stop her mind from working through all the questions she had been trying so hard to squelch.

She had seen what happened to people who failed their Testing Day. It was as if something dark had twisted their souls and began to slowly eat away at them. Her mother was the end result, and she could see in Enith's anger and Kallaren's power-hungry stare that they were on a dark road as well. She just had no idea how to stop it. Could the Jyres have done this? Or is it a natural consequence of whatever they had done in the forest to fail?

The thought haunted her, and for a moment, Michalethia's chest seemed to tighten as her breath grew shallow. She tried to catch her breath, to force air in and out of her lungs, but it all grew worse as panic set in and tears poured out. She let her pencil fall to the tabletop and set down her notebooks as quietly as she could. Eyes wide as silent cries racked her body, Michale lowered herself to her knees, weeping as she felt her body and soul crushed under fear. It was worse than when her mother tried to drown her; this came from inside of her.

The panic lasted for a few more minutes until she closed her eyes and focused on breathing slowly, reminding herself that she was here in the library, breathing, even if this perfect life was suffocating her.

***

CHAPTER 8
SYRA

Syra knocked quietly before entering the room, smiling at Michale'thia's form sitting by the window, staring out at the Botani mountains like always. A change of room didn't seem to change her at all. Neither did marriage, Syra chuckled under her breath, moving the basket of dresses onto her hip as she entered the large room and opened the closet door.

Her toned arms lifted each dress gingerly, hanging them in an order that would make choosing a dress daily quicker. She absent-mindedly hummed a soft tune, its melody carrying her mind away to that night's nightmare again. Whatever this white magic was, it saved her every time, and she was beginning to lose her fear of the night.

It was exactly eight years ago on this day, that her small, ten-year-old self, terrified and sickly, collapsed on the beach near the castle walls, finally escaping her father's hand. Syra winced at the flood of unwanted memories of the twisted forest she used to call home.

She had been sure death by monsters outside of the forest would be better than staying in it. When she had escaped and been thrown on the ground before the king and Queen of Anaratha, waiting to be eaten or crushed under their feet as her father used to warn, she had been shocked when she received insults and sneers but was told she could remain if she was a maid to the young princess. They didn't know their worst punishments in Anaratha were trivial compared to what she had seen in the dark Jyre Forest.

She had nodded fervently to the king and queen with wide eyes then, fearful and unsure of what the princess would be like but convinced anything, even death, was better than life under her father.

When she was introduced to a young girl only one year older than her, half covered in mud at the time and struggling to reign in her glare as her friend bragged about winning their mud fight, Syra's heart breathed a sigh of relief. She smiled at the memory. Michale'thia had always had a fire in her spirit in her own way, only covering it up more and more as time went on. By the age of ten, Alethian royals were officially watched for any immoral act, and for Michale'thia, somewhere around age eight was when her parents had hired a tutor to stand over her and chide her if she ever let loose an imperfect action.

Syra suddenly started as the mud-covered boy in her memory of their first meeting came into focus. Light brown skin, dimples, an impish smile.

It was Luik.

She had rarely seen the boy again after that, and to this day had never thought to connect him to the Prince of the Brends she had heard about. She shook her head, smiling to herself at the thought of the wild prince.

Later that day, Michale'thia had shut the door to her room, sat Syra down and, seeing Syra's frightened reactions to any movement, served *her* tea. Syra remembered Michale talking about everything she could think of in her life, teaching her everything she knew about the Kingdom of Anaratha for close to two hours before stopping and looking at her closely. Then, the young princess had tucked a stray curl behind her small ear and told Syra with no uncertainty that they would be best friends.

Syra smiled at the thought of young Michale'thia, with the button nose and dimpled chin. Still humming her tune, she forgot for a moment Michale'thia was still in the room.

"Syra," Michalethia's voice startled her out of her memories, "will you sit with me?"

Syra could see her friend's face as she crossed the room. Her tan skin looked paler, and even the soft freckles on her high cheekbones looked as if they wanted to disappear today.

She felt her mood darkening at the thought of Michale's coming Testing Day. She pulled her legs up to her chest as she sat down, pushing her hair behind her shoulder and waiting quietly. It always took longer than it used to when they were young, but Michale would eventually share her thoughts.

"What will it be like?" Michale's eyes pleaded with Syra.

"You already know, Michale. It will be dark and full of temptation." *The exact thing you should be running from, instead of to.*

"No. If I fail. If I succeed. Something great will change tomorrow and I'm ready neither for change nor for things to stay the same. To succeed means the rest of my life will be lived with this crushing weight of moral perfection, yet if I fail, I live with the crushing weight of shame. How can I bear it tomorrow?"

Syra was silent for a moment, lost in thought as she gazed out at the Indigo mountains in the distance, contemplating something. A determination finally settled in, and she answered, piercing Michale with a stare as she felt the familiar hum coming to life inside of her, like a bright light guiding a ship back from the sea.

"It will be good. You will make it. And someday, the weight will be lifted."

She knew it.

***

The next morning Syra's finished her routine grimly. Today was the Testing Day, and she couldn't shake her anger over the danger these royals put themselves in for the sake of finding their perfect heir. Did their history books tell them nothing? Or were they just too arrogant to see the true danger her fallen people posed? Two years ago, she had gathered her courage and snuck up to Prince Enith's room, begging him to forgo the test. She had thought she was in love with him back then. He was a gentle soul at heart and had kindly taken her hands and assured her all would be well.

When he returned though, he was anything but. She saw the shame that lurked just beneath the surface of his eyes, and she noticed the way he never looked at her anymore, even if forced to ask her for something. He had experienced the darkness of the beautiful, dangerous Jyres, and it had broken him. How could she allow this to happen to Michale'thia?

Having quickly washed up and thrown on her dress, Syra rushed to the princess's room with a simple breakfast and tea, doubting anything would be eaten.

She knocked quietly and entered, not surprised at all that Michale was already awake and curled up in her bed, staring out the window.

"Here, your breakfast. And after that, I can begin preparing you for the party." Syra couldn't fathom why the royals chose to throw a ball *before* the test for the chosen royal. It made her sick.

Michale continued to gaze at the mountains, as if refusing to eat gave her some kind of control in the world. Funny, that a possible heir to the throne could have so little.

Syra huffed and, spurred on by her anger over the whole Testing ceremony, planted a hand on her hip.

"Michale'thia Aleth Digar- Thorn."

Michale turned her head to look at Syra with wide eyes.

"Whether or not you want it, today you will walk through the most dangerous place on earth and experience perversion and darkness you have never known before. You will possibly break, possibly die, and definitely be exhausted. If you do not eat you risk failing only because your physical body did not have the strength it needs to say no, and believe me when I say of all the reasons you may fail, you would most hate it being because you could not summon the self-discipline to eat your breakfast. So please, eat."

Syra rarely spoke sternly to the princess, and never in her years of living there had ever dared to speak to a royal as an equal, but today's coming events combined with the odd energy she felt after last night's dream, brought her ample reason to.

Michale stared at Syra dumbfounded for a moment, and then seemed to shake herself out of her reverie and accept the blunt chastisement with grace. She picked up her fork and began to cut into the eggs.

Syra studied the princess for a moment longer. Her high cheekbones gave her beauty a fierceness which her dark auburn hair only accentuated, but there was something in her eyes—a sadness or loss, mixed with a fire that had not yet been put out—that made her so different. She wasn't blind to the realities of the world, though perhaps she was sheltered. But she also wouldn't give in to the way things were, and that fire made her different from other royals. She would make a formidable, lonely queen, if only this test didn't change her.

"Syra, I haven't wanted to ask this of you… I know you endured much in that forest."

"Ask it, my princess. Your brother would not listen when I spoke, but you must."

"How do I make it through whole?" Michale frowned at her own question and began pacing the silk laden room.

"I don't want to lose myself in there, like so many others who failed have. I am afraid if I fail I will turn into a bitter version of myself, like so many before me, and if I pass I will have to live a life silently killing myself inside for the sake of perfection. Please, tell me how to make it out alive."

Syra paused, realizing she had never exactly thought about why she never became dark and twisted like her kin in the forest. She was never overly intelligent, or strong, or anything. The dark deeds relished by the Jyres had just never tempted her, even though she knew nothing else. What did it all mean?

"Michale", she stared at the floor, ashamed to be so useless, "I don't know how you should do it. Just *do* what is good, no matter what your emotions say in the moment. Don't even move an inch toward whatever tempts you, and never let yourself think too hard on it. Even with all of this though… I don't think I *did* anything to not be darkened by my people. The darkness just never had a draw for me the way it did for them. I think..."

Syra was unsure how much to tell the princess.

"You think, what?" Michale leaned toward to her maid as if the lost words were imperative, eyes afire and pleading.

"Michale, I do not know what's happening to me. I have dreams that seem real, and in them I feel this strong presence of something inside me." She shook her head, knowing she sounded like a lunatic. "The other night, the... thing, the presence... it left a mark."

She pulled up her sleeve to reveal the white, glowing mark on her tan skin.

Michale gasped and gently examined the circle. Her gaze hardening as she stepped back.

"Syra, have you noticed any other signs? Anything you can possibly think of."

"No… I don't know. I am not trying to do this!" She kept her eyes down, feeling like a child caught by her scolding mother.

Michale watched her for a full moment, her arms folded across her chest.

"You must be honest with me. Do you truly not know what this marking means? Did they not teach you in The Jyre Forest?"

"I..." She hesitated again, knowing this would only unleash a new wave of panic in the princess. She had gone too far to stop now.

"In these dreams—nightmares, horrible nightmares—I am back in the forest... and... and my father finds me and speaks to me. But it's too real to be a dream, I think he is somehow really there. He is still looking for me. He told me there is magic in me. He seemed to understand what it felt like and said he would teach me to use it. But I will never go back to him, I promise!

The things he has done to me... to others, and would do to the world... I have never heard of a more evil person. In my dream that night, I was afraid, and suddenly a wave of white water crashed over us both and I woke up. It saved me, and now it has marked me. What is it that has claimed me?"

Michale's strength seemed to leave then, and she sat slowly on her bed. Her mouth parted in disbelief. Without a word, she quickly strode over to her desk and picked up a file of papers, sifting through them until she found one and began to read. Syra knew Michale studied the ancient texts, but she hadn't realized she studied them *this* much. From the number of notes on each page and the filled notebooks open next to them, she had to be putting in many hours every day.

"Here it is," she pointed to a place in the middle of the page and paced as she read.

"In the third hundredth year of the world, the sons and daughters of the Ancient Brothers were bestowed the ancient power from their veins. The deep magic was distorted and perverted by many, but few individuals, a small remnant, claimed to feel the true call of the Spring and dedicated their lives to using the power for what the Ancient Magic intended. Light set them apart and they became both disdained and revered as prophets of the Ancient Magic, dreaming and having visions of terror and hope."

Michale set the paper down and closed her eyes for a long moment, before pacing the room again, stopping every so often at her desk or the bookshelf to pick up another page of notes, only to set them down again, not finding what she needed.

Syra was too stunned to speak herself, trying to work through what the text had meant.

When Michale spoke, her voice was barely above a whisper. "Syra. Who was your father?"

Syra's took in a shaky breath, knowing she was about to admit her longest kept secret. "He is King Maendon, ruler of the Jyres."

Syra watched Michale cover her face with her hands, as if the gesture would stop the truth from being real. She took a deep breath and regained her composer.

"Why didn't you tell me?" Syra's heart threatened to crumble at the hurt and betrayal Michale'thia bore at that moment. And Syra didn't blame her.

"Michale, I was so afraid." Syra's voice cracked along with her resolve, as the terror of her father surged forward.

"I thought if I told *anyone* I would be sent back, and I can't go back to him. I would rather die." Her last words came out through choked sobs as she held her stomach, terrified of losing her friend.

Michale knelt down next to Syra and wrapped her arms around her, letting her own tears fall.

When they had both regained their composure, Michale'thia spoke with quiet awe.

"Syra, these markings mean you have power from the ancient Spring passed down to you. And not just any power, but the protection of the Ancient Magic with it. You are not just a Jyre mix-blood, you are the only living prophet we know today."

***

CHAPTER 9
MICHALE'THIA

Michale'thia sent Syra down to her own room to take the day to rest. She tried to convince herself it was out of benevolence, but she was still hoping Syra would learn of a way for her to get through her upcoming test.

Two maids entered and began the tedious work of drying her hair and preparing every stray curl to portray perfection. The women finished her hair and moved to begin putting on her makeup, only to be stopped by Michale.

"No. Today, we do something different."

"I know."

Michale'thia startled at Syra's voice. When had she switched the last maid out?

"Princess, today you will not look soft or beautiful or alluring. You will look fierce and ready for battle because to battle you will go." Syra caught her eye in the mirror and smiled.

Michale's eyes sparkled back. Exactly.

A sudden knock on the door and then a swishing of skirts signaled the entrance of the queen. Syra bowed and backed away slightly, refusing to leave Michale'thia alone by her mother.

Michale greeted her mother with silence, staring at her without emotion.

"Michale'thia, I- " Queen Ellar stood a few feet away, searching her daughter's face for some untold sign. Her mouth opened and shut again as if trying to speak but unable. She swallowed and lifted her chin.

"Do not fail today. Our kingdom needs the Heir. I have raised you to be strong. Do not disappoint me."

Michale sighed inwardly, realizing only now that she had been holding her breath, holding out hope for *something* loving from her mother. Anything.

But she was disappointed, as always.

"Yes, Mother. I will be strong."

The queen eyed her for a moment longer before turning sharply and leaving the room as suddenly as she came in.

Michale watched the door creak as the final thud of its closing resounded in her ears. Who had her mother been before the forest?

Since birth, her country had heralded itself as moral superiors in the land of Elharren because of its pure-bloodline. They didn't mix in marriage like the Brends Kingdom, lurk in the dark like the Jyres, or run away like the Botanis; neither did they become weak like the Drands, or fill up on greed as the Syllrics. And who knows what the Loharians even do.

They hoped for the Perfect Heir to fulfill the prophecy's rule, and meanwhile, they themselves strove to live without moral blemish. That made them good, didn't it? But was her mother good? Was *she*?

Michale'thia turned and sat back down in front of the mirror. Both she and Syra were silent for the remainder of the morning.

***

While normally the maids would retire to their rooms until it was time to help their ladies out of their clothes, Michale threw a dress at Syra and told her to make her hair presentable. She needed a friend by her side today.

The pair posed a striking picture. Michale'thia, princess of the greatest kingdom alive, her Anarathan tanned skin glowing and complemented by the sparkling, gray, shift-like dress she wore, uncommon to the palace. It was Michale's secret purchase from the last Syllarian trade day. The dress bared her arms fully, showing a hint of her shoulder, and then draped down until it gathered at her waist, falling once more to the floor. While most women in the room wore their corsets and large, round skirts, for once at a ball Michale could breathe and move. The dress complemented her form and allowed her comfort without throwing out the beauty.

Syra had added some light coal mixed with ground bark at her cheekbones, as well as charcoal lightly around her eyes, making her appear daring and commanding. Instead of looking like the pretty princess the palace longed for her to be, she was a fighter ready for battle.

Syra needed very little to look stunning. The simple white dress Michale had ordered for her mimicked Michale's, but lay in simple elegance, without finery needed to be stunning on her beautiful frame. Syra's white hair was pulled in a loose braid behind her head, very clearly trying to be plain while making Michale the sight to behold, but failing impossibly.

Apart, they were astonishing, but side by side the two heirs of light and dark neither stole beauty from nor gave it to one another. They seemed more akin to a sunset and sunrise appearing all at once, filling the human soul with too much emotion to bear. And together, they made their way to the ball.

The ballroom was lavishly decorated with candles and garden plants, holding the three hundred royals who lived within the main palace, all dressed, powdered and ready to hold their breaths in anticipation of this newest royal who could be their salvation.

When the two women walked in, a hushed whisper traveled through the room, hardly a child dared to move. Michale maintained her strict gaze as she sought to look at every pair of eyes in the room. She wasn't sure when she became so hardened toward the frippery surrounding this test, but she realized she was. Maybe it was from the long talks with her brother, or the many nights wondering who her parents could have been had they not been twisted by that forest, but either way, she was angry. She had no choice but to go, and no good to her came of it.

"Michale'thia! Daughter of my heart." King Jorran's voice boomed merrily from across the room as he raised his arms, as if to embrace her at such distance.

"I dare say, child, you will make the Dark Forest itself run in fear today!"

The crowd chuckled as the anxious tension began to dissipate.

Michale eyed her father and smiled, "My dear king, I hope it does."

And with that, her father's laughter let loose and the music struck up once again as everyone seemed to accept that her entrance was over. Michale made her way through the crowd, greeting royals by name and responding to the same question again and again.

"Are you ready for this test? You could be this kingdom's savior, you know."

Of course she wasn't ready. She wasn't even sure it was a good idea anymore. Standing ten feet away, she caught sight of Kallaren and groaned.

She turned to find any other stuffy royal when he suddenly appeared at her side, a hand on her shoulder.

"Michale, please. A word."

His blue eyes bore into hers and he tilted his head to the side, toward an emptier corner.

She tore her shoulder away, subtly and continued walking, letting him follow her to the far end of the large room.

"Kallaren, I do have quite a few things on my mind tonight, you know." She stopped and rubbed her temples lightly. She had less than an hour left.

He stood beside her and lowered his voice, "Why have Botani come?"

Her brows shot up, and she looked at him with disbelief.

"We have not seen a Botani warrior for three generations. What are you talking about?" She eyed him suspiciously.

"Well, it looks like the mysterious mountain kingdom may be making an appearance for your Testing Day. Even they want to see if you fulfill the prophecy." He smirked and nodded his head to a cluster of large plants on the opposite side of the room.

It took a moment for Michale to notice anything off, but then she began to see the green and browns of the plants take form into something altogether not plant-like.

He was darker than even the Brends, with skin akin to the purest chocolate. His jaw was strong and shaped with a short beard, and his hair was unlike anything she had ever seen, braided back along his head in a multitude of braids with half of it gathered high behind his head in a string while the other half lay on his back and over one shoulder. The warrior's eyes bore into hers as he held onto a spear in his hand, not threatening but watching. Carefully watching.

For a moment, the world paused, and all was silent except the slow beating of her own heart. Countless years she had stared out her window at the Indigo Mountains, finding comfort in their blue peaks. She had ached to go for reasons she couldn't explain and too often shrugged off as restlessness, but now her eyes seemed caught in a trap of his, and she could only describe the yearning for those mountains as something grave and mysterious. It wasn't a moment of infatuation or attraction, it was something deeper. Like catching of glimpse of the home her heart longed for.

Michale shook her head to snap herself out of her thoughts. She was being ridiculous and needed to confront the interloper before a scene began.

With the ball focused on her, there was no way she could move about freely and not be noticed, and she didn't trust Kallaren at this point.

But Syra could do it.

Michale looked around for her maid and found her not far away, attentive but discreet with her hands clasped in front of her. Syra nodded at Michale's brief explanation and quietly slipped away around the crowd.

"Anarathans!" Michale startled and whirled around to look at her father, standing regally in front of his throne.

Not yet, it must be too early. Please.

"The sun has moved to its third mark downward, and it is time. Today, my beloved daughter will walk through the Dark Forest and be tested for any moral fault. She will enter in, and we will cease eating and speaking, as is the way of our ancestors. As the prophecies proclaimed, our kingdom has been granted the Ancient Magic's blessing as long as the purest Alethian bloodline is on the throne. But even this is not enough to fully satisfy the dark mistake our ancient ancestors made when drinking of the Spring. We now wait for one royal to prove their incorruptibility and take the throne as the Perfect Heir we have long-awaited. It is then that we will throw the longest feast in our history and raise a resounding shout, glorying in our everlasting paradise."

The crowd around him shouted in agreement, and her father began the traditional benediction that would send her off into The Jyre Forest.

"Michale'thia, may you be ever pure."

Michale bowed her head to the king and closed her eyes, allowing herself one brief moment of silence. When she looked up, her eyes glistened with determination. Any lingering doubt or fear was swept away in the face of danger.

Michale turned and marched from the room, pulling pins out of her hair and gathering it into a practical, loose bun at the nape of her neck. Passed by the small changing room readied for her, and donned her trousers and a lightweight, long-sleeved white tunic for the journey.

The Jyre Forest was several days' journey from the palace by foot, but if she kept a steady trot on her horse, she could make it in a day and a half. There would be guards stationed at hourly intervals along the way, each with a fire signal to light as she passed. And when her test was complete, Syra would meet her on the forest's other side, where they would have a few hours of privacy to ride and talk before riding back by each guard again, who would take down his fiery torch and follow her home.

In her bag, she had packed a waterskin and her notebook, hoping to take as many notes as possible about The Jyre Forest after she was finished. Guards met her at the gate with her horse bridled and ready to go, murmuring 'good luck'" as she gracefully jumped into the saddle and took off, riding away from the ocean and toward the forest.

CHAPTER 10
BELICK

Belick's body was frozen in the *il'sone* way, feeling every word and breath from the world around him. His fingers tapped his spear methodically, counting the seconds over and over again. Watching every face in the room.

One, two, three, four…

He tapped.

Why was he even here? The Botani had cut off the rest of the world for this very foolishness, and yet the elders had sent him of all people to "watch." Watch what? He wasn't to know. Do what? He wasn't told. Belick scoffed at the memory. Perhaps it was a test of his strength. Everyone knew he despised the *deganes*, possibly more than most.

The aggressive music made it hard to focus, and Belick had to physically stop himself from rubbing his eyes. He was a formidable warrior and could win a spear fight against many of the men in his village, but he had never trained to battle a thousand instruments and a hundred thousand colors all in the same place. It was disorienting.

Through the cacophony of celebration, one thing was still. Belick's eyes seemed drawn by a thousand strings to the woman dressed in silver, who stood like a quiet mountain against the crashes of a stormy sea. She wore her elegance simply, with much less to prove than the other women in the room who obviously made up for their modesty in skin with extravagance in dress.

He stopped tapping as her eyes searched the decorative greenery and found him. She showed no fear or surprise, just staring at him with an expression he couldn't quite read, and that disturbed him. Who was she? He scowled inwardly at his timing—if only he had arrived earlier, he would likely know more answers. The woman reached out and touched a girl behind her, catching Belick off guard as the second girl's white hair spoke of obvious Jyre blood. Were the Jyres here too? Were the two kingdoms on friendly terms? That would mean ruin.

He stiffened as the white-haired woman discreetly moved around the outside of the ballroom. She was coming toward *him*!

"Anarathans!"

Belick's eyes moved toward the front of the hall as the unexpected shout rang through the room, and the music paused. The king stood looking directly at the woman in silver, who seemed to plead silently while the king obliviously ranted on.

"The sun has moved to its third mark downward, and it is time. Today my beloved daughter will walk through the Dark Forest and be tested for any moral fault..."

A light touch to his arm signaled she had arrived, and he turned his head slightly so he could better see the girl, tightening his grip on his spear as he took in her features. A picture flashed through his mind of Jyre men and women thrusting swords through his people, but as quickly as the image came, he pushed it away. He had seen many Jyres in his day, but this one held an odd resemblance to an old friend he would rather not be acquainted with again.

She was young, or innocent perhaps would be the better term, but with eyes that spoke of ancient depths. Looking at her more closely, he wondered how young she could really be with such depth in her eyes.

"Botani." Her voice held the Jyre lift to it, making normal words sound slightly rounded.

Refusing to look at her, he stood tall, watching the room.

"Jyre."

"Princess Michale'thia Aleth Thorn requests that you explain your presence here, and seek to be discreet in your movings."

The girl faced the dancing royals and spoke quietly through barely moving lips. There was something to her—certainly not her hair or angelic features—that could be trusted, making his own head swim with confusion. She was a Jyre, yet he couldn't deny that she didn't quite match those he'd known. She moved with gentleness in every step, as if she didn't want to hurt even the earth with her presence.

"The Botani elders have... felt a change of sorts... a strange change in the air. I have been sent to find out what is happening."

The girl tilted her head to the side and glanced at him, waiting for more. He stared stubbornly ahead, not wanting to admit he had the same feelings toward the mission. There should be more to it than this.

Finally the Jyre girl—wait, those freckles—the Jyre-Alethian girl, spoke.

"Something is changing, Botani warrior, and there is much for us two to speak on. Right now, I must prioritize my mistress and meet her at the forest when she returns. Will you wait for me?"

Belick hesitated for a moment, weighing her words, then made a quick decision.

"I will not wait. I will come."

***

CHAPTER 11
MICHALE'THIA

Don't think on anything too long. Just keep walking.

Michale breathed in as she stared at the looming forest before her. It was time to get this over with.

She checked her water skin for the seventh time before stepping through a gray archway, shaped from bent branches. It was dark in the forest, unnaturally so, and the air felt stale, thick and heavy somehow, as if it was trying to push her down. There was no breeze, just cold, which seemed to seep into her bones.

The mangled limbs of once beautiful trees creaked as they shifted toward her, aching to dig their talons into her skin. Even the dirt path before her seemed to writhe like a snake more, weaving and shifting menacingly, tricking her senses. Shrieks wailed in the distance, and Michale'thia looked around with wild eyes, suddenly very conscious of how alone she was.

She took a breath, feeling it catch in her throat as she *swore* she saw large dark shadows moving in the trees, and heard the faintest whispers growing and quieting, like swells in the sea. The air began to grow heavier and heavier, somehow sweet, and Michale could feel her own thoughts growing hazy. So this was how they...

Michale stopped in her tracks, unsure of where that thought was going but wary of the ground, which she swore was actually shifting around her, trying to keep her there. She continued walking, determined to not let fear keep her frozen in place, each step a small victory. Disembodied voices whispered from the brush above her, vague shadows passed on either side. Michale didn't know when it started, but a fog began to thicken until she could barely see. When it thinned, Michale found she was no longer alone.

Lining the pathway on either side of her were men and women, walking toward each other and intertwining limbs in passionate fury. Michale'thia kept her eyes down, something deep inside begging her to watch and catch a glimpse of what it looked like, but she fastened her eyes to the path and walked onward, ignoring the tension building in her own body. The scenes were wrong somehow, twisted and perverted—not depicting tender love, but something much closer to an addictive lust that *desired* to take and use rather than love and cherish. As she kept walking, feeling the pull grow stronger with each step, the whispers began again, but this time, she could make out their haunting words.

"This is your only chance to freely give in to your body..."

"When you return, there will never be this freedom again..."

"Join us..."

"No one will ever find out..."

Michale'thia tried to tune out the noises around her and quicken her pace. Suddenly she tripped over a root, arched upward from the ground in wait for her, and went sprawling across the forest floor.

When a hand reached out to help her up, Michalethia's eyes shot up in surprise. Kneeling before her when she didn't rise was a man whose beauty she could only describe as perfect. Flawless in every way. His pale skin and white hair were set on a precisely chiseled face, and his deep green eyes twinkled as he smiled playfully.

"Are you alright?" His words were soft and smooth, oddly melodic amid the creaking forest around her. She couldn't help but feel her stomach flutter when his eyes roamed her face, entranced by her very being.

She shook herself out of the spell, trying to gather her thoughts.

"I-I am fine. It's just… dark in here."

He nodded in understanding, his hands moving to her arms with familiarity as he looked into her eyes.

"It is dark, but I'm here with you. Come with me."

His hands gently caressed her arms, moving to her cheeks and making her head spin. Something about this felt wrong… What was it she had to remember?

Michale was frozen beneath his touch, her breath catching as his eyes moved to her lips and began to pull her closer.

"I would listen to every thought and dream, and we could build a small house, far from everything." He continued to speak softly, cupping her face in his hands.

It was everything she wanted. To be seen and loved, and left to live a simple, beautiful life. And Dagen hadn't given that-

Dagen. Anaratha. No.

"No!" She stepped back, breaking the trance and trying to look anywhere but at his face, only to find the images of lust and passion still lining the road around her.

"I mean, I am married. And I need to be going."

When she finally did look up, no one was there. No one moved on the side of the road or stood before her. She was alone again with the murderous looking trees looming above her.

Michale'thia shuddered. How close had she just come to giving in? She shivered again, feeling like the cold and dark were seeping into her bones.

The silence was eerie, and with each step she became more anxious, wondering when the forest would unleash its next test.

Unable to keep track of the time, Michale walked in silence, not knowing how far she had walked or how often the temptations would come.

When the whispers began again, Michale braced herself mentally for whatever they would bring. Who were they? Were they real people, or was this some kind of trick?

She heard a crack or a footstep from the shadows in the trees ahead and froze, unsure of what would come. Emerging from between the trees was a tall woman, with a crown of auburn hair floating down her back and sharp confidence in her chest.

Her mother.

"Well Michale'thia, you managed to pass the first temptation. Good." Her eyes narrowed, hard and unfeeling as she stared at her daughter with disdain.

"Come here, child."

She held out her arms to her daughter, and Michale'thia could feel her feet moving of their own accord, bringing her closer and closer to her mother's snakelike smirk.

As Michale'thia entered into the hug, she was suddenly thrust down into what she believed was a puddle in the road, but had turned into a deep well of water. Michale'thia grasped at the edges of the hole, fighting desperately to get out even as her mother's hands pushed her deeper in, her beautiful face smiling the entire time. Michale's lungs burned, and she could feel the panic rising in her chest as the weight of the water stole any chance of breathing from her.

This couldn't be happening again. Was this to be her life? Fighting constantly just to *breathe*?

As she fought desperately, she found a small foothold nestled into the side of the rock and began searching the dark water for more. They were just high enough for her to be able to step into them and push herself out against her mother, hopefully knocking her back enough to give Michale time to climb over the side and onto dry land.

With lungs burning, she dug her feet into footholds and pushed herself upward with as much force as she could muster. Her head exploded through the surface and she threw her weight sideways into her mother, hearing a grunt as they both tumbled to the side. Michale scrambled to gain her footing, sucking in air quickly while trying to get as far away from the queen as she could. Her head pounded, and she could feel blood trickling down onto her face.

Her mother lay crumpled by the pool, grabbing at her bleeding nose and screeching in anger.

"I promise you, Michale'thia, I will be in every shadow, and every nightmare! You will never have peace with me here! I will turn every friend against you until you are the only one left, alone, weak, and the greatest failure our kingdom has seen!"

The queen had stopped holding her nose now, her lip curled as hatred poured out of her eyes, her face bloody and crazed.

That's when Michale'thia saw it. Nearly covered by dirt, and rusted along the edges, was a large knife set in an intricately designed golden handle. Her mother saw it just as she did, and Michale'thia jumped to grab it first, coming face to face with the venomous woman as she did so. The whispers continued to come in waves from above, sometimes deafening, sometimes barely audible, and the darkness lay like a cloth around them.

Michale held the knife at her mother's throat, staring into her crazed eyes. In that moment, she realized something.

There was no love left inside of her for the wicked woman who bore her 19 years ago, only pure, hot hatred. And Michale could stop it all. She could stop the torturous games, stop the fear, and stop the cruelty. With one flick of her wrist, she could give back to her mother all the darkened queen had done.

Her hand shook as she raged inside, *wanting* so much to see the life drain from her mother's eyes, if only to find peace at night again. Or to finally have justice. Or to finally feel powerful.

Michale blinked. She wanted power enough to kill a human being. The realization stilled her.

She hated her cruel mother… but she was still a human. Still worthy of life...

Michale'thia turned and pulled her arm back, launching the blade into the forest somewhere, then took one last look at her mother's snarling face before running down the path. She hadn't made it a hundred feet when the whispers stopped in perfect unity, and Michale'thia looked back to find her mother and the puddle in the distance both gone.

Mind racing, Michlae continued nervously on, now more confused as ever with her still-wet hair and clothes proving the last temptation was real to some extent. She was exhausted already, ready to drop to the ground and sleep, but she continued walking lest the creeping trees catch her.

Fatigue was setting in, a weariness she had never experienced before, and a headache making every movement more painful.

The path before her snaked around a grouping of trees and Michale'thia silently begged for an end to this. There was a deep mental ramification to resisting, but there was also a physical one, and she wasn't sure how much more she could take.

When she rounded the corner, careful not to come too close to any of the trees, the sight before her stunned her into a full stop.

There, in the middle of the path was a man, quite beautiful in his middle-aged years, sitting at a table covered in food, dressed in the finest clothes and waiting. For her.

The man smiled knowingly at her reaction and rose to meet her. Michale'thia wasn't sure if she should politely stay or run and just forgo whatever this temptation would be, but the man's long stride had him in front of her before she could decide.

He stretched out a hand in greeting and gave a small bow.

"My dear Michale'thia." He gave her a fatherly smile. "I have waited a long time to meet you."

Michale shook her head, trying to clear the fog in her mind a little more before responding. He saw the motion, and his eyes widened apologetically.

"Oh, I'm sorry! Here, this will help those effects wear off. We need you in clear mind for our dinner."

He held out a small vial of light pink liquid and laughed when she hesitated.

"Don't worry, if I wanted to kill you, I would have had ample time to do that, here in my kingdom."

With shaking hands, Michale grasped the vial and took a sip, then waited for a moment, looking warily at the man. When her headache began to slowly dissipate, she drank the rest, feeling everything come into focus again and a small bit of energy return.

He smiled, his green eyes brightly contrasting his white hair. At least her history books weren't lying when they said the Jyres and Botani people were the most beautiful. This man looked otherworldly.

"Better?" He held out his arm to escort her to the table. Every warning bell in her mind ringing, but she saw no way around it. This was her test, and she had to play by their rules.

"Much needed, thank you. And what should I call you, since you already know my name?"

He smiled, "You can call my Oren. It's what my friends call me."

Oren pulled out a chair at the small round table for her, and she took a seat. The food in front of her was brighter and smelled more savory than anything she had experienced outside of the forest, and her mouth began to water as her stomach ached with hunger.

Oren's laugh sounded genuine, and he motioned to the food, "Please, fill yourself up. We have the finest cooks here."

Michale'thia gave him a smile of her own, working toward making herself look more relaxed than she was. She counted eleven different plates to choose from, each filled to the brim with foods. She opted to try three and see how she felt after that. No use putting more on her plate if she was about to be poisoned.

She cut a small oval-shaped piece of meat and watched with interest as a yellow sauce flowed from the inside, complementing the crisp outer layer.

Tilting her head, Michale looked up at Oren with what she hoped was polite curiosity, not the fear she actually felt.

"So, Oren. You put quite the effort into this shared meal. What did you wish to speak of?"

Oren smiled knowingly, wagging a finger in the air lightly as he dabbed his chin with a napkin.

"You *are* intelligent. I thought so." He set his napkin down and straightened.

"I want to make a deal with you, Michale'thia. One that will benefit both of us."

She struggled to keep the disbelief from her face. Why would he ever believe she would make a deal with him? She had been taught since birth, through every nursery rhyme and school lesson, to *never* make a deal with the Jyres. It would, in the end, cost much more than you bargained for.

She set her fork down without taking a bite and placed her hands in her lap, a smile of her own on her lips now. She could play his game.

"I'm listening, Oren."

He studied her, his eyes tightening ever so slightly around the edges.

"I know you have been searching for the truth behind Anaratha's prophecy." He smiled at her startled expression and continued. "And we both know there is more to the prophecy than your kingdom understands. I have access to every scroll with every prophecy revealed in this forest, and I am willing to give them all to you."

Michale's smile fell, and she leaned forward, a hard glare now on her own face as the game seemed to fade and the real conversation began. How could the *Jyres* have more knowledge of the prophecies then they did?

Her mind was scrambling to understand, not finding a single plausible answer on her own.

"But, it is not going to say what you hope it will say. There is no Perfect Heir. There is no hero coming to bring you back to the Age of Perfection. In fact, the only way we will get back to the Age of

Perfect is if the Ancient Spring is found again, and we have the power to create once more."

His eyes looked over her shoulder into the distance as his own thoughts took him somewhere else. Then blinking, Oren smiled at her.

"I would need something in return, however. Here in this forest, we have been creating a way to simulate the Age of Perfection, and we can create the joy of it in your kingdom as well, with you on the throne. *Only* you would know the truth of the prophecies. To the rest of the kingdom, you would be the Perfect Heir they are looking for, and with our help, of course-would lead them into their desired Age of Perfection. It will be beautiful, indeed." The words began to sound like silk as he painted the picture before her.

"There will be no more arguments, no more pain, no more hurt or pretending. Your people will live in absolute joy, and you will lead them. All we would want from you is full cooperation and alliance. In exchange, you will have full knowledge, full power, and full prestige. We would simply be...in the background."

Michale's head swirled as his words muddled everything she had once believed, both confirming and distorting what she had known. There were too many pieces to this, too many questions.

"How does your... simulation work?"

He shook his head, lifting a finger to his lips.

She rubbed her temples, trying to make sense of it all. The prophecy was a lie. They would not ever get to the Age of Perfection. At best, they could have the false pretense and live happily, and she could *finally* answer all the questions she had yearned to understand.

But it would all be a beautiful, terrible lie.

Was a lie worth the happiness of her kingdom?

She paused, trying to slow down and breathe. What if *this* was a lie?

The Jyres built their entire kingdom in this forest by taking what was good and twisting and mangling it for their own gain.

The reminder from countless history lessons echoed Michale'thia realized her decision was already made. She could not let her kingdom live under a pretense of goodness, and she could not bind them to the Jyres.

As if he knew her answer the moment she thought it, Oren's own face contorted into a wicked mask of anger. Michale'thia stood, raising her chin and throwing a defiant look back at him.

"I must be going."

Michale'thia walked away, every muscle tense and expecting to be attacked at any moment as the air once again began to grow heavy, and the whispers returned in their ebb and flow. The ache in her body returned, and the exhaustion settled back in, even worse than before, bringing tears to her eyes. She didn't know how long she had been in the forest, but it felt like days. And by the look of it, she still had a long road ahead.

***

It was through a haze that Michale could see the light. Small and unwavering, growing larger with each inch forward she dragged herself, but it was there. She was finished. Tears rolled down her cheeks as overwhelming relief pulsed through her veins, giving her strength to move forward.

Michale passed by an especially gnarled tree, almost feeling sorry for the twisted creature. At least she could escape. The trees here had endured this place for thousands of years.

How many temptations had there been? Fifty? Sixty? She dragged her pack behind her, with the long-empty waterskin rattling on each bump in the ground. Would there be ten more tests before reaching that beloved exit?

She forced every step forward, slowly gaining speed as the archway to the light bid her forward. As Michale'thia finally stumbled through the light-layden archway out of the Dark Forest, a roaring tore through her ears, and searing pain began to radiate through her body. She clutched her head, panting, unsure if the screaming she heard was her own or Jyre beasts.

Minutes passed until her vision cleared, and she found herself collapsed on the ground, barely able to take another breath from exhaustion. Laying there on the dry edge of the Loharan Desert, tears poured down her cheeks and a sob caught in her throat. She cried for the pain she had endured, for the images she had seen, and for the desire she had felt every single time to give in. She now knew without a doubt the darkness was inside of her.

All at once, two thoughts sank in, one like a weight lifting and the other like a thousand boulders crashing onto her chest.

She hadn't given in. She had passed her Testing Day.

But she had wanted to give in every single time.

Michale's eyes widened in horror, and her mouth opened and shut as if to plead with the threads of reality to change her fate. She was the Heir her kingdom had been waiting for, and yet inside she was the most vile creature to ever walk this earth. She couldn't be the Perfect Heir. Did an heir even exist?

Delirious with exhaustion, Michale pushed herself off the ground and began to walk. Instead of following the edge of the forest, where she knew she would meet Syra, she walked slowly away, toward the desert. Anywhere but toward the kingdom she was soon to destroy.

She couldn't tell anymore what time it was or which direction she was heading. All Michale knew was that it had been hours she was dangerously thirsty, desperate for the water that had long since been gone from her waterskin. Why did the air feel like sand? Or was it her mouth sticking to itself? She fought the blackness hovering at the edge of her vision as long as she could until it finally her, taking her consciousness with it.

***

Muted voices murmured above her, and Michale felt something nudge her leg with a grunt. She attempted to open her eyes but found even that too hard. Her head was pounding, and her body ached. She groaned, and in response, small hands lifted her head, and she felt water pour down her throat. No, not water, something scented. The muted sounds became clearer as the pounding began to subside. Whose hands were these? And what did they give her?

"Navaid, unpack the horse and make a fire. Navaid! Hurry, child!" An old woman's crackling voice came from Michale's left, followed by swift feet scurrying away and rustling a bag close by.

Michale began to open her eyes, fluttering them at first until she was finally able to keep them open longer and look around. The woman in front of her had long black hair pulled together by a string behind her neck, and though her face was lined with wrinkles, her skin still looked strong, ready to meet any task. She sat with her legs crossed, looking down at the small bowl in which she was crushing herbs to make a paste, humming as she went. Michale took in her hardy clothing and realized she herself was freezing. Where was she? Panic set in, and she made a feeble attempt to get up before realizing the drink that had helped her feel better could only do so much. The older women's eyes flicked up to her when she moved, narrowed in disapproval.

Michale started. Her eyes! They were tilted slightly in the Loharan way. Was she...? She hoisted herself up onto her elbows, ignoring the pain, and looked around at the never-ending desert before collapsing back down again, forgetting she didn't have a pillow beneath her and moaning in regret.

The old woman's leather face appeared above her, an eyebrow arched and lips puckered.

"Don't be foolish, child. You are too weak. And don't fuss with me, this is for your good." She spoke with a commanding abruptness and began to smother a thick, green paste all over Michale's face and shoulders. Michale gasped and quickly realized that was a horrible idea as she breathed in what she believed was the most putrid smell in all of Elharren. She gagged for a moment, heaving as her stomach tried to empty out the nothing that was in there.

"Stop, girl, relax your body. You will get used to the smell, and it will help."

Michale tried to not breathe in, but her lungs eventually won out over her nose, and she tried not to make a face at the old woman as she hobbled back over and began to wipe the paste off with a rag.

Despite the volatile smell, Michale no longer felt pain in her body and suddenly had the energy to sit up and gingerly stand. The young boy shot glances at her from the corner of his eye as he added things to the pot over the fire.

Michale tried not to stumble as she slowly made her way over to it and sat down, losing herself in the flames. She had passed the test, but something felt wrong. She didn't feel any great power or assurance that she was her kingdom's savior. If anything, she realized more than ever that she was muddled with darkness inside of her. What was she to do? How was she to rule perfectly, imperfect as she was?

"Your face is too sad for a girl your age. You should be happy." The old crone lifted a stick she had found and waved it toward her with false menace. Not getting a smile or laugh from Michale, the woman sat down and sighed, leaning forward with one eye widened as she studied her, as if getting closer to her would give her answers.

"Why are you here?"

Michale sighed and threw a rock into the fire.

"I am here because I am not what I should be. And I don't know what to do."

The boy poured water from a small goat skin into the pot and stirred it above the crackling fire. The old woman waited for her to continue.

At this point, Michale doubted the pair were robbers or kidnappers but wasn't sure how much she could trust them. The woman's frankness put Michale at ease, but her own ease said nothing about what was true. The forest had taught her that much.

"What are *you* doing out here? And what should I call you?" She tried to turn the questions toward them.

"I live here, and we travel often to gather herbs for healing. I am Ni, and this is Navaid, my grandson. Now that you know we aren't here to harm you, tell me why you are out in the desert dying, royal Alethian."

Michale cursed her features. Did everyone on earth know they took this stupid test? The fire cracked in front of her, and she found solace in it while she spoke.

"Today," she paused and looked up at the moon, "or yesterday, was my Testing Day. It is our Anarathian tradition and the prophecy's bidding, as we search for the one perfect person without moral failings who can rule the kingdom and satisfy the Ancient Magic."

When she mentioned the prophecy, Ni scoffed lightly under breath. Michale looked up at her.

"And you failed," she said flatly.

Michale lowered her eyes to the fire again, feeling the weight of a thousand worlds on her chest.

"No. I passed. I am who my kingdom has been looking for."

She kept her eyes on the fire, suddenly all too aware of how she must look in her ragged clothing, now covered in dirt. She expected an outburst or astonishment, or really anything except for the silence she received.

Michale finally mustered the courage to look up at the old woman, and almost burst out in laugher at her unique facial expression. Her eyes were narrowed, and her lips puckered out as she craned her neck forward, studying Michale. At the moment, she looked more akin to a frog than a Loharan healer.

Moments passed, and the woman seemed to find whatever she was looking for, giving a curt nod to herself and sitting back again.

"You are not what your kingdom needs."

Michale didn't know why she felt offended at being told what she knew to be true. "Then what does it need? I didn't give in to a single temptation. I-"

"Girl, I will not tell you again. You are not what your kingdom needs and you Anarathans know less than you think about the Ancient Magic." Ni smacked her mouth shut in emphasis of her last word, refusing to say more.

Michale scowled, "And how would you know? Have *you* been studying the ancient texts for hundreds of years? Anarathia has built our entire kingdom on following the Ancient Magic and..." Her eyes widened in realization, and she glared at Ni.

"How do you know what we know? Are there spies in our kingdom?"

Ni cackled at the thought before sobering again and staring into the fire, muttering about not needing spies.

What the older women said next would change Michale's life and ultimately, everything she once knew.

"Ti kilna sho li amehe Oen."

It was only a whisper, barely even audible, but the earth itself seemed to pause and listen. Michale's heart stopped for a moment, and she felt like the air had been sucked out of her lungs.

Children wait for the Perfect One.

The phrase that ended every fragment they had of the prophecy. On top of it being *in* the prophecy, it was *always* added to the end of the scrolls, for reasons much debated by scholars in Anaratha.

Michale's mind whirled; for Ni to know the phrase by heart meant she had to have studied the ancient language and prophecies. Which meant the Loharans must have ancient scrolls too. This entire time Anaratha thought they alone held the secrets of the ancient texts, not knowing the Loharan's had been hiding some of their own. Were they different?

Michale stood and tried to contain her desperation.

"How do you know that phrase? Do the Loharans have ancient scrolls?"

Ni's face had already closed off again. "I cannot answer your questions. Eat, girl. You will need it for your journey home."

"Please, at least tell me if there is more to the prophecy than we know!"

Ni's lined face stared blankly at her, and Michale'thia feared the old woman would refuse to answer at all, but then she spoke slowly, measuring every word.

"You know less than you think in Anaratha."

Michale'thia sat stunned. So they were wrong. Her kingdom was wrong, and the Loharans knew it as common knowledge. Her whole life had been dictated by this one prophecy, and it may not even be the full picture.

Navaid quietly handed his grandmother a bowl of fragrant soup and then brought a bowl for Michale before ladling himself a portion. They ate in silence as Michale worked through what she had learned. If Ni was just a wandering healer woman, their scholars must be far more knowledgeable than those in her own kingdoms. The Loharans had disappeared long ago when Lohan did and held themselves up in the desert, where few outsiders choose to live. Some believed they guarded the Ancient Spring, while others accused them of being cowards, hiding away from all conflict and wars. Either way, she needed to come back and find their people. Her kingdom depended on it.

"Please. I need to know what you know about the prophecies. Can I come with you? Back to your people?"

The woman cackled, "They would not welcome you, Royal Anarathan. You may not come."

Michale'thia leveled the woman with a stare, not willing to back down.

"My *entire life* has been dictated by the test. I passed but found no joy in it, only the greatest weight of knowing I *am still tainted* inside. I will go back and be crowned the Heir to the throne, and my people will rejoice in our eternal utopia that I am *supposed* to lead us into. But we both know it won't work, will it? Somehow, our hundreds of years of study has brought us to the wrong conclusion. Ni, if I do not find the truth, my kingdom will crumble." Michale'thia looked down, tears welling in her eyes as she realized the truth behind her fear. "And it will be my fault. I *need* to know the truth."

Ni studied her for a moment.

"We do not have all the answers. We wait for Lohan to return. If you can make it to our people, I will ensure you are at least fed and cared for—but I cannot promise you will be welcomed. If you get there, you are on your own. I will not stand against my own people. Travel at night when it is cool. There," she pointed up at the night sky, "follow that star north, and we will find you."

Michale looked at the star, committing it to memory as much as possible. It was brighter than the rest, known by her people as the "dreaming star," which never moved and helped sailors know their direction. She had never studied the stars much, but it would seem she now had a reason to.

She nodded and thanked Navaid for the food, wincing at her aching muscles before standing to start her long journey back home. Her hair had all but come out of her bun, now gently flying across her face in the dusty breeze against her dirt-smudged face. She would certainly be a sight to behold when she arrived.

The sun was beginning to rise already and she knew by now Syra would be frantically looking for her. It was time to go home and face her kingdom.

CHAPTER 12
BELICK

The wind whipped across their faces as they raced west toward The Jyre Forest. They had been riding for west for a day in silence, stopping to rest for a small few hours before waking again to head around the southern part of the forest, then north again, where Michale'thia should emerge on the other side somewhere.

It was all a guessing game now, infuriatingly enough. From what Syra had explained, every royal came out different, just as every Test ran a different course. Some came out within an hour, still holding the same amount of energy as when they began, while others lasted an entire half-day before stumbling out, barely able to walk. They should have left there hours ago, but between Belick waiting to move until people had cleared out of the ballroom and the guards deciding if a Jyre should go toward the Dark Forest, they had left later than Syra would have liked. Belick could see her biting her lip nervously, glancing at the setting sun every so often. It would be dark soon. By now, the princess had been in the forest for hours. This test was a foolish notion. Belick shook his head in disgust.

"Botani warrior, we need to ride faster. The princess may already be out of the forest."

His only response was to lean down and whisper a word to his horse that spurred him into a gallop. Her horse naturally followed lead and they sped on through the twilight.

***

Belick had not been so far from their mountains in a long time; he had forgotten how difficult the world down here was. There was a mustiness to the air he despised, and the people chased after every fanciful belief. He needed to be back in his mountains, where he could breathe.

Since riding closer to The Jyre Forest, though, he had felt a foreboding he couldn't shake. This land was evil and had seen many evils.

"The Well inside of me trembles, with rage or fear I do not know. *Oounehle Oen, masulan ien.*"

He whispered the ancient prayer, befitting for this place. He kept his eyes sharp, ready for an attack at any moment. Syra seemed unsettled too, afraid even, constantly looking toward the forest as if it would jump out at her and plunge her into its dark foliage. It wasn't normal. The trees loomed with a crooked arch in their trunks like disfigured men, their bark scarred with lines, their branches sharp and curved like talons to ensnare any who dared enter. Someone had twisted and perverted the Ancient Magic's creation here, and Belick was afraid it could never be undone. Sadness swept over him at the thought.

Why would the Anarathans choose this for their best?

He reined his horse and sidled up to Syra, wondering what she must be thinking.

"You are from here."

"Yes." She kept her eyes ahead, refusing to look at him.

"But you do not have the darkness the forest has. How can that be?" They had slowed their horses now that they were on the final stretch of the forest ridge, giving their horses a much-deserved break.

Syra shrugged her strong shoulders and didn't elaborate. Why were women so difficult? They talk about all the wrong things and then are quiet when they should talk about the right things.

"How are you so different from your people?" he pressed. He had a theory, but he didn't want to give anything away until he was sure.

"I do not know."

Belick continued to study her, knowing there was more to it.

"Syra, your people have twisted and mangled creation for thousands of years, and yet here you are, a Jyre who, from what I have seen, doesn't even want to hurt the grass beneath your horse's hooves. How are you not like them?"

Minutes passed before Syra spoke so quietly her words were almost lost in the wind, her large green eyes somber as she looked at him.

"I believe it was not me. I wasn't like them even from birth, but even if I was, something… something called me away. It started when I was young, but *somehow* I was born tied to this outside world, hating the Delvior and all they do. I have tried to understand it, but I do not. All I know is I began to have nightmares where my father visited me, looking for me, and a white light, like a wave, would save me. I woke up with this."

She held out her arm so he could see the marking on her wrist, and he gasped. Belick muttered words in Botani she couldn't understand and kicked his horse forward, leaving her watching his back in confusion.

He had suspected the Ancient Magic had called her, but this? This would mean she was a Spring Warrior, one of the very highest honors in his kingdom. The Spring Warriors heard the Ancient Magic's call and spoke its words to the people, guarding the Spring and administering it to the earth. How had a Jyre girl gotten the marking? Was this a perversion of the Jyre people?

He shook his head in anger. It could not be. There is no faking the Ancient Magic's touch. What's more, he didn't feel the same darkness in her as he did the forest. Belick couldn't deny she seemed exactly like the other Light Warriors. Pure. Gentle.

A scream rang out behind him, and Belick whipped around to see Syra surrounded by a group of Jyre men, knives in hand and ropes seeming ready to pull her off her horse and drag her in. His training kicked in, and he wheeled his horse around and into a gallop. How had he gotten so far ahead of her? The Jyres had to have been watching for this moment.

The air left Belick's lungs as one man stood out among the rest. Taller, and strikingly beautiful. A man he had hoped he would never see again. Belick kicked his horse into a gallop, fear and rage too tightly mixed together for him to sort out.

Belick watched in a blur as the man suddenly tensed and screamed something, lunging at her.

Then the world exploded in white.

***

Syra

Terror pulsed through Syra as she registered her father's looming form. Her horse danced nervously as she frantically looked for any space between his men to escape, but they knew her well and circled her tightly, ropes and knives held at the ready.

No, no, no! She couldn't go back! Her breaths came in short, panicked spurts as her father inched closer.

"I told you I'd find you, daughter. It was only a matter of time." His wicked grin was beautiful and terrible, and Syra fought for calm as memories surged. She would die before going back with him.

He approached her slowly, every movement and word speaking to his authority.

"Syra, my child, calm yourself. Why did you run from me? I promised you *everything.* I will teach you how to control the magic in your veins, and together we will do great things."

At the word 'control' something inside Syra rebelled, rising up and swelling within her chest. It was not to be controlled. Syra closed her eyes too, for the first time, welcoming the magic she has so often tried to quiet.

"You will rule beside me and learn to love the way we rule the earth. Syra, look at me!" His own voice had taken on a frantic edge, but she could barely hear as the roaring in her ears grew.

His steps quickened, and he lunged to grab hold of her, but it was too late. The magic burst free, exploding in hot furry, and everything went white.

Syra found herself on the ground ten feet away from where her horse, the only thing miraculously still standing in the heap of men scattered about her. Her father lay unconscious and bleeding from his nose a few feet away from where he had been, and his men were strewn about on the ground, some in grotesque angles. Syra stood shakily, panting as she bent over and emptied her stomach. Her body shook uncontrollably, and she wasn't sure she could walk. Syra turned at the sound of footsteps running toward her, afraid at first her father had woken, but relieved to see Belick run to her side and kneel down beside her with his waterskin. He silently lifted it to her lips and helped her drink. As the shock began to wear off, sobs overtook her. The moon was at its highest point, and the trees rustled in the wind. Belick scooped her up and walked over to her horse, guiding it away from the bodies, gently setting her on top as if she might break.

He stood there in front of her, quiet and troubled, before patting her horse and walking back to his own, silently committing to ride beside her for the rest of the journey.

Syra's head began to clear, and she pondered through the events that had taken place. The explosion… it was… she *did* have magic. And it was alive inside of her, listening and moving. Everything in her dreams had been real…

Belick was unharmed, but every other man lay about on the grass, dead or unconscious she did not know. Somehow, the Magic had only affected them, and she wasn't sure if she felt comforted at the thought or unnerved. This wasn't something she could entirely control.

The pair walked on through the night in silence, searching the forest's edge for any sign of the princess. Could she have been taken by the dark king too? Fear welled up in Syra at the thought, and she redoubled her efforts to find Michale'thia.

Hours passed with no sign of her, and they had already had to turn around and retrace their path after going too far. Syra could barely keep her eyes open and swayed in her saddle. She tilted her head back and looked up at the starry sky for a moment in hopes of waking herself up a bit. As her gaze lowered back down to the horizon, she gasped. There, from the Loharan Desert she saw a figure limping toward the road.

She nudged Belick and pointed, both waiting quietly.

Syra whispered, "It doesn't matter if it is her or not. Whoever it is needs help."

Belick nodded, and they broke out in gallop toward the limping figure. As they neared, the full moon's light revealed Michale'thia's features and her tattered riding clothes, and Syra nearly wept with relief.

The princess was found. They would bring her home. When they came close enough to see her face though, Syra knew something was wrong.

***

CHAPTER 13
ENITH

Enith woke in his chair on the balcony with a start. He had barely slept the night before and had spent the past three days, nearly driving himself insane, pacing his bedroom.

He looked out over the land, as he had done over and over again this evening to see if any of the five fire signals they could see had been put out yet, signaling her return. But they had burned on infuriatingly through the night, lighting a bright line to The Jyre Forest.

Her worthless husband hadn't even shown up yet, the pig's arse.

Enith called for kauf to be brought and drank the bitterness down before pouring another cup and rubbing his eyes. It had been years since he had slept well. Two years, actually. Since his own Testing Day.

Trumpets suddenly shook him from his thoughts, waking Enith more than the strong drink could. He threw off his wrinkled clothing, quickly donning a fresh shirt, and begn jogging down the hall toward the courtyard, slowing into a dignified walk just in time to meet the king and queen on the steps outside the door. His mother looked him over and gave him an endearing smile, coming over to him to take his hand.

"My son!"

He pulled his hand away, putting some distance between them as he watched the fireline. Refusing to look at her.

"Mother."

Her face hardened, and she dropped her hands to her side.

Enith could hear her beginning to sniff and looked over in time to see her wipe tears from her eyes.

"Enith, please, a mother cannot endure-"

He held up a hand, cutting her off from her theatrical scene. Enith spoke quietly, every word coming out hard and crisp.

"I am not one of your palace fools, Mother. I know when you are faking it, and I will not be manipulated. Tell me what you want and leave me be."

She blinked in surprise, and the tears stopped immediately, replaced by a dark smile that twisted her lips more than lifted them.

"Very well. There are matters we need to speak of. We are working *hard* here to better this kingdom, and your support is vital."

Enith scowled. What could they possibly be trying to do to better the kingdom? No part of him cared to side with her or hear her plans, so instead, he continued watching the fireline, allowing the hour to pass in quiet.

The fireline finally approached the outer gates of the palace, and Enith could feel his own heart beginning to race. It was not the same eagerness of his kingdom- hoping Michale'thia would be Heir they had waited for, it was fear. Fear that her sweet fire would be ruined if she failed. That she would become like him, drowning in anger, soon to be like his own mother.

The gates were now open to their fullest, and Enith craned his neck to catch a glimpse of his sister.

He squinted and took a step forward, mouth dropping in surprise. Was that a...

The queen hissed beside him, and a hush came over of the crowd.

Michale'thia had arrived with a Botani warrior.

The warrior rode beside her on one side, with Syra on the other, both watching her carefully as she swayed in her saddle, barely managing to keep upright.

The crowd parted, and whispers began to spread like wildfire through the kingdom.

The princess went to her Test and returned with a legendary Botani warrior at her side.

His father pushed his way through the crowd with his councilmen trailing behind, and the Botani slid off his horse before slowly helping her off as well. Enith would be annoyed if he couldn't see even from a distance how weak she was. Where was her bloody husband?

It looked like she could collapse at any moment. What happened in there? Enith barely held himself back from rushing to her side, knowing she already had enough people surrounding her.

The crowd quieted, and the king's voice echoed across the courtyard.

"Daughter, Princess Michale'thia Aleth Thorn, did you walk in the Dark without blemish?" It was the traditional phrase asked of every contestant after their test. They may be royals with the status to rule, but they also had to stand before an entire kingdom and admit their failing if they didn't pass the forest's test.

Everyone held their breath as they did every Testing Day. Enith fidgeted as he waited, wishing she would just answer but seeing an internal struggle going on inside of her.

Then slowly, she looked up and met her father's eyes, and with a clear voice that would ring across the land, she gave the answer no royal had ever been able to give before.

"I have walked the Dark path and stayed pure, for the sake of the Ancient Magic and the kingdom."

The roar began slowly, from those closest to the Princess first, then slowly building as it moved outward down to the last soldier on the wall. The rallying of the kingdom was so great the farmers in the foothills only needed to hear the shouts to join in themselves and rejoice that their Heir had been found.

It was an eternity until the shouts of joy subsided, and her father spoke the next traditional words steadily, only the rocking of his heels betraying his excitement.

"Come forth and show the truth."

She stepped forward on shaky legs and held out her arm. The king's councilmen stepped forward and took her arm gingerly, looking up and with wide eyes at the king.

The one who seemed to lead the group exclaimed, "She does not have the mark of condemnation! She is pure!"

And the crowd once again erupted into cheers. The king pushed his way past the councilmen to see for himself, before engulfing his daughter in a hug and spinning her around, oblivious to the look of pain on her face.

Springs, she must have been through Jyren's grave. Enith looked down at his own mark of failure, with a pang of anger. Those who failed bore the sign of it for the rest of their days. Legend said it was a sign that a piece of your soul was forever attached to the Jyre people. He shuddered at the thought.

The entire kingdom joined in for a day of celebration. People pulled out instruments and played in the streets, feasts were spread on every corner, and dancing ensued late into the night. Enith watched from his balcony, confusion and frustration clouding his thoughts.

This is what the kingdom had been waiting for, now that it had come, he wasn't so sure he wanted the prophecy to be fulfilled. But then, he didn't want everything to be destroyed by the Ancient Magic. And his sister? Enith found no fault in her, but he also didn't want this role for her. Give it to anyone else. Let her be. Let both of them be.

A knock rapped on his door, and he strode over to throw it open. Surprised by his visitor, Enith grabbed the man by the shirt to throw him against the wall.

"Where in Jyren's Grave have you been." He was breathing heavily, glad for a place to pour out his anger.

Dagen grabbed his hands and pulled them from his shirt, his own anger rising, tempered only by understanding.

"I got here as fast as I could, Enith. Luik's kingdom is not exactly an easy place to order. It has been a raging battle there, just sneaking away nearly cost Luik and I both our lives."

Enith forgot his anger, "Luik's here?"

Dagen shook his head, "No, he had to stay in his kingdom. But he did manage to get me out in what we both thought would be perfect timing." He wiped his face with his hand, leveling Enith with a stare.

"I am her husband, Enith. I would be here for her. Now, tell me what happened."

Enith launched into a brief retelling of what he knew, which wasn't much at all.

"Are they letting anyone in to see her?" Dagen asked.

"No, not even me. Syra is tending to her, but I don't think Michale is even awake. The doctors have been in and out all day."

"I have to see her." Dagen turned toward the door, ready to storm the bedroom if he had to.

"Dagen, wait." He turned only slightly, making it clear he wouldn't be dissuaded.

"She passed. Which makes her the Heir to the throne, effective the moment the king's advisors saw her unmarked skin. You are now in line to be king. And I am pretty sure there are quite a few things that are needing to be done about that."

Enith felt his own heart break as the man sat down slowly in a nearby chair, eyes wide with shock. He didn't know Dagen well, and he still thought he was a swine for not being here sooner, but the look of confusion and grief that crossed his face was all too familiar. Dagen didn't want to be king. Enith guessed the man had secretly believed no one in their lifetime would actually pass their Testing Day. He would have been free to live at his estate, free from gossiping royals and suffocating palace life. But as sure as the seasons change, so did history, and Dagen was swept up in it.

Dagen looked up at Enith, seeming a broken man. "What do I do?"

Enith grabbed his hand like he would to help a sparring opponent rise and pulled Dagen up, clapping a hand on his shoulder.

"Go see Michale'thia. Then, when you both rise in the morning, figure out this new life together."

***

In the days that followed, Enith waited for something to change. Anything. To feel better somehow, or for their entire kingdom to be pulled in one swift motion into another land where everyone would be happy. But nothing came. He cycled between drink, sleep, and jogging the outer walls of the palace. The servants knew to wake him if Michale woke, and there was nothing he could do now.

He checked the clock and groaned. It was the fifth hour of the day, with the sun just starting to turn the sky shades of blue. He had been up for hours already, brooding and pacing. Enith changed into his training pants and a looser shirt, deciding it was high time he began his exercises again.

Jogging past the palace walls, he wondered in irritation if his squadron was keeping up with their own physical strength. They'd better be, or he planned to teach them a good lesson the next time they sparred.

Enith realized he would need to replace his fallen soldiers and felt sick to his stomach. So was the way of life, especially a soldier's life. Unless everything changed like it was supposed to.

Picking up speed, he bounded around the castle's corner wall, making his way toward a small hill a half-mile out that he usually ran before ending at the waterfront. Today, he bounded up the incline, thankful for the cool morning air, and stopped at the top of the hill to take in the view.

Below on the beach, he saw movement, a flash of white hair, and Syra jogged out of the water, taking a few minutes to catch her breath, before beginning a series of movements in repetition. Enith's eyes widened as he recognized the drills as military training. What was she doing?

He crept down the hill and into the tree brush, hoping to get a better look. Did the guards know about this?

Syra moved with grace, making the harsh stances he taught his men look more like a dance than a fight, but still doing each one with more precision than he could usually drill into a soldier. Suddenly wishing he had brought his own training gear, Enith quietly made a move to leave.

"You can join if you want."

His face heated at being caught, and he turned around to face his shame. Syra just looked at him though, her expression revealing nothing, which seemed to be her way. She beckoned him with her head to the open stretch of sand in front of her.

"You want me to fight you?" he asked and laughed in surprise.

"Spar with me. Your anger needs to get out somehow."

He shot her a glare, unimpressed by her uncanny ability to perceive things others didn't, but took a ready position across from her and unsheathing his own short knife.

"Feet a little wider, and hold your knife arm higher." He begrudgingly instructed.

She did as he said, carefully repositioning her body.

He took a half-hearted swipe on her left side and was easily blocked. He tried again near her leg, but this time was blocked and knocked back more aggressively than he had been prepared for. Enith narrowed his eyes, wondering what her game was.

"What has you angry inside?" Her voice was soft and to the point.

He refused to speak, instead, throwing three rapid attacks at her, landing only one. That would bruise. She took a step back but didn't flinch.

"Enith, you walk around tense, as if every injustice eats away at you-"

"It does!" He went into a series of attacks then, swiping at her arm while kicking toward her knee, then turning just in time to try to land an elbow but finding that blocked too. He grunted, slowly moving up his skill level from how he would fight a novice to how he would fight one of his men after a year of training.

To his surprise, her own speed picked up, and she managed to deflect everything he threw at her, then landed a kick on his chest that knocked the air out of him. Anger boiled in his veins, and he stood up quickly, moving into his starting position again.

Her chest was heaving as she re-tied her long hair back, shedding her long-sleeved shirt for the sleeveless tunic underneath.

She pointed her knife at him, eyes unwavering and speaking in between breaths.

"You've been angry since your Testing Day."

Sweat dripped from his forehead down his face, and he shot her a glare again, ignoring it.

"It's none of your business, Syra. Let it go."

She swiped for his head, catching him off guard, shocking him with her speed and her audacity.

He knocked her hand away, feeling the rage build.

She circled him at a few feet's distance, her knife lifted like a pointing finger.

"You are angry because you are part of the injustice."

Rage exploded in Enith's chest, and he let his full skill surface, in one swift move spinning left with a jab, then faking a top swipe only to drop and kick her legs out from under her. His knee pressed against her chest, and his knife was at her throat, marking him the winner of the sparring session.

They stayed frozen like this, both trying to control their heavy breathing without breaking eye contact.

"Enith, what did you do in the forest?" It came out as little more than a whisper, but the question blew through him like a strong wind, cooling his anger and leaving all that was behind it. Pain. Grief. Images from the darkest day of his life.

"I killed you."

***

Enith sat on the beach next to Syra, his legs drawn up slightly, and his arms rested on his raised knees, twisting a blade of grass between his fingers.

"It was an image, maybe a hallucination. It was you or my people's respect, and I chose the adoring look of every royal." He hung his head, barely able to even talk to her without feeling sick to his stomach again.

He laughed, almost delirious at the irony. "And look where that has got me. I hate this kingdom now, and I act as if I hate you." He shook his head, staring at the ground.

Syra sat next to him, gazing out at the ocean, an unreadable expression on her face.

Her silence unnerved Enith, and he finally gave in, glancing her way. How could she look so at peace? The wind blew her white hair across her back, and the sun had always seemed to favor her more than others.

"Bloody..." he growled, tossing away the blade of grass and lifting himself off the sand. She was beautiful. An enchanting, otherworldly, beauty. He had withstood all the women, every lustful sin imaginable in that bloody forest, and still he had somehow lost her.

"I'll go-"

"I forgive you." He stopped, surprised. She continued, "I think it would have hurt more back then, when I was still lovesick for you." She looked at him, her large eyes somber but a half-smile playing on her lips.

"But now it is not your past actions that have murdered our friendship, it is the anger you have hidden behind since." She stood to face him squarely, eyes boring into him.

"Figure out a way to let this go, Enith. Resurrect this friendship. We have only gotten this far because I pushed, but I will not push again. You are a man, push yourself."

She turned then and walked away, leaving Enith drowning in a mixture of hope, shame, and love all at once.

***

Enith opened the door to the War Room and entered, already annoyed to have been summoned by his father for a meeting at all, much less while Michale'thia was unable to attend.

Around the room sat the normal advisors, all looking especially giddy now that the Heir had been found, and his father looked especially satisfied as if his daughter passing her Testing Day could be credited entirely to him.

"Ah, Enith, there you are. Let's get started." Enith silently took a seat by his father, folding his arms as he waited for the purpose of the meeting to be revealed.

His father took a moment to look at every person in the room with a smile, placing his hands on the table in front of him.

"We are finally here. We have found the Perfect Heir of the prophecy, and our kingdom will finally be ushered into the Age of Perfection." He paused for a beat, his gaze taking on an intensity Enith rarely saw in his father.

He nodded toward Lord Thilan, who gave a curt nod back and folded his hands in front of him, his square jaw seeming to jut further out with all eyes on him.

"It is time to take our place in this world, as leaders and servants of the Ancient Magic. It is time for the cleansing of the land, a ridding of all that is impure and opposed to the Ancient Magic's original design." Enith held his breath for a moment, a creeping sense of dread digging into his stomach.

"Men, it is time we rid the land of Elharren of all mix-bloods."

Heads began to nod as men around the table gave their affirming grunts, immediately livened at the statement.

Enith sat back in shock, looking at his father and those around the table, *sure* this must be a sick joke of some kind. When no objections arose and discussions on how to execute the "cleansing" began, his stomach churned. This was no new idea. They all agreed without any question or surprise. This had been quietly discussed over luxurious dinners and pious prophecy readings, slowly seeping into the minds of every man in the room until the thought was no longer just normal, but enjoyable.

Enith rose to stand, using every bit of self-control to keep himself from flipping the table over in rage. The room went silent, and he could feel the heat of his father's stare.

Where was his sister's diplomacy when he needed it?

"What gives us the right to even think about murdering thousands of our people?" He spoke carefully through clenched teeth, his blood pumping hot in his ears as the faces of families he knew all over the kingdom sprang into his mind.

Lord Thilan glanced over at the king, then spoke carefully to Enith as if placating a child. "The Prophecy is clear. We have gone over it time and time again: the Perfect One will lead the pure into the Age of Perfection," Thilan looked around the room, "and only the pure."

"Have we not seen the Ancient Magic's wisdom in this already? Mix-bloods do not have the propensity for moral goodness that those with truer bloodlines do. The more muddied the blood in an area, the more crime seems to run rampant in that quarter of the kingdom. The mixing of blood was against the design of the Ancient Magic and is an abomination. It is that simple."

Lord Thilan hesitated for a moment, choosing his words carefully as he reasoned with the angered prince, looking like he very much believed every word he spoke.

"As hard as this will be, we can only bow to the Ancient Magic's will. This is the time to be strong. To soldier up and lead, Prince Enith. As commander of the army and the brother of the Heir, you have great influence here. We need you to be with us, not divisive."

"He's right, son." The king spoke up, a gentle, warm tone to his voice this time.

"These will be difficult times for us, but we are called to be strong in the face of this sacred challenge. We will rise from this stronger, and soon we will bask in a perfect land once again!"

Enith clenched his jaw so hard he thought it might break. He looked around the room at all the men nodding in agreement to Lord Thilan's words.

Closing his eyes as his mind raced, a lump formed in his throat, and he swallowed down the string of curses about to jump from his mouth.

This next moment could make or break their future, and he had to play it well.

Eyes grim, he sighed and nodded, folding his hands and sitting down.

"You're right. Serving the Ancient Magic is not a task for the weak-hearted, and we must stand in unity to do Its will. No matter the cost. Let us plan this well. No mistakes and no holes. If we are going to be strong, we are also going to be smart. I want to lead this march."

CHAPTER 14
MICHALE'THIA

The sun rested in the morning sky, gently pouring in through the window like the soft swells of the ocean below. It was as if the land itself was at rest knowing the Heir had come.

Michale woke from a deep sleep to the steam of hot tea dancing beside her and warm smells of sweet breads imploring her stomach. The spring breeze floated through her open window beside her bed, and she slowly pushed back the colorful array of blankets and pillows. How long had she been asleep?

Starving, she sat up with shaking arms and took the plate of food onto her lap, eating small bites while she waited to see if her weak stomach would handle it. After a few minutes, she scarfed down the next two rolls, emptying her tea with them.

Michale rubbed her eyes and laid her head back against the chair, still exhausted and weak. Her eyes roamed over the room and halted as she realized that every surface was covered in flowers and gifts of all shapes and sizes. She walked slowly around the room, tracing presents with her fingers and smelling flowers.

Her old self would have loved this: the fruit of her laborious life being shown through the love of her people. But in this bright room filled to the brim with light and color, Michale'thia, now titled Perfect Heir, savior of the kingdom, knew that if she were to rip open her own chest, they would see a dark and mangled thing. Someone who wanted to murder, lust, and take everything for herself at any cost.

She was just the most self-controlled at hiding it.

This must be why so many came out of the Dark Forest changed. On top of seeing your most twisted desire, to then give in and murder, or betray, or abandon…to be shown that version of yourself and forced to admit it… She shook her head, eyes glazed over as they looked out toward the Indigo Mountains.

Michale blinked. The Botani people. Whatever happened with the Botani warrior? She was just about to ring for her maid when Syra slipped in the room, stopping when she saw Michale awake and then running to envelope her in a hug.

Michale smiled down at Syra as they stepped apart, about to ask about the Botani, but Syra spoke first.

"How are you? They said you would wake hungry and weak, you ate the food I set out, yes?"

Michale nodded absently, stifling a yawn.

"How long was I asleep?"

"Two days, Princess. The kingdom has been rejoicing and waiting eagerly for your crowning."

"And the Botani? Why was he here?"

Syra hesitated for a moment, clearly unsure how much to say.

Michale'thia raised a brow, "Syra, enough. Tell me what he is doing here."

"Belick's kingdom elders are... gifted with the Ancient Magic and felt there was a change coming. He came without knowledge in hopes of finding answers and found us. You." She avoided Michale's eyes, fidgeting with her dress.

"And..." Michale could tell there was more.

Syra sighed and explained the events of their journey in as much detail as she could, resigning herself to whatever came next. Michale silently processed everything she had heard. The Botanis have been hiding a source of magic, the Loharans a source of knowledge, and the Jyres somehow produced from their wicked line a magic-wielding prophet with more goodness in her than anyone Michale had ever encountered. Worst of all, the other kingdoms seemed to laugh at Anaratha for their interpretation of the prophecies. Nothing sat well with Michale, and she folded her arms across her chest. For her plan to work, she needed someone else on this team as knowledgeable as she was on the workings of the kingdom and the ancient texts. She groaned at the thought, knowing exactly who fit the criteria and rubbing her temples in an attempt to rid herself of her oncoming headache.

"Syra, this... light explosion you spoke of. It will protect you in tremulous circumstances?"

Syra shrugged her shoulders, unsure.

"Well then, you will just have to be ready to defend me with all your morning training if the need arises."

Syra's eyes widened in surprise, "You know-"

Michale laughed as she walked toward the window.

"Of course I know. I used to get up early to do training of my own… just in the library." Michale grinned.

"Syra, can you find Belick, Enith, and Dagen? I think we all need to talk."

Syra nodded, giving a half-smile as she answered.

"Belick should be easy to find, but Enith was called away to a meeting. Dagen has barely left this room the past two days but just left to take a bath and freshen up when you woke. He will be back soon. But you may want to put something more decent on before letting anyone in." Syra's eyes flickered to Michale's sleeping robe, causing Michale to flush and laugh, realizing how tired she still was.

"Right, I need proper clothing."

Syra grinned and called a bath to be brought in, arranging her clothes and eventually doing the tedious work of pressing her hair with towels to dry it.

By the time Michale'thia was ready to see people, she felt normal again. Or at least, as normal as she could feel given her new status as Heir of the Propehcy. Dagen was the first to arrive, lighting up at the sight of her and quietly shutting the door.

"You're awake." He smiled as he crossed the room.

She stood as he neared, allowing him to take her hand while trying to stamp out the sudden shyness she felt creeping in.

"Yes, well, I suppose I had to wake up at some point."

Dagen laughed then, the tension in his shoulders releasing and his easy spirit returning. He drew her into a careful hug, having seen her bruised body and fatigue.

He gazed down at her, "I barely know you, and yet the relief I feel at your wellbeing is deeper than I can express."

She smiled up at him, thankful for his tenderness.

Dagen motioned toward their favorite spot on the balcony, smiling when she followed him out.

They took a seat at the small table overlooking the waters and sat in silence for a minute, each working through something in their own mind.

"Dagen, I need to te-"

"Look I don't think-"

The newlyweds laughed at their timing.

"You first, Michale'thia."

She took a breath, preparing for the worst.

"I passed my Testing Day," she glanced at him, confirming her own thoughts, "as you have heard. Which makes me the Prophesied Heir, and you the king. But during The Test... I ..." She struggled for a moment, unsure how much to tell her new husband.

But looking into his eyes, she saw no trace of doubt or pride in her position, just open desire to listen. This was a man she had *chosen* to trust, and it was time she started doing that.

Dagen squeezed her hand gently, running his thumb over the back of it in comfort.

Michale continued, confidently this time, "I think our kingdom may not fully understand this prophecy. And...I may not be what this kingdom needs. How can I be perfect, when all I did was control myself better than others? Is that perfection, or is that compliance? And even worse, I still have no idea how I am supposed to lead our kingdom into the Age of Perfect. Nothing has been revealed to me, and there is nothing in the texts I have read about it." Tears brimmed in her eyes as she let her guard falter for a moment under the protective gaze of her husband. Her eyes searched his, pleading with him to understand, "Dagen, after my test I wandered into the desert. I was lost. I met a Loharan woman, and she confirmed there are more prophecies… I have to go find them."

Michale stood quietly, watching him process her admission.

Dagen just looked out at the ocean for a quiet minute, undisturbed but thoughtful.

He looked at her and gave a half-smile, squeezing her hand gently and speaking softly.

"My father and I have long suspected we had things mixed up. I'm with you, Michale."

Michale took another breath and plunged in.

"I am about to speak with Syra, Belick, and Enith about this, but I believe I need to go to the Loharan Desert and find the other prophecies. I cannot lead without them. If I wait too long to go, I am afraid I will be asked to make a move toward the Age of Perfection, and have no answer for my people. The Syllric's have sent people into the Loharan Desert for weeks and found nothing, which means they have devices that can keep them alive in the desert for longer periods. We will pass by there first to see what we can find and then make our way to the desert.

I need you to go back to your estate after I leave and find all the texts you can of where specifically in the desert the Loharans are located, anything about their dwellings, or how they stay alive. Take note of whatever you can that might be helpful. I will send you with one of my father's messenger birds that we use to communicate with the Syllrics. It will fly directly to a tavern I have heard him talk about, and I will find it there-"

"You are going to find them *now*?"

She nodded, "I have to, Dagen. I don't know how to usher this kingdom into the Age of Perfect, and I don't even know if I believe in my own station anymore. This can't wait."

He nodded in understanding, still looking perplexed.

"Do you want me to leave?" came a voice from the doorway.

The pair jumped, and Dagen drew his sword faster than Michale'thia thought possible, stepping in front of his wife.

Belick let out a booming laugh then, his white teeth stark against his dark skin. Dagen glanced back at Michale with confusion and awe. He obviously had not been told about the Botani warrior.

Belick only laughed harder, wiping tears from his eyes. It took him a good minute to regain his composure and straighten his body back up.

"Oh, my friend, I like you. You did what a brave warrior would do!" He extended his hand with an ease and openness Michale had not seen from him yet.

Dagen let out a laugh of his own and smiled, grasping the other man's forearm and bringing a fist to his chest. The Botani's eyes widened, and he tightened his own grasp, doing the same.

"You know the Botani way?" There was an eagerness sparkling in his eye, and Michale could already see a brotherhood forming.

Of course, Dagen would know 'the Botani way', she rolled her eyes lightheartedly.

"My friend, I only know what I have been gifted to learn. You are a beautiful people. I have a feeling I wouldn't have gone far in a fight against you, though. What is your name?"

The warrior smiled, his spear arm dropping to his side, "I am Belick, and I have come down the mountain to learn why the winds change."

Dagen nodded solemnly, seeming to understand precisely what the Botani was speaking of.

"Well, you seemed to have found that out then." Dagen considered Belick, as if anticipating something in his response.

Belick's eyes narrowed and he answered flatly, "No. I have not."

He glanced at Michale quickly before returning his gaze to Dagen.

Dagen's shoulders tensed again, and Michale wondered what hidden meaning he was finding in this whole exchange.

"I see. I believe we will come to that conclusion too."

Belick nodded with new respect, stepping back from the doorway and into the room.

A knock on the door pulled Dagen away to sign papers, and Michale moved into her sitting room to start the next discussion with Belick and Syra.

Michale jumped right in to explain her Testing Day and the problems at hand, revealing her own personal fears about their prophecies and her suspicion that the Loharans have what they need. When she finished, Syra sat back quietly, eyes wide as she contemplated everything Michale had just said.

Belick folded his arms, thoughtful as he spoke. "Your kingdom will not like this. For hundreds of years they have expected the Heir to lead the kingdom into their perfection, and this would mean their *only* hope is lost."

He tapped his spear as he continued. "Panic will erupt if they find out before having a different source of hope. You may be accused of fraud or even destroy all belief in the prophecies."

Syra caught on quickly, lips parted as the weight of his words sunk in.

"He is right. Your kingdom has believed this way since the beginning. It is easy for outsiders to understand, but for a people whose entire lives have been built on this understanding of the prophecy… it will not go over so well."

Michale gave a small smile as she studied the cup in front of her, speaking slowly in case her next idea scared them all away.

"The kingdom does not need to know. If I were to disappear for a time and find the prophecies, my parents would likely cover up the absence to prevent panic, and I could find the texts we need and come back with answers."

Michale looked up to find Syra's eyes wide in surprise. Belick, on the other hand, was smiling broadly, letting out a short laugh as he thumped his spear on the floor.

"This is a great idea!" His deep voice enunciated every word in the Botani way.

"We take our journey, find the truth, and you get back to your kingdom, and I get back to mine."

Michale nodded, trying to quell the excitement building in her. She turned to Syra, not wanting to make a commitment without her being on board, but was met with an indifferent shrug.

"I'll go where you go."

With trepidation in the air, the next hour was spent sorting through every detail they could think of, going back and forth between various route scenarios.

After the details had been worked out, Michale sat back and sighed. The day was yet young.

"I suppose it is time to speak to Kallaren. Let's hope this goes well. Bring him, please. Tell him his future queen would like a word."

Syra's only response was to grimace before leaving the room to carry out her orders.

***

A knock from the guard signaled Kallaren's arrival, and he sauntered into the room wearing his finest jacket and sword, chest puffed out, and his signature smug look painted onto his face.

Michale'thia paused a moment, taking in his demeanor, before returning her attention to her notes, her small table in her sitting area now littered with papers and texts.

Kallaren waited politely for a moment, but his confidence waned, and he began to squirm in the silence, obviously expecting a besotted princess rather than a busy soon-to-be queen.

"Michal-

Michale put a hand up in the air, "Stop. Don't speak. Stand there until I am ready."

She continued to scribble some notes on a page, navigating between three different sources for what she needed.

"Look I-"

Michale's head snapped up sharply, and she cut him off with a glare.

"No, you don't. You are entitled to nothing and can stand there until I am ready, Kallaren. Now be quiet. I just need a moment longer."

She bent over her texts again, underlining a sentence and jotting down a note before sighing and moving it aside, beckoning Kallaren with her hand to sit.

By this point, he seemed more like the unsure boy she used to know than the overconfident brute his father had formed him to be. Good. It had worked.

Kallaren and most other royals in the palace rarely saw her in anything extravagant, since she usually opted for simple and comfortable. Wearing one of the new, completely gold-layden dresses she had received within the past few days was an easy and effective way to startle them all into the realization that she was now queen.

"Kallaren, as much as I loath to bring you here—and let me be clear, I do loath to have you here—you are incredibly good with the ancient language, and I may need your help. I need an ally right now that I can talk to in *complete* confidence."

She looked into his eyes, hoping that what she said would sink in, and hoping even more her theory was right.

"You are not your father, as I am not the same girl who entered the forest. Let us work together, for Anaratha's sake."

He nodded and looked away, clenching his jaw as he hid the shame in his eyes, obviously thinking back to their encounter in the hallway weeks ago. She breathed a sigh of relief and worked to keep her eyes from straying to Syra, who had taken shortcuts to be back before Kallaren entered the room.

"I am afraid our beloved kingdom does not have all the information it should. I think it's possible we only have part of the prophecies, and are missing a significant piece. I cannot rule as Heir of the Prophecies without knowing what the other pieces say. I believe the Loharans have the other prophecies, and the Botani at very least know of them."

Kallaren frowned and folded his arms, skeptical of her wild theory. This was not what they had been taught in Anaratha.

"How would you know the Loharans have the rest, if there even *is* more? And you realize this could put your claim to the throne in danger, right?" He arched a cocky brow at her.

Michale poured herself some tea, truly believing talking to a delvior would be more enjoyable than this.

"After I came out of the forest, I wandered into the desert and met an old Loharan woman. And when I was in The Jyre Forest I realized..." She paused, unsure of how to proceed.

Kallaren's eyes were suddenly glued to his lap as he finished her thought in a whisper, "You realized all the temptations came from inside of you."

Michale couldn't meet his gaze either, and the two royals sat in the quiet for a few more moments until Kallaren spoke again, arrogance once again dripping from every word.

"So, you need me." He smirked, "Of course you need me, Michale."

She rolled her eyes and decided to just continue.

"I'm planning a journey with a few handpicked people, to find the remaining prophecies in the Loharan Desert, and I want you to come. I need someone with knowledge of our interpretations, as well as an understanding of the ancient language to help read the prophecies once we find them."

He crossed his arms with an annoying smile pulling on the side of his mouth.

She drummed her fingers on the table while he played his little silent game. He was too much like her mother for comfort.

"How do you know I won't corner you again?" His eyes sparkled with dark amusement, and she wasn't so sure about bringing him along anymore.

Syra didn't wait to be asked before coming to stand beside Michale and with a blank face, staring directly into Kallaren's eyes.

Syra's voice was almost monotone with anger, but she looked completely at peace.

"If you hurt her, Kallaren, I'll kill you. And believe me, we Jyres know how to make death a good time."

Michale'thia almost jumped, looking over at Syra in surprise, not knowing what to do with the sudden dark-Jyre version of her sweet maid. Kallaren stuttered and began fixing something on his jacket, and Syra flashed a grin and wink Michale's way, sending relief flooding over her as she realized her maid was *also* an exceptional liar. She hoped.

"Additionally, you will not be the only man with us." She felt her own smile growing as she pointed behind Kallaren with her eyes, to the corner of her room where Belick stood in dark glory, his face fiercer than normal and his knuckles tightening on his spear.

His voice over-pronounced each word as he ground them out, seething.

"You are a lowly dog, and can join us only until I decide to kill you."

Michale exhaled loudly, tired of all the threats going around.

"So, Kallaren." She smiled and tilted her head to the side. "Do you want to join?"

Kallaren had just given a curt nod when the door slammed open, and Enith strode in, jaw clenched tightly shut.

He barely gave Kallaren a glance before grinding, "Get out."

"Whoa, I was invited-"

Enith had Kallaren's shirt in his hands within seconds, and his fist pulled back, ready to swing if another word was spoken.

"If I have to look at your face for a minute longer, I swear it will be too bloody to recognize by the time you are out of this room."

Kallaren's own eyes widened, recognizing the dark anger Enith usually held on his shoulders now raging in his eyes. Kallaren stepped back, fear evident on his face, and gave a quick nod to Michale before scampering off.

Michalethia's own heart raced at her brother's barely contained fury.

The door had just thudded shut when Enith spat out his news.

"They are planning to murder all mix-bloods."

The words echoed hollowly in the room, followed by a silence strong enough to kill. No one moved. No one could. This changed everything.

***

Michale stormed through the halls, her dress trailing behind her in its own fury. Belick had stayed back with Syra to protect her, and Enith, having been briefed on their plan to leave, now strode beside Michale, matching her pace easily.

She wore her crown high on her head, and each stepped echoed in the halls as they neared the War Room, where Enith had left the group of men to work through their plans. The doors to the room were just at the end of the hall, and Michale had full plans to show these men the anger of the Ancient Magic itself.

Suddenly, Kallaren slipped out from the War Room and began nearly running toward them, eyes frantic.

"We have to go. Now."

Enith stepped forward, about to grab him up as the traitor he was, but Kallaren gave him a hard look, urgency clear in his eyes.

"Enith, this isn't a game. We leave now, or we won't have the chance to. Go, I'll explain on the way back to your room. We can't let them know you are out here."

Michale could almost smell the fury coming from Enith's eyes, but his soldier kicked in, and they turned around, now struggling to keep up with Kallaren.

Kallaren spoke as he walked, "My father called me in. The plan is to take the next two months to prepare, and then they will kill every mix-blood in this land." Michale followed as fast as she could, struggling and to piece together Kallaren's hurry and what he had said.

"What does this have to do with us leaving?"

Kallaren stopped suddenly in the middle of the hall, turning slowly to her without quite meeting her eyes.

"If you disagree, they believe it will be because you have gone through too much and are not in the right mind yet to lead. And if Dagen does not agree, it would only be because he is working against the Ancient Magic and thus would need to be eliminated."

Enith sucked in a breath, and Michale brought a hand to her mouth, fear now coursing through her veins. She looked past Kallaren at Enith, and a silent understanding passed.

"Let's go. We need to move now."

***

It took the next two hours to pack their things. Michale helped Syra tie together the bags of dried food and put them in packs, while Enith was out spreading the word among the servants to start finding places to hide. Dagen returned, and they filled him in, his shock echoing through all of them once more.

"Have they gone insane? They can't just murder these people, *my people.*"

"I know, Dagen, and we have to stop them. We can only do that by getting to Luik's kingdom and warning him. If what Kallaren said is true, our birds will be shot down before they ever reach him."

"And why are we trusting Kallaren?"

Michale threw down the bag she was packing and stood to face him.

"Dagen. Please. There's no other way. Go home, find the information we need, and send it to us as soon as you can. We should be at the tavern in the Syllric's trading port in one week's time. Kallaren is risking his own life telling us all this, and we don't have time to sit and ponder if it's some twisted game. We have to move quickly. Enith has bought us precious time, but if we go the southern route around The Jyre Forest, my father and the whole army will see where we are going.

The northern route through the Syllric trading post, then through Luiks kingdom will give us provisions we need right before entering the desert from the east, where I met the Loharan woman so it can't be far from their permanent dwellings. It will take a week to get to the Syllrics, and then another four days to Luik and the Brends Kingdom if we keep a good pace. After that, it's only a few days' ride around the northern tip of The Jyre Forest before we reach the Loharan Desert." She looked at everyone in the room.

"That puts us in the desert in two and a half weeks' time at the very minimum."

Enith shook his head, folding his arms as he did.

"Neither our horses nor feet can keep that pace, Michale. We will have to stay in a tavern in the Syllric trading post for a night or two, at least. We can buy other horses if we can sell ours, but we will need to take another break in Luik's kingdom. That will put us closer to three weeks."

Michale nodded, calculating their time frame.

"That can work. We would still have time to find the Loharans, do our research, and hopefully be back before any plan is executed."

The small group stood there, preparing themselves for the task ahead. A Botani. A Jyre. A royal heir who passed, and two who failed. All prepared to flee for the pursuit of the truth.

Michale looked at the group, knowing what she asked was great.

"Our only hope is that the Ancient Magic is good, and has decreed good things. And that is what we need to find."

They nodded, each person pulling themselves together again by the healing strands of hope. They all had to be stronger than the doubt of betrayal right now.

***

Night had fallen, and Michale's head was threatening to explode by the time she closed her door and dragged herself to bed. She had met with at least five different advisors seeking to gain her favor and explain what *small* changes could be made to make the kingdom perfect, two councilmen who obviously needed to ensure their piousness was understood, and at least a dozen different palace staff members asking questions about her upcoming coronation and ball.

Syra instructed the maids to discreetly let it slip that Michale was still unwell, and was planning on taking some of the sleep remedy the doctors had prescribed so she could sleep through the next day.

Kallaren made it known that he would be traveling to visit his father's estate tomorrow, and Enith gave notice to his father and his advisors that he would begin scouting the surrounding countryside and marking the best strategies for eliminating mix-bloods.

At this rate, Michale would get about three hours of sleep before they snuck out with the early morning travelers, who usually left the gates at long before the sun rose to get a head start on their journeys. Syra knew from experience that at the end of their shift, the overnight guards tended to be tired and more relaxed about who went out, only critical about who came in.

Michale wasn't sure where the Belick was, but he would meet them outside of the gate, leaving presumably the same way he had come in, unseen. She still needed to hear how he had managed that.

When she finally laid her head down on her pillow, the sun had long since gone down, and the kingdom slumbered peacefully, not knowing that in the morning their beloved Heir would be gone.

***

Michale woke to a gentle shake from Syra and immediately slid out of bed and into her tunic and trousers. She had spent the night tossing and turning, unable to let go of the excitement of what was to come. They pulled on hooded cloaks and quietly left the room, trying to avoid the places they knew guards would be stationed. After exiting the courtyard and entering into the main streets of the city, they wound through the alleyways until they reached the western gate. As Syra predicted, the guard was unphased by the groups of travelers already milling about, and barely took notice of those who were leaving.

Despite the smooth travel so far, Michale felt like she had been holding her breath the entire morning.

The pair moved slowly along the path heading north for a few paces until they saw the large form of Kallaren, meandering along the road with two horses and plenty of supplies in hand. They caught up to him and matched his pace with no more than a quiet nod, wondering where Belick could be. True to his word, Belick appeared with two horses of his own, also amply supplied, and the four seemed to visibly relax. They all knew the consequences of Michale being caught at this point. Uproar. Scandal. Accusations of treason. Nothing good would come of it.

Michale and Kallaren had talked through every angle and knew their parents well enough to predict what moves they would make after reading Michale's note, explaining her absence as a need to visit the countryside. They would see through it but would play along for the sake of the kingdom.

When the group was far enough from the castle, Syra and Michale let their hoods down and sighed with relief, looking at each other and laughing anxiously for a moment. They were really doing this.

"Thank you all. I know this isn't easy, and won't be easy, but...thanks." Michale honestly couldn't come up with any good reason the Botani and Syra should be here. Both seemed to gain nothing from this, and yet here they were. Quietly committed.

Kallaren's voice piped up from the back of the group then, breaking the silence.

"So what *is* your name, Botani?" All three pairs of eyes were suddenly on him, his fingers frozen in the middle of drumming on his spear.

He glanced back at Kallaren, but continued scouting the area for any threats as he answered, "I am Belick of the Ngari People." His jaw clenched, and his chest puffed out—or was it always that way?—and he brought a fist to his heart.

"Who are the Ngari?" Kallaren pressed. "I didn't know the Botanis claimed different lineages." His interest obviously piqued at the thought.

Michale smiled, thankful she had thought to endure Kallaren on this trip. He had terrified her in the hallway that day, but it would seem her gamble was correct: Kallaren didn't crave power; he craved knowledge. His *father* craved power, and since he had already failed his Testing Day last year and with it any hope to bring his father the ultimate power, the only way he could have righted his standing again was if he found a way to marry the one who would become Heir.

The two men began to talk back and forth, and Syra moved closer to Michale, bowing her head to speak quietly about the journey ahead.

Two days passed before Enith came riding up from the east, having taken a far route around the hills to meet them without being seen. He trotted up on his horse and rode in the back, a silent guard for their small journey.

Michale turned back to look toward her kingdom, blinking back tears as she rode away, mourning the years lost and all the ages of her people falsely held together with the hope of a lie.

CHAPTER 15
BELICK

The sun shone on the dirt road, crowded with travelers journeying to Anaratha to catch a glimpse of the prophecy's fulfillment. The green hillsides surrounding them were scattered with farmers in their fields and small towns where simple lives were lived merrily, where each evening was spent watching the breeze sweep the dross of the land away.

With each step north, Belick's chest squeezed with a yearning to be home in the southern Indigo Mountains. He could claim a kind of alliance with his fellow travelers, but his home called to him as strongly as the songs his mother used to sing, or the cries of victory his father roared after a good hunt. But something was changing in Elharren, and it wasn't just the elders in his village who could feel it.

Kallaren's questions began to wear on him, and he lapsed into a content silence by their fifth day of travel, thankful for the quiet and not caring if Kallaren was bothered by his lack of responses. Instead, Belick allowed the wind to carry his eyes over the rolling hills, reminding him of both sweet memories and blood-drowned wars. They had another day's worth of walking before they made it to the trade city, and he begrudgingly looked forward to seeing all the exotic goods.

As he looked around, his eyes paused on Michale'thia. She wore men's trousers that had been fitted to her body and a loose tunic tucked in, her hair flying loose from the long braid set across one shoulder. She talked with her brother with grim joy now, holding the weight of a kingdom on her shoulders, as he too had done. The girl had withstood the Jyres though and desired truth over prestige. He found himself slightly in awe of both Michale'thia and Syra. Both seemed to wield great strength in their souls and somehow remain untouched by the desire for power in itself.

"Wipe that look off your face, Belick, she's a married woman now." Kallaren teased, clearly amused to catch the Botani off his guard.

Belick grimaced and shook his head, not realizing how his own gaze could be interpreted.

"She is not for me, and I am not a man who takes pleasure in desiring what is not his. Not even in my mind." Belick shot Kallaren a hard look, annoyed to find Kallaren not taking him seriously.

Kallaren sighed and guided his horse closer to Belick, lowering his voice accordingly.

"Practically every man in the kingdom has tried to get her attention, but she'd never have it. She would walk the loneliest halls and spent most of her time studying. Because she's so perfect, her standards for men were too. She only married because she had to, and even then, I am pretty sure she just picked Dagen because he is as much a goody-goody as she is."

Belick raised an eyebrow then, slightly amused that this Alethian who claimed such high intelligence could miss so much. From what he had seen, the young couple clearly had something between them. A small candle of a flame perhaps, but one that would surely grow into a passionate fire.

"Whatever you say, Alethian."

Kallaren's brows drew together in confusion, but he shrugged and kept riding, also watching Michale.

She turned her head then and spoke over her shoulder toward them, "Belick of the Ngari People, will you tell me about your home?"

Suspicion filled him for a moment before he looked at her side profile and saw something familiar. She spoke of the Botani mountains with unusual reverence and desire. It could only be one thing.

Belick had heard of the mountain's magnetic pull but had never been down the mountain to see it, even if he had met others who experienced it. Once in a while, someone would climb the mountain without a guide or any knowledge of the terrain and show up at their gates half-frozen, with broken bones and a half-starved stomach, claiming they felt a pull so undeniable they would take any risk to be there. Belick swallowed, knowing what beckoned them there, and suddenly worried he would not be able to keep his kingdom's secrets much longer. But if she was feeling the pull as well, that meant she belonged there. The Ancient Magic itself called her toward it.

He nodded to himself and looked back over at Michale, who was now staring at him oddly, obviously having witnessed his silent internal struggle.

He hurried to answer then.

"The mountains are covered in greens, purples, and blues. And then, when the sun rises and touches my mountain, the blues and purples meet fire, and my Papa once said he is sure the sky itself becomes jealous of the great beauty. I have a rock on a ledge I found that overlooks all things. I see your kingdom, but you look so small. And I see the ocean for miles and miles! It seems like it never ends!"

He lowered his voice and whispered, "And then to the west, I have seen something in the distance. The land stretches out as far as the eye can see! We thought our land of Elharren was all there is, but no, there is much more across the Loharan dessert. I have seen it."

Belick would have given everything to keep the wistful look of amazement on Michale's face. He continued.

"When I was younger, my mother would wake me before the sun rose, and stuff me with warm *pelluahs*, ones with pig meat inside of them, and then I would race to catch up with my father as he went out for the hunt and we would find the best deer for dinner. My father was the Captain of the Spear Warriors, and had the best aim in our kingdom—until I grew older." Belick flashed a playful smile.

"The deer would cook in a hole underground all day long, filling our house with the smell of what we couldn't wait to eat. Then, at some point in the day, my father would make my mother very, very angry, and she would plant her hands on her hips with the strength of a tree trunk."

He turned to her while walking, putting his hands on his hips in his best mimic of his mother, "And she would say, 'Oombieri Ngaro, if you don't leave my house I will fight you and skin you like a delvior," Belick straightened and gave a gentle laugh as he looked out in the distance, seeing everything in his mind as if it were happening right then.

"And when she said that, her voice would get deeper, like she was an angry bear growling its last warning." His laugh echoed through the foothills like an orchestra of trumpets resounding their joy. He tapped his temple and gave Michale a knowing look she was sure to not understand.

"So then my father would leave and come back with a new flower every single day for her. Every color and every shape, he always finds a new one on our mountain somehow. When he would walk back in, she would try to hide her smile, but I know she is always happy for the flower. And she acts surprised every time."

Belick was still grinning at the love story he saw every day—and not just a love, but a strength and a courage. He thanked the Ancient Magic every day for the gift of this family. A family he couldn't see.

His mood ruined, he sighed, remembering that the others were all listening.

The dirt path rumbled from passing carts as people journeyed in the opposite direction. Belick glanced over at Michale, surprised to see her eyes misted over. But then again, it shouldn't be a surprise at all if he had thought about it. Her soul was tethered to the mountains too.

"I wish I was there," was all she whispered, and the two walked silently onward.

***

The sunset began to darken their path, and the pleasant breeze turned malicious as early winter wind flew in. The small group walked closer than before and headed toward one of the small towns to break until the next day, making their way to one of the only inns they could find.

The room was dimmer than they expected, with lanterns strewn about, their lights tinted by colored glass. In a corner, a short man with a full beard played a smooth instrument, unlike anything Belick had seen in his day. The strings were touched by a stick of some sort, or was it a small bow? Whatever it was, the music was long and drawn out, beautifully filling the room.

Another man with strong Syllric features, dressed in a fine suit, gave the group a nod from the front of the room as he continued his conversation with another guest. They took a seat at a gold-painted table in the corner and waited, not noticing at first when the music stopped, and all eyes turned in their direction. An eerie silence ensued, and Michale and Syra looked at each other before turning around in their chairs.

Some looked at the group in horror, others in open interest. Belick shook his head, realizing how far they must be from the city.

"Why are they staring at us?" Kallaren whispered over to Michale'thia, who shook her head in confusion.

Syra looked down at her lap, refusing to acknowledge the situation, and Belick scoffed, unable to believe the others really didn't understand.

His voice was loud and free as he bellowed, "It's because I am black like the night, and she is white like the moon, man! Of course they are staring, we are too beautiful to be traveling with you!" His white teeth shown as he sat back and laughed, causing the crowd to hoot and roar in laughter also. The musician took the laughter as a sign to start the music back up, and the room seemed to accept that acknowledgment as enough for them.

The Anarathans' faces were frozen in shock at Belick's statement, only making him smile wider. He looked over at Syra and saw a slight smile playing on her lips as they shared a knowing look. Unbeknownst to their companions, they had received looks of terror and awe their entire journey so far. It is easy to miss the discomfort of others when you are wrapped in the arms of your own comfort.

He sat back as he realized a profound sadness. He would return to his people and be loved, a brother of blood. But Syra would never know that homecoming. She could not return to her evil kin, and as much as he would like to bring her to his mountains as the Spring Warrior that she was, she would only stand out more amongst his dark-skinned people, even though she would share in their bond. How sad, to be so alone.

His brows lowered as he made up his mind, daring to reach back into his past and risk his identity for the sake of bringing another into a family, as he had been.

"Syra, give me your hand." His eyes held hers, a stubborn edge daring her to argue with him.

She bent her head to the side and studied him, seeming to read something in his soul. Finally, after a long study of his face, she nodded in agreement and gave him her hand. He didn't know how, but somehow she had understood his intention. Enough to be at peace with what he was about to do.

Belick turned her hand over gently, all noise quieting around him, muted by his clear focus. Something like a soft melody of wind entranced him as he brought his knife up to his hand and made a small incision. Then, as gently as possible, did the same to her skin. The melody stirred within his heart, and he barely registered the muted indignation of Michale'thia and Enith. Instead, he brought Syra's hand to meet his until their blood mingled.

The melody roared to life, and the wind in his ears rushed madly about, and he swore right then that she glowed. Did she hear the same music?

In the same quick instant it had started, it was gone. Everything quieted, and they both returned back to that place in the small tavern, in a small town, on a journey someday to end.

His voice was choked as he returned her hand.

"There. Syra Ngaro, I have made you my blood sister."

And without surprise, or anger, or fear, Syra looked up at him with tears in her own eyes and smiled.

***

Several bowls of steaming soup and watered-down wine later, the tired travelers dragged themselves up the stairs and to their rooms. The men decided to cram into one room, while Syra and Michale took the room next to them.

Enith began what Belick would deem a lengthy, feminine process of washing his face, arms, and feet before donning his sleep shorts and settling in. Belick moved toward the window to look out at his mountains one last time before he unrolled his mat on the floor, warmed and ready for sleep by the ale.

The walls creaked as they pushed back against the howling wind, and Belick was about to drift off when Enith spoke up from his bed.

"What was that today? What did you do to her hand?"

Belick's irritation calmed as he realized how odd the scene would look even to his own people. The rite had not been performed in centuries, and he hadn't even been sure it would work. But it did. He could feel it.

"I made her my kin. By blood," he answered, hoping that would be the end of it. He was already exposing too much about his people, and this came dangerously close to information he could not let outsiders know.

"But how does that do anything at all? She still has her own blood and lineage. It's a nice thought, but it seems more mystical than anything else." Enith seemed to remember himself and rushed on, "But I respect that you do it, it must be an important ritual for your people."

Belick turned onto his back and rested his head against his hands. "Centuries ago, in the time of the wars, this was done to unify those that could not otherwise be unified. It is called *sunago*. To bring in. Like the Ancient Magic brought us in, no matter our rebellion, so we bring in others. There is something more than tradition in this. There is a heart bond. It is said that this bond brings a depth of love for the other that one only feels for closest kin. And now, I would give up everything for Syra. She is my sister, my own soul. I would protect her with my life."

Enith lay still on his bed for a moment, then Belick could hear him shift as he rolled over. He was still for the remainder of the night. Not long after, Kallaren entered the room, kicking his shoes off and grunting as he dropped his body onto the room's second small bed. He was snoring in minutes.

Belick settled into a deep rest that night, the rest of one who had found a piece of his lost self and brought it safely home again.

***

CHAPTER 16
ENITH

It was almost midday when they reached the city of the Syllrics, its streets bustling with activity. Enith had been to their trading days often and even met dignitaries when they passed through Anaratha, but he had never been to the Syllrics' city itself. His father often spoke of them with respect, but his mother always tensed when their names came up.

Colors of every kind dressed the people, who walked by quickly in groups, often carrying supplies in baskets or large jars. Enith recognized many of the spices lingering in the air but found his mouth enticed by a whole new set of aromas he had no name for. Belick was looking grim and slightly sick, muttering something about too much noise, leaning on his spear subtly. Michale and Syra huddled closer together than usual, frightened by all that was going on around them, and Kallaren stood with a disgusted look, not enjoying the smell of spices as Enith did. Enith felt more alive than he had in a long time,

The countryside of Anaratha held a beauty to it, and his days with his comrades were filled with mornings of hard work followed by lengthy naps in the afternoon and evenings spent enjoying their drinks as they forgot the day's work, willing to wake up in the morning with aching heads in exchange for a night of dreamless sleep. But nothing compared to crowds for him. New people, new places. Something about the mannerisms of a stranger or the new design of a basket fascinated him more than all else. His mother used to be the same way. She would venture out into the streets with him just to buy from the local bakers and farmers, often being pulled away by little girls for stories and hair braids. She had been magnificent.

Enith's spirits fell as he remembered the slow change he had seen in her. She had birthed him soon after marrying his father, only a half year after her own Testing Day, and he could remember her gentle touch and love for the people from his younger years. By the time Michale'thia was old enough to care, she could see nothing of the mother he used to know. Just the dark, conniving woman who was left. Was that to be his own fate?

"Finally. Here we are!" Enith turned about, taking it all in. "And what beauty it is." He couldn't keep the smile from his face, and he turned to try to hide it. He didn't want to look like a schoolboy.

Women walked with scarves covering their hair and lower face, leaving a mysterious air about them as their eyes gleamed mysteriously at him. The men walked around with a type of sword at their belts that had a bend to the blade but looked ruthless nonetheless. A cutlass. He had always wanted to train with one, just to compare it to his usual blade, but his father had always disapproved, wanting their military to keep their traditional straight swords.

Enith turned to the group, taking in their wide-eyed hesitation and letting a laugh escape.

"Come on, Michale'thia, all those books and you weren't prepared for this?" He smirked at her playfully and continued.

"Let's find the market. It can't be far with all these wonderful smells."

He began walking toward where he thought the heart of the city would be, eventually finding an open square with booths of every kind lining the inner square, each beckoning those passing by with savory aromas.

All five wandered off and found different stalls to buy food from, meeting back at a central fountain where water poured out from a beautiful marble rendition of Syllric the Shrewd. A small gold plaque had been set in the stone around the fountain, on which was inscribed:

Syllric the Shrewd

traded his bowl for his food,

followed the leader until he could lead,

then killed his brother too.

Come, children, come,

and learn the trickery

of Syllric, who stayed alive

and bore our destiny.

Enith frowned at the implications of the plaque. Syllric was no hero in their textbooks, and he couldn't comprehend calling children to be tricksters like their storied forefather. And Syllric killed his own brother?

According to Anarathan history, Syllric was the dark-haired, light-skinned Ancient brother who had created stones of every kind. From jewels to building blocks, Syllric basically started all industry and trade, gaining a name for himself as a shrewd dealer among the nations. When Jyren declared his intent to find the Ancient Spring again, Syllric and Brendar had both followed at a distance, hoping to also drink of the well so as not to be left weak. After the Ancient Brothers disappeared, a plague devastated the Syllric people, which scholars suggested may have come from their own doing, mixing materials together and digging in places they shouldn't have touched, but nevertheless, those left in the seaside kingdom became rich with the gold of those who passed, and they somehow turned it all into a thriving business of trade. Some even said they took their ships to other lands to get the spices, but no one knew for sure.

The Syllrics were a smaller kingdom, but supplied most of Anaratha's military supplies, staying neutral for the sake of trading with anyone from any political background. Enith had heard from his father that their new chief, Nasir, had taken greed to a new level, wanting anything he knew the other kingdoms valued and even setting up a spy system in other kingdoms to best gauge what they most desired and then raising the prices on those good. Nasir was smart, he'd admit that.

The group ate in silence as people milled about them, making purchases and haggling in loud voices. Enith had chosen a soft bread folded in half to hold seasoned meats, cheeses and vegetables, with a dip with hints of garlic and cream.

After he had wiped his hands and dusted off his trousers, he stood and stretched, feeling revived by the culture around him.

Belick, who only looked a little better than before, stood unsteadily and took up his spear. "We should be gone from this place."

"What? No. We need to stay at least one night for the horses. Besides, I'm sure we could find something of use in these booths." He racked his mind for more reasons to stay, thankful when Michale chimed in, standing and dusting the crumbs from her own trousers.

"Let's just take it one hour at a time. If we do stay, Belick, perhaps you could secure for us a place to sleep. I am sure the inns fill up quickly with so many people here."

Belick tried to mask his relief and nodded, obviously ready to turn in, then grimacing when Kallaren spoke up as well.

"I'll head back with him." He gave no reason for doing so. "We will meet you all back here at sunset." Kallaren gave another nod, and the two disappeared into the crowd.

Enith looked over at Michale and Syra, a smile on his face.

"Well, I have heard rumors of inventions here that are *life-changing*. Even one that allows sailors to tell the north and south from their pocket." He held out his arms after straightening his shirt. "Would you ladies allow me to escort you around the city so our lives can be changed?"

Michale laughed at his exaggerated chivalry, and Syra smiled slightly, interested herself in what this city may bring.

They wound their way through the streets, finding too many small shops to choose from. As they continued away from the square, the shops began to evolve, looking more polished, decorated with whites and golds rather than the multi-colored tent covers the inner city shops paraded. Enith walked by one window and noticed devices of every kind lining the tables. He clapped in delight and swung the girls around toward the door, receiving laughs in return.

The door glided open, and a small bell announced their entrance, bringing a thin, tall man with obvious Syllric descent to greet them.

"Hello, how may I be of service today?" The man kept his hands behind his back and offered a small bow, greed already gleaming in his eyes as he took in their Alethian heritage.

Enith took on a formal stance, ready to deal with the businessman.

"Good day, sir. We are browsing for any devices that may aid us on our long journey. We will be continuing for the next few days and could benefit from many different things. What do you have?"

The man nodded as Enith spoke, as if this was a common request. He turned and moved down the row of display cases, motioning with his hand to the various devices.

He picked up one. "This one was developed by some of our brightest minds. As you can see, it's small in nature, but when activated, the crystals inside give a light that allows travelers to see their path in the darkest night." He set the glass globe down and turned to another device, this one a flat metal case slightly larger than a coin. "And here, this one has the ability to show the direction using a new rock type, and its reaction to another rock in this same family." He flipped open the lid to reveal a round face and an arrow. The arrow spun slowly, choosing between North, South, West, and East. Enith's eyes glowed; now *this* could be useful.

"And how much is this direction device worth?"

"This one is highly valuable. It is priced at 200 gold coins." Enith almost choked. That was a hefty price and would leave him barely able to buy food for the next week. Sighing, he decided it may be worth it. He could scrape by on bread and hard cheese.

Just as he was about to agree, Syra laid a cool hand on his arm, stopping him.

"Good sir," she said. She was doing that eye thing she did sometimes that made a man feel uncomfortably known. "We would give you 50 gold coins, no more."

The man barely batted an eye, acting as if it was Enith that had spoken. "I will not be robbed, no less than 150."

Syra was undeterred. "We can possibly stretch to 60 gold coins."

"This is thievery! *Sir*," he focused his emphasis on Enith, obviously frustrated by Syra's voice in the conversation. "I can go no lower than 120."

Enith, at that point, had caught on and realized his mistake.

"I am sorry, our greatest bid is 80 gold coins. I understand that is too low for you, so we will be on our way."

The group began to shuffle out of the shop, making it only to the door before hearing the owner's voice call out.

"Wait! For you only, I can do 80 coins. Come, my friend, come. Let us settle this account."

Enith hid a smile and walked over to the man and began finalizing their purchase.

They walked out of the shop, excited about their new device, and began walking back toward the center of the city, having already spent hours shopping and ready once again to eat.

The stomping of horse hooves began to thunder, approaching the inner square the same time Enith and the girls did, and the crowds around quickly moved to make way for the coming entourage.

Enith, Michale, and Syra followed suit, stepping into a doorway and waiting for the guards to pass. The stomping grew, and Enith craned his neck to see what was going on. Guards in white suits with gold sashes rode horses in a tight formation, wearing an odd fashion of hat on their head. Leading the group was a man with red markings on his sash and a sharp face that boasted a full beard. He scanned the sidewalks, obviously looking for someone, or danger. His eyes met Enith's, and he stopped, looking over at Syra and Michale before frowning in disdain. The large man called for a halt and directed his horse over to them, amidst the now quieted crowd.

He pointed and spoke with a clear, loud voice.

"You three. You are to dine with Chief Nasir tonight. Come with us."

Enith was so surprised he could barely move. Was this just happenstantial, or had Chief Nasir somehow known they were in the city?

The guard eyed him warily, his teeth bared in what couldn't quite be called a smile.

"If you would please, Prince." His arm was raised, directing them toward the group of soldiers.

"I guess we have no choice," Enith murmured to the girls before striding with intentional confidence in the direction the man had shown them. The girls followed suit, and the horsed soldiers began moving at their leader's command, continuing back the way they came.

The women whispered in low voices to each other as they slowly made their way toward the higher-end shops they had seen before, toward a large white building with golden spires topping rounded structures. Enith stared at the structure in awe, wondering how they had even been built. He had never seen anything like it! They live inside of giant domes, perfect and gleaming in the sunlight.

Steps covered in gold welcomed them, and they stood dumbfounded at the intricate designs inlaid at every turn. They were passed off to a butler who had been waiting for them and were led through the great palace.

The inside of the building outshone the outside even. Green, tropical plants lined the halls, and golden lamps hovered near every corner, holding the rocks he had seen earlier that gave off light when activated. The tile was cream marble, and their steps barely made a noise as they walked under what seemed like hundred-foot ceilings, arching up high toward a window-filled dome. They made wonderful use of natural light.

The group found themselves before two large doors, carved with scenes from historic battles and stories. When the doors opened, they were ushered into a lavish room, with large, plush pillows gathered in various areas as colorfully dressed men and women sat, chatting and eating from plates filled with fruits and cheeses. Even here, the women's heads were covered, though more loosely, and with faces were fully shown.

One man lay at the front of the room on a large pillow, a gold ring around his head, drawing the attention of all the others, like a magnet. He rested his body on one arm as he plucked off some fruit with the other, chatting amiably with the men around him. A woman sat quietly next to him, dressed in a dark blue skirt and a long-sleeved shirt that looked cool rather than warm. Loosely braided hair could be seen beneath her loose headscarf, and her eyes were lowered to the floor, hands complacent in her lap.

The man looked up when they entered, grinning as he stood and beckoning them to join him. His jawline was strong, and his eyes gleamed with intelligence.

He rested a hand on his cutlass and hurried them forward with the other.

"Come, come, friends. Join me. We shall eat and talk."

Enith hesitated, but took a seat on cushions in front of Nasir and awkwardly tried to look as comfortable as his host, moving so Michale and Syra could sit too.

Their host's face darkened slightly, and he seemed to avoid looking at the women.

"My friend, I believe you met my father once, Chief Norj. Before his passing, he spoke kindly of you and your father. As the chief, I will extend the same kindness to you as my father would." His dark eyes flickered hesitantly to the women before returning to Enith's face.

"You are not from my country, so I will allow you to continue with your traditions, but it would be better for the women to sit beside us. There, you see." He pointed to where the woman in blue had placed herself a few feet away, and he smiled, adding sharply, "Silently."

Enith sucked in a breath. So this was why his mother disliked them so much. She had worked to make him busy any time his father met with the Syllrics, only failing once to keep him away from them. Now he understood why. By their standards, she was nothing.

He panicked, unsure what Michale'thia would do at the slight, but breathed a sigh of relief when she and Syra quietly moved to sit beside the other women, who looked up with gray, piercing eyes.

The man smiled again, comfortable at last.

"So," he plopped a large grape into his mouth, "what brings me the pleasure of hosting young royals in my country?"

Enith took his cue and took a grape of his own, staring at it for a moment before popping it in his mouth.

"We are traveling and decided to see what your city offers in the way of goods. So far, we are pleasantly surprised. You have been keeping many glorious inventions from us." He smiled widely, allowing his admiration for the to place show.

Nasir roared with laughter, taking to the compliment well as he beckoned the woman in blue to bring more food. She shot up and pattered away, returning with servant bearing trays of food and more wine.

"That we have!" He touched his nose, "We cannot give everything away. Now, what brings you on a journey? And please," his mirthful eyes held a dangerous undertone, "You are my friend so you can be honest."

Enith thought fast as he worked through the various meanings the chief's words could hold. He figured at this point there was nothing to do but tell as much of the truth as he could.

"Our kingdom has found the long-awaited One, who will rule with perfection and lead us into a gifted future. She is here with us now." He motioned toward Michale.

"But we believe there may be something we are missing in our prophecies, and we journey to find answers." He ate another grape and met the cheif's shrewd eyes, gauging his reaction.

A grim look came over the older man's face and he nodded knowingly, looking at Enith with new respect.

"Yes, yes. I have heard of this 'Heir who passed the test. And that she is a woman. You are right to question it. The Ancient Magic would not choose the inferior half of us as the Ruler. I am glad you see the weakness of your kingdom and your ways before it brings ruin.

We have our own prophecies, did you know? And I believe they call for a man, strong and mighty, who will tear down walls with his bare hands and build up nations with his shrewd mind."

He grinned up at the murals painted around the room, of a man with a cutlass removing heads from bodies and stealing treasure for his people.

"You see, it could not be a woman who is the answer. They do not have the muscle or the intelligence. They would swoon at the mere thought of the work the Warrior must do. It must be a man." He nodded in agreeance with himself, seeming perfectly at ease saying such things in front of the women. Enith heard a sharp intake of breath from Michale and silently begged her to go along with it. They were on dangerous ground right now, dining with a man powerful and greedy enough to capture them and sell them for ransom.

"Where do you travel?" Nasir asked casually, eating another few grapes and picking up a piece of cheese nonchalantly, as if he had no real care for what they did. Enith could see the underlying curiosity, though, his waiting for a reason to pounce.

"We go to the desert to find the Loharan people. We believe they may have ancient texts we did not know of."

There it was. At least he hadn't needed to lie.

Nasir smiled then and chuckled.

"We have long believed they hold secrets and have sent many of our men to find them. None have returned with anything, and many have died in the desert. I will give you my advice: do not go there. You will not find anything. We are not even sure the Loharans still live."

"We are determined to go, sir, even if we risk death."

The words were like a magic phrase, opening up the chief's face with a broad smile, almost proud.

"You are a man! And you have told me the truth. I count you my friend—what is mine is yours. How can I help your journey?" he asked, then raising his brows as ideas sprang to mind.

"We will give you camels, and supply you with food and drink, as well as the clothing you will need. And I know, my friend," he paused and smiled, "that if you do discover anything, that you will tell me so we can hold the truth together."

The chief absently signaled to the woman beside him, lifting his finger without looking at her. She rose at the command and waited silently.

"Drinks. We will have a toast." She picked up the wine jar beside the chief and poured for the men. As she poured for the chief a drop of wine flew from the pot and landed tragically on his coat.

The woman stopped, frozen in terror at what would come next. Enith watching curiously as the scene began to unfold. To his horror, the chief's hand drew back and flew across her face, sending the jar flying from her hands and knocking her backward to the ground. He then rose and picked up a wooden stick at his side, standing over her.

"Ilytha, my sister, you will learn to do better." He raised the stick and brought it down forcefully over her back, which arched in pain as silent sobs racked her. He lifted the stick again and brought it down once more across her legs. She took the beating silently, and Enith stood, unable to decide how to end this without losing the ally they had just made. Michala's hands covered her mouth to keep from sobbing, and Syra's eyes were locked on the ground away from the scene.

Enith barely had a moment to think through what he was about to do before standing up and rushing his words out.

"Chief Nasir."

The chief paused with the stick still raised in the air and looked at Enith, furry pouring from his eyes.

Enith thought fast.

"Why waste your energy on such a lowly creature? I have a better way to punish her rightly. Let us play a game. A game of swords. And if I win, I get to keep her and punish her at my will." Springs, he was getting at good lying.

A dangerous silence screamed in Enith's ears as he waited to see what Nasir's reaction would be. The chief's was a stone wall, unmoving and unfeeling. Then it began to crumble into laughter.

"Let us play!" He threw down the stick to remove his coat, and the dance began.

Swords were drawn, and servants scurried in to clear the room for the duel. Both contestants smiled, energized by the competition, but a tension crackled in the air, lurking beneath the surface on both the chief's and Enith's cheerful faces. The men held their swords up together, as Syllric tradition demanded, and with a clang of a gong, the swordplay began.

The chief lunged forward and hacked his cutlass downward with surprising speed and force, knocking Enith back a few steps in surprise. The large man smiled and took a few steps back, giving Enith time to regain his composure again. Face aflame, Enith took up his stance again and this time prepared for the onslaught to come, still barely managing to parry the chief's attacks in time. The men moved together in a dance of attacks, blocks, and dodges toward the east wall of the throne room, where Enith found himself quickly running out of space to play defense. The chief's brute force was enough to terrify a man; one missed strike would bring death instead of the winning game move they had agreed upon. The gongs kept time for the competitors, and Enith knew that with twenty minutes having passed, his time was approaching quickly. No matter a man's strength, everyone eventually tires.

Sweat poured down Enith's face, and he could see the chief's bravado beginning to falter also. He had put on a good show for his citizens and flaunted his strength, but not played to last a longer sword game.

Parry after parry Enith allowed himself to look the fool, watching the angle of the chief's arm closely, waiting for it to drop ever so slightly, the tell-tale sign that exhaustion was fast approaching. Enith had pushed his way out of the corner, gradually moving closer to the center of the room again and somehow managing to assault each other without breaking any of the decorative vases and plants decorating every pillar in the room.

Then, in one beautiful moment, Enith saw the drooping arm he had been waiting for and brought out his own strength in force, tactfully aiming for the weakest areas he had taken note of.

Nasir was surprised but recovered quickly, frowning at being on the defense so suddenly. Enith focused his attack on the left side of the chief's body, side-cutting and slicing downward with precision until with one strong move, he put everything he had into a left turn and a right-sided cut directly where the other man's throat would be. Nasir moved too quickly to defend the side he was accustomed to defending and fell prey to the tactic. Enith's sword rested at his throat.

The room was silent except for the heavy breathing of the two men, both trying to catch their breath without seeming too exhausted from the exchange. Enith waited, refusing to lower his blade yet, unsure of what the next few moments would bring. A man never challenged a king in front of his people, and if he did, he certainly didn't win.

The chief's chest heaved as his eyes pierced Enith's with a dangerous glow. Seconds ticked by, feeling more like minutes, and Enith began to strategize his escape if the guards were called on him. Would he kill the chief?

Slowly, a laugh began to rumble through the room, echoing against the far walls and high ceiling. Enith looked around for the owner until he realized the sound was coming from Nasir himself, who dropped his cutlass and opened his hands in surrender.

"You, my friend, are a brave man! None of my dueling partners dare to give their best. But no—you have defeated me fairly, and even with a bit of trickery. Ha! The winner, and new owner of Ilytha, Princess of the Syllrics!"

The servants and nobles lining the walls cheered along with their chief, as Enith laughed anxiously, ready to fall on the floor in exhaustion, but knowing the image of manliness to the chief was more important.

The chief threw his arm around Enith's neck and rubbed his head as a father would do to a son, then lead him over to the woman whose eyes were fastened to the ground, hands shaking slightly in front of her.

The chief paused and grinned at himself for a moment before turning to face the room with hands on his hips.

"What better way to give a gift than to make it permanent. My friend, I will make it so that no one can take Ilytha from you. You will be her final master. Bring the traditional cords! And all our best wine! Ilytha, be gone and bathe yourself—tonight we dance and feast!

Enith smiled at his luck—not to own the woman, but for Nasir to be so willing to give her away and make sure she could never be taken. He didn't plan on telling the chief, but once they were out of the gates, he would set her free and even ensure her a fair place within their Anarathan walls.

Nasir ushered him through a door that led into a large room where a bath was dragged in, and Enith was left with no fewer than six servants who invasively scrubbed every part of him and poured scented oils over his head, ending the odd tradition with a white robe tied by a purple cord around his waist, clearly setting him apart from the rest. Knowing now that he had challenged the chief to the princess made him swallow a sudden lump in his throat. He had expected to take the woman he thought was a servant girl and run, but he guessed these formalities he saw now would only be right for royalty. Where had Michale and Syra gone off to?

A servant soon came to escort him into the main hall, which seemed to have magically been filled with flowers and candles, wines, and golden jewelry spread out as decor on the tables.

The chief sat in a plush chair, his finest robe spread along the floor around him, and Ilytha at his side, her head covering changed for one made of sheer purple lace. Nasir stood when he saw Enith and opened his arms to embrace him, making Enith laugh at the sudden comradery he showed. He should challenge people to duels more often.

"My friend, today is a good day."

"A good day indeed. You have provided quite the feast for us." Enith grasped the man's arm one last time, overwhelmed with thankfulness and relief. "Your generosity will be remembered."

Nasir threw his head back and laughed, seeming to find humor in his words. He led Enith toward a fire in the middle of the room, where he motioned for Enith to wait as people took their seats around the table, dressed in silks of every color.

He stood by… he grimaced, realizing he had not fully caught her name. She stood like a stone, her head down, covered from her head to her feet in some way, clearly refusing to look at him. But he guessed that made sense, he realized, she had lived an entire life being taught she was nothing.

A loud bell rang, and voices quieted as the chief made his way to the front of the room, coming to stand beside Enith. He held out a large rope in one hand, and a small string in the other, giving Enith the stronger of the two and Ely… the woman, the string.

"Today, my sister leaves my command and will be under the rule of another for the rest of her life."

Enith fought not to grimace.

"He is a warrior, a trickster, and he is worthy of being her master." Nasir smiled at the crowd and winked, "I have tested him myself!"

Laughter rang through the room before settling again into a respectful silence as the chief continued.

"Enith, teach her obedience, as the Ancient Magic requires. Be strong, and provide." He patted Enith's shoulder, giving it a squeeze before moving toward his sister.

"Ilytha, do your duty well."

Head still down, she gave one single nod, lifting the string up with trembling hands. Enith watched, intrigued by how seriously the people took the passing of what they considered property.

In one sense, the women were nothing, but in another, to pass them along to another master meant an entire feast and ceremony, showing they had an incredible value of a kind. Even so, Enith felt dirty, owning a person even for just a few moments.

Nasir took the end of the small string from Ilytha and the large rope from Enith and tied the string around the rope, holding it up for the room to see.

"And so Ilytha is tied to Enith. May it never be undone."

The room erupted in cheers, and the chief motioned for Enith to join at the table. Enith hesitated for a moment, unsure of what to do with Ilytha, and opting for a "do nothing" approach, relieved when she followed.

Enith was about to take one of the only open seats on the side of the large table, but Nasir stopped him with a smile, pulling out the chair at the head of the table for him.

Alarms began to sound in Enith's mind for the first time since their duel. Something was off. Nasir would not give a foreigner the most honored seat at the table without reason.

He moved toward the seat, muscles tense now and ready for anything. Was Nasir putting on a show this entire time? Is this when he would be attacked for challenging him in front of his people?

Instead, the chief sat on his right side, Ilytha on his left, and servant poured them all glasses of wine, filled to the brim.

Nasir raised his glass and put his left hand on Enith's shoulder, seeming to wait for something. Enith nearly jumped when he felt Ilytha grab his hand under the table and thrust it upward, pointing toward her own shoulder with her eyes.

Slowly understanding, he placed his hand on her shoulder, and Nasir cheered. He raised his goblet up, and the others all followed.

"Let us toast! To many good years ahead, tied together with the kingdom of Anaratha, to my new brother Enith, and to a marriage that will benefit us all!"

Enith choked on his next breath of air and froze, eyes widening as the people around him all drank deeply. He looked down at his expensive robe, then at candles and jewels, then the petals covering the ground where they had stood.

No.

Sweet bloody Springs, what had he done?

CHAPTER 17
MICHALE'THIA

Having been "escorted" from the palace directly after Enith won the sword match, Michale'thia and Syra had wandered around the city for an hour before finding their original meeting place where Belick waited, concern etching his face at their late arrival without Enith.

Michele now paced her small room at the inn they had found, waiting anxiously for her brother to return.

Syra stood by in their small bathroom, unwrapping the dusty scarf from her head and pulling her hair into a loose bun on top of her head.

A knock sounded at the door, and Michale rushed to open it, visibly frustrated when it was only Belick and Kallaren.

"He will be fine, Michale'thia," Kallaren said with too much attitude for her taste.

Syra gave a wry smile to herself as Belick came behind Kallaren and slapped the back of his legs with his spear, rumbling, "Let her worry about her brother in peace."

Kallaren yipped and glared at Belick, taking the rebuke in silence.

Michale peered between Syra and Belick for a moment, noticing more and more some kind of odd... connection between the two. Syra was always perceptive and seemed to see beyond this world, but now it was as if she responded to things Belick said or did just a small moment before he actually did them. As if she sensed Belick's intent before he acted on it. She shuddered, thinking of how complicated that would get when they both married separate people. She supposed they could just marry each other though. Michale smiled at the thought, then grimaced as she realized the union would probably be a horrible match.

Belick came and squatted down next to Syra, and Kallaren lowered himself down into a chair, folding his arms across his chest.

"So he challenged the Chief."

Michale nodded, looking out the window now.

"And they ended on friendly terms. And he won the woman?"

"Yes Kallaren, as I told you."

Ignoring her obvious annoyance with him, he kicked off his shoes and sighed, leaning his head back against the wall.

"Well, I for one can't wait to hear how this all ended."

Time ticked by slower than usual as each member of the group let their mind wander toward the journey ahead.

Michale'thia stayed at the window, her mind straying to her parents. What were they doing? Had Dagen found anything useful?

She rested her chin on her hand, wishing she had thought to bring a few books to study.

A knock sounded at the door, and Michale jumped up alongside Kallaren, who had the door open by the time she had crossed the room. A young boy stood before them, smiling up at Michale'thia with a small gap in his teeth, and handed Kallaren a note before bowing and scampering off again.

Kallaren opened it for him and Michale to read, bringing the candle closer.

Meet you here in the morning.

- E

Michale wanted to laugh and scream at the same time. How typically unhelpful of Enith. She opted instead for kicking the men out to their own room so they could all get some rest.

Nearly collapsing into bed, she quickly fell into a deep sleep, eager to be on their way the next morning.

***

Wind blew the shutters against the wall, adding a clattering to what may have been a peaceful morning had Enith not ran off with a Syllric Chief all night. And had Luik not been in danger. And had she not found out so recently everything she grew up believing was a lie.

Michale'thia groaned as she sat up, her disoriented mind clearing only to find a disorienting reality. She glared at Syra's empty bed, not sure why she felt so disgruntled other than missing her morning breads and kauf.

Sore from the lumpy bed beneath her, she slid her feet onto the ground and made her way to the washbowl, rinsing her face quickly before tying her hair back in a bun before trudging out to the main tavern hall.

Seeing Kallaren in the corner alone with an empty plate of food, Michale headed to the bar to order breakfast of her own and a cup of kauf, delighted to hear they had their own special spiced sweet cream.

She took her food and sat down at the rickety table across from Kallaren and shot him a questioning look.

"Where are Syra and Belick?"

Kallaren folded his arms and nodded toward the door.

"The creepy twins are out training. Have been since before I woke up."

Michale nodded, knowing Belick had likely been training daily too. She honestly felt better about Syra training with him around anyway.

She took in the quiet chattering of the room for a moment before sitting down to eat the soupy meal before her, trying to hide her nostalgia for the palace sweet breads. Michale took a long sip of kauf, warmed and pleased by the almost spicy tones to the cream. The wind continued to wage war against the side of the tavern, suddenly flinging the door open.

Michale stood, almost spilling her drink as Enith entered in followed by Belick and Syra. She left her table and threw her arms around him, about to let him have the full force of her anger when she noticed the covered woman behind him. Nasir's sister.

Michale arched a brow at the woman, now glaring at her with a keen fury. She hadn't seen *that* last night at Nasir's.

Enith looked at his shoes and shoved his hands in his pockets, taking a deep breath and swallowing before he plunged in.

"Michale. Syra. Uh. This is Il… Ilytha. My wife."

Michale'thia stared at Enith. Waiting for a smile or wink or *something.*

He rushed on, keeping his eyes on the floor.

"I didn't know- I thought it was a simple transfer of property to them, and then I'd set her free with a house in our kingdom or something…" He threw his hands up, his frustration spilling over.

"I didn't know! But she is here now, so we have to deal with this." He folded his arms and glared at Michale'thia, who was somewhere between laughter, despair, and going back to bed.

Keeping herself composed, she glanced over at Ilytha, whose brown eyes continued shooting daggers into her.

Syra stepped over toward Ilytha and gave her a gentle smile.

"You must have had quite the day then. Come, let us go wash up. My name is Syra."

Syra's smile seemed to be just what Ilytha needed, and her body relaxed as she looked at Enith with a blank stare.

The prince was rubbing his face, getting ready to order some food when he froze, realizing his wife had been staring at him.

"Uh. Yes? I mean, can I help you? Do you need something?" he stammered, searching his pockets and coat for something that could solve the problem.

Syra smiled at Ilytha, squeezing her hand and addressing Enith.

"Can she come with us to our rooms?"

Enith stared at them in bewilderment. He then squeezed his eyes shut for a moment before taking a quick breath and turning to face Ilytha. He put his hands awkwardly on her arms, looking at her as intently as possible.

"You are free. I do not own you, and you are not property. So… don't ask me. Just… uh... go do it."

He dropped his hands from her arms and sat down, letting her be pulled away by Syra, who was now directing her toward the stairs. In a sudden panic, Enith sprang back up. "Wait! Ah… Another thing. We aren't married. I didn't agree to be married, and you didn't either… so we uh… aren't. Okay."

Michale had never seen her brother so flustered and out of sorts, but she *had* seen women deeply hurt, and Ilytha's now was the walking emblem of pain and wrath. Her eyes narrowed into slits, and she turned on her heel, head held high as she walked to their room.

Michale'thia planted a hand on her hip and raised her brows at her brother, a million snarky comments coming to mind.

"Don't." He held up a hand and shuffled off, glowering at the creaky floor beneath him.

She took a seat back at the table and looked up at Kallaren. Both tried as diligently as they could, but seeing each other's battle, could no longer hold it in. He threw his head back and laughed, and Michale did the same, holding her stomach as she wiped tears from her eyes.

They were finally able to regain their composure just as Enith sat down at the table, joined by Belick and two steaming bowls of soup.

Belick looked at Enith solemnly and opened his hand to reveal a small chunk of cheese.

"The owner gave it for you. As a wedding gift." His own dark face split with white as his booming laugh filled the tavern, and Michale lost all restraint again, laughing until she could barely breathe. Enith's dark mood lightened as he saw her struggle, and he joined in until they all sat back in their chairs again, tired and bewildered and amused.

Michale gave Enith a grin and threw an arm around his neck. "She *is* beautiful, you know. I don't think I had much hope for you marrying anyone at all, so this looks like a step up to me!"

He threw a mock glare and a piece of bread at her as he continued eating.

"But really, Enith, how did you end up *accidentally* getting married?" Kallaren leaned in as he spoke, eager for a good story.

Enith groaned and rested his hands on his face, as if trying to forget the whole thing happened.

"Nasir beat her, and he was going to keep beating her, so I challenged him to a sword fight, with her as the prize. I won, or so I thought, until his sly, beady eyes found some kind of profit for himself in the whole thing. He made it sound like he was just making the transfer of possession permanent." He closed his eyes and groaned again, laying his head down on the table. "I should've known when he said 'permanent'."

Belick gave him a thump on the back, "You were being honorable. Fate has a way of working itself out. Leave it be and rejoice. You have a wife!" He chuckled, eating some of his soup in between smiles.

Michale laid a hand on her brother's arm reassuringly. "I'm proud of you, Enith. This was a hard result, but I don't see how you could have said no." She took another drink of kauf before continuing. "Well, it is time we find our way to The Merilean. Dagen should have sent the messenger bird by now, and we need to be on our way."

Kallaren pushed his bowl of soup away empty, taking a drink before looking at Michale'thia.

"Where is this Merilean anyway?"

"It is just outside the inner marketplace of the trading city on the north side of the kingdom. We'll have to ask around to find it, but it is supposed to be a well-known tavern among the traders here. Nothing about it stands out, and nothing to make a new person entering anything to think twice about. My father prided himself on this setup."

The group immediately sobered at the mention of the king and finished up the meal in silence. A screech of chairs and tired sighs were all that indicated they were leaving as each head out to pack and load up their horses again.

Michale stopped her brother before they parted, giving him a small bit of much-needed woman-advice before climbing the stairs to her room.

She opened the door, entirely unprepared for the scene in front of her. Ilytha lay on the floor sobbing while Syra tried ardently to console her. Syra looked up at Michale with pleading eyes, having exhausted all her own comforting words.

Michale stood there for a moment, walking through the last interactions before Ilytha left. She shut the door and planted her feet.

"Ilytha, get up. We need to talk." She wasn't surprised when the women stopped sobbing to glare at her, pure disdain pouring out.

Michale rolled her eyes, trying to stamp down her annoyance. She had no time for pettiness right now.

"Come on, get up. Sit in that chair." She motioned with her eyes to the chair at the small desk in the corner, raising her brows when Ilytha didn't move.

Slowly, the Syllric princess moved toward the chair and took a seat, her eyes now glued to the floor, yet not without their heat.

"We are going to talk about three things," Michale off with her fingers. "First, why you look like you want to murder me all the time. Second, why my brother married you—"

When Michale said the word 'brother', Ilytha's eyes widened, and her cheeks reddened with shame. Realization dawned on Michale too. She imagined how awful it would be to see a woman come and wrap her arms around Dagen after they were just married. She hadn't even known Dagen, but *that* would have set a very different tone for their marriage. She softened at the thought. The two of them weren't so different.

"I see," she sighed and took a seat on the bed across from Ilytha. Syra came to sit down on the floor near them.

"Yes, I am his sister. I'm sorry, I didn't realize..." She winced, thinking of her own emotions had it been her. "I would have explained if I had known you didn't know. Enith is my brother and one of my closest friends. The *closest* being Syra." She smiled at her friend, who gave a smile of gratitude in return.

"Well then, third, is where you will be after this. Ilytha, you *must* know we do not act the same as your people. Women in our country can move about freely and can say no to marriage. They are *people* just as much as men. Well, sort of." She thought back to the many marriages she had seen so centered around childbirth.

"My brother saw you being mistreated, and he did whatever it took to stop it." Michale looked Ilytha in the eyes for a moment. "He was willing to risk his life to save you. *That* is how valuable he thinks you are. We think you are. But it is not because he wanted marriage, it's because he wanted your freedom."

She could see tears welling in the woman's eyes.

"Ilytha, this isn't about him wanting you or not. Or seeing you as worth keeping or not. His conscience—and his sister, I might add—could not let him live with owning another human, and he does not want a forced marriage either. His plan is to set you up with land of your own and a house, plus a small monthly stipend. It would be enough for a simple and comfortable life, and it would be yours to do whatever you want with. You would own it and yourself."

Ilytha didn't stop crying like Michale thought she would. And she didn't thank Michale or look overjoyed. She pulled down her headscarf, revealing beautiful thick, black hair, braided down her back.

She looked at Michale, the kohl around her eyes almost completely gone now, and gave a short nod.

"I am to become like you. An Anarathan. That is what Nasir told me. But I did not expect to be thrown away like trash. Trash taken from one man and thrown out by another. To my people, I will be soiled, unwanted—*even* by foreigners."

Michale held in a sigh. She had been doing so much of that these days.

"I know how it is to your people, but right now you do not have a choice. If you stay, your people will view you as unwanted. If you come with us and try to force this marriage, you deprive my brother of the freedom to choose you. Wait, Ilytha. If you want to come with us, *come.* We want you, and I will welcome you as a sister. But if you come, you cannot wait to be ordered about, and you must give my brother space as a single man. However, if you do want to be set up in the countryside in Anaratha, we can have that done in a week, as well as find people for you to stay with in the meantime.

Michale knelt down in front of Ilytha, whom she now could see had a beauty to her sharp features and a softness behind her hardened eyes.

"You are more than a servant. You are more than a bride. Ilytha, all that has changed now is that you must live that out, and that is a more daunting task then being nobody, perhaps. But you can and must do it."

Something settled in Ilytha's face as she searched Michalethia's, as if she were testing the Anarathan's words to see if they were true.

She came to her decision and stood, dusting off her shift as she did.

"I will join your people."

***

The sun had just reached its halfway point to lunch when the horses were packed and ready to move out. Michale was surprised to see Ilytha fully prepared to journey with them, and even though it meant having fewer horses than people, she meant what she had said. The woman had been traded and torn from her life, something that could never be undone, and Michale planned to make sure she felt welcome wherever she decided to be. She was also just glad the glares had stopped.

Belick fastened the last straps and began guiding the new horses he had bought down the road, having claimed they would need to each have their own if they were to quicken their pace. It wasn't lost on Michale, however, that his horse was a beautiful and large warhorse, better fit for a warrior his size.

Kallaren had Enith deep in conversation in the back, and the three ladies walked side by side in the middle of the convoy, glad they had taken Ilytha's lead and braided their hair and covering it with a scarf to avoid it being blown about by the wind.

They arrived in the northern trading city a few hours later. The streets were bustling and filled with clouds of dirt riding on the cold wind, but the colors of the city seemed just as brilliant. After asking three different people and getting three different responses, the group *still* hadn't found the tavern, and Michale was starting to give up hope, already working through how they could manage without the information.

Without warning, Syra suddenly stopped, turning her head sharply to the right as if listening to something.

Enith and Kallaren nearly collided with her, still deep in conversation, but Belick had stopped too, looking in the same direction.

"What's wrong?" Michale turned to her friend, whose quiet nature suddenly had a stubborn air to it, her brows creased and muscles tense.

Michale's concern grew as Syra didn't answer. A mix of emotions crossed her face as her eyes searched the empty street around them. She began to walk through an alleyway toward a small stone-built tavern with a rickety sign too faded to tell the name. The others followed on instinct. Then, very quietly, and without taking her eyes off the building, she explained in a low voice, "There is both great darkness and great light in that place. I can't explain exactly… but, I need to go in. I have kin in there."

Kallaren raised his brows and scratched his head, "Well, sounds like a good reason for us *not* to go in actually. Come on, we have enough to worry about."

He walked a few paces back toward the road and stopped when he realized no one was following, muttering under his breath about "fools looking for trouble".

Enith stared at Syra's face for a moment too, seeming to find something there worth heeding.

"Let's have a drink," he said.

Michale tore her eyes from Syra and slowly began following her brother, trepidation setting in.

The wind blew the old sign against the wall, and Michale was able to see the name as she neared. The *Merilean*.

Eyes wide, she followed Syra and Belick through the wooden door, her nerves tight with anxiety.

Lamps lit the small tavern, and even at this early hour, half the room was filled with travelers and Syllrics alike. A single woman bustled around, chatting with those at the tables and taking empty glasses.

Kallaren had decided to stay outside, which suited Michale just as well. The rest of them took a seat at a table near the door, Belick, Syra, and Enith, all positioned where they could best see the room.

It was too early in the day for music, and the low rumble of discussion took its place. Michale sat with her back to the rest of the tavern, working to not turn around. Beside her, Ilytha seemed tenser than normal, not that Michale knew her well enough to know what 'normal' was, she supposed.

Minutes ticked by, and they sat quietly, drinking the Spirits they had ordered for appearances' sake and waiting for something. Michale was just about to suggest they leave when Syra straightened to attention, her eyes fixed on a man leaving from the kitchen area at the front of the room. He was tall and well-built, possibly ten years older than Michale and her friends, but handsome. Remarkably handsome. His dark hair seemed to draw even more attention to his well-defined, clean-shaven face. He kept his head level as he walked to the door, seeming to not notice or care about anyone else as he left. Michale wasn't sure, but she *almost* saw his eyes flicker to their table, as if wanting to look at them but trained to seem indifferent. Something was off indeed.

Syra's eyes were wide as he left the room, and her voice hushed, talking quickly. "He is a Jyre. I don't know how, or if he is a mix-blood, but he is of my people."

Eyes widened around the table, and Michale looked at her brother, both of their faces hardening as they connected pieces of the puzzle in their own minds.

Enith looked around the room and spoke quietly, leaning in now to be heard.

"What is a Jyre doing here, coming from a kitchen of a forgotten tavern?"

The question only led to more questions. Michale suddenly had a thought, turning her attention to Ilytha.

"What do the Syllrics have going on with the Jyres?"

Ilytha's brown eyes were fastened to the table, and Michale'thia could see the war tearing through her. She knew something.

To Michale's surprise, Belick seemed more concerned than any of them, taking on a dangerous look as he eyed Ilytha.

"Answer, woman." His low voice rumbled, "We have no time for this."

His stern voice seemed to take her back to her upbringing, and she replied on command.

"Not many people know this. It is a secret of my people. They have been trading with the Jyres for years now, giving resources for money. It has made my brother very rich."

The words almost knocked Michale'thia out of her chair as the implications of this news began flashing through her mind. She looked at her brother once again and could see him also registering what this meant.

His eyes darkened, and his hands clenched as he ground out, "Half my men died from where those resources are going."

Ilytha didn't respond. Syra seemed distracted already, looking across the room.

"Enith," Michale spoke softly, "this could mean war. If the Syllrics are funding the Jyre creations, nothing would be stopping the Jyres from making more and more delviors." Her mind followed the progression of thoughts, and she gasped.

"They would have what they need to build another Dark Army."

They stared at each other for a moment, sitting in the realization of their changing world. How long had this been happening?

Michale breathed. She still needed Dagen's message. Squaring her shoulders, she rose from her table and made her way to the side of the room, passing the owner and whispering something discreetly as she continued on toward the woman serving drinks, making a small show of ordering something for her table.

It took longer than she expected, as they waited at the table for what seemed like an eternity, but then the serving woman appeared with drinks, passing them all out and slipping a small letter to Michale as she did.

Michale knew not to open it now and instead slid the envelope into her jacket, taking a casual sip of her drink.

She smiled at the group, feeling victorious.

"It would seem odd if we left the moment we received our drinks, so I suppose we will be staying a while longer."

They sat back and drank in silence, each mulling through the ramifications of all they had just learned.

Kallaren suddenly burst through the door, running to their table without care for who was watching.

"Guards are headed this way, and they don't seem happy."

Enith caught Michale's eyes. His expression turned grim as he realized their mistake.

"The Jyre spy knew we were here. He must have informed Nasir that we found out about his little trade deal with the Jyres."

The door slammed open, and Syllric guards poured into the room, drawing swords and looking around. When the head of the guard saw their table, he pointed to them, ordering them up.

Enith rose and drew his own sword, and Michale'thia could see he was itching for a fight.

The guard sneered at the group, unimpressed by their numbers. "Drop your weapons and come with us. I won't ask again before I decide to bring back your lifeless bodies instead."

Belick stood with his spear in hand and gave a broad smile, his laugh booming.

"Well then, friend," he spun his spear around to face the soldiers, crouching down as he did, "you may try."

Fighting erupted, and Syra backed the women away to a place in the corner.

The Captain of the group swung at Enith's head, missing as he ducked and brought his own sword sideways into the Captain's gut. The large Captain cried out in anger and kept swinging his sword. Belick threw his spear at a guard, then grabbed the man's dropped sword and attacked another, nodding to Kallaren, who had drawn his blade and joined in immediately, now face to face with two guards of his own.

They were outnumbered, with six guards now enraged by the fall of their brothers. Kallaren could barely hold off his two, and Enith was still striving against the Captain, knocking over tables and chairs as they went.

Michale's eyes caught movement in the back corner of the room, and to her dismay, she watched as a tall man, Alethian in every way, a yellow-haired woman dressed in armor and wielding a sword herself, stood from their table. The man took the straightest path to the remaining guards and tapped one on the shoulder, delivering a solid blow to the jaw when he turned around, while the woman crept along the side of the room and in one swift movement let loose two arrows, then dropped her bow and attacked another man, sidestepping a thrust and kicking him in the gut before bringing his own sword hilt down on his head. Enith had just finished with the Captain when he saw the newcomers, but his only response was to nod to the man and continue with another soldier. Belick came to Kallaren's aid, and the two guards fell before them.

All at once, the fighting was over, and all that could be heard was the heavy panting of those still standing.

The yellow-haired woman picked up her bow and took back her arrows from the men, and the Alethian man looked around with a smile, faltering for a moment when he saw Belick. Michale swore there was recognition in his eyes, but before she could ask about it, he spoke up.

"Well then, they'll send more, and we won't want to be here when they do. I'm great with a sword," he winked at the group, "but not good enough to fell 50 guards on my own."

The woman folded her arms and looked toward Enith.

"Do you have horses?"

He nodded and moved to the door, everyone else hurrying behind.

CHAPTER 18

SYRA

Syra rode with Ilytha down the road away from the trading town, riding at a gallop for a few miles before slowing and moving off the path into the trees, trying to put distance between them and any coming guards. Belick stayed in the back, periodically turning around to see if anyone was coming, and the new Alethian man and woman took the lead. They seemed to have an idea of where they were going, leading them slightly off-trail to continue their fast trot out of sight.

Hours passed in silence, Michale'thia contemplating the future now with eyebrows furrowed while Enith clenched his jaw as he tried to pull himself out of the past and back into the present. Then there was Kallaren. Seemingly unphased by the news of the rapid delviors and unworried by the pursuit. Interesting.

Syra nudged her horse toward the right, taking Michale's lead as they followed the strange couple down a path and into a tangle of trees.

Syra craned her neck, trying to see the couple more clearly. She had never seen anyone with *yellow* hair. Not white, not brown, but clearly a color in itself. She bore no freckles or other Alethian features and carried herself with a casual confidence one rarely sees in women. She didn't wait for the men, she just did things herself.

The man though… there was something there, like an echo of recognition or kinship. She couldn't pinpoint it, and she was sure she had never seen him before. Was it the Ancient Magic?

Coming up on a small dwelling amidst the trees, probably only big enough to house two people, the horses stopped, and the couple slid off. Syra looked around for the first time, taking in the scene before her with surprise.

All around the house, wildflowers grew in abundance. Vegetables sprang up everywhere, as wild as the flowers, and the trees around seemed to grow together to create this secret haven away from travelers' eyes.

As she looked around, something began to stir inside of her. It was just a flutter, nothing more, but her hands itched to reach out and grab the earth, bringing forth flowers of her own. She could see them in her mind, white petals and long green leaves giving off hues of blue near the end.

"Syra, I think we should follow them in." Ilytha's words tore Syra from her trance, and she looked around in bewilderment. The two women were the only ones still outside. Had she really lost herself for that long? Syra hopped off her horse, moving to help Ilytha down, but the other woman waved a hand, sliding off on her own.

Syra took the horse's face in her hands and smiled, "Go crazy. This place is good."

As if understanding her, the horse snorted and trotted happily over to a cluster of grass to munch in peace.

They entered the house to find an astonishingly bright room. Syra looked up, appreciating the window they had somehow placed in the ceiling, bringing in more natural light than she knew could be inside a house. With just a round table, some cooking space, and a bed, it was simple. The flowers and plants lining the wooden walls made it feel almost identical to being *outside* the cabin, as if they loved the outside world so much they invited it in. Syra smiled—actually, that's exactly what it seemed like.

The woman had taken off her armor and now stood at the cooking area beside the man in simple trousers and a shirt, her hair braided on one side down her head. At this close distance, Syra could see other smaller braids woven throughout her hair. What an odd, beautiful woman.

They made a small fire on the stone counter and boiled water for tea and kauf, which they served around the table. Syra peeked over at Michale, whose face was lit with excitement at the thought of drinking down something warm after such a day.

The princess looked around the room, "I know this must sound presumptuous and ungrateful, but would you happen to have cream too?"

The woman chuckled and opened a small square door in the ground, bringing out a flask of white cream, whiter than Syra was used to seeing around the castle.

Seeing her surprise, the woman explained, "It is made from a large nut that grows in the trees. Inside is a water-milk, and if you separate it out, it brings a naturally sweet cream I love. Try some."

She passed the flask around the table, and almost everyone took part, smiling at the soft sweet taste. Belick alone rolled his eyes and drank his kauf black, unimpressed by the couple.

Syra could feel something off in him. Ever since he had performed the ceremony, she could sense him in a way. Nothing so specific as his desires or emotions or exact thoughts, but *him*. She shrugged to herself, confused by the whole thing but content with it.

Michale finished her kauf before leveling their hosts with a stare, setting down her cup, and folding her hands on the table as if *she* owned the place.

"Now. Who are you two, why did you help us, and Springs, Belick," Enith's eyebrows shot up at Michale's choice of words as she turned to give the Botani an exasperated look, "will you please tell everyone how you know these two?"

Belick froze, looking like one of the royal children caught mid sweet bread steal.

The Alethian man came to his rescue, though, taking a seat beside the woman and resting an arm on the back of her chair.

"My name's Nethaenial, but Nethaen is easier. And this is Rienah, my wife." He smiled over at her, and she gave him a sweet smile back, making Syra like them even more.

Nethaen spoke slowly, as if contemplating each word then.

"We had been watching that particular tavern for the past year. We've seen the Jyre coming and going, and we had been paying the serving woman to gain information on their meetings. We saw he noticed your group, and when I snuck out to follow him, I overheard him tell the guard that the 'Anarathan guests' had seen him and needed to be taken care of. They really didn't want you knowing about that deal they have going on."

He looked at his wife with a questioning look, receiving a shrug in return.

"We try to ambush the carts before they get to Jy's forest. Or, the Jyre Forest as you know it."

Ilytha's eyes widened in shock.

"It was *you*? My brother has been driving himself mad trying to figure out who is behind the ambushes. He would rage on and on about the small army sending in spies to his palace, and then overtaking his guards. But it was just you?"

Rienah smiled widely, winking at Ilytha, "Wisdom and bravery will always outdo greed. Plus, we know the land pretty well."

To Syra's surprise, Ilytha shot a wide smile back at Rienah, the first Syra had seen out of her.

"As to… Belick. We have met in the past. Quite a long time ago. He doesn't want to admit we were friends for fear I may tell all his embarrassing stories to the world."

Belick looked around and found a wooden figurine on a shelf next to him, tossing it at Nethaen and successfully hitting him square in the forehead.

He raised a brow as Nethaen rubbed his forehead, still smiling, "You may be able to tell embarrassing stories from the past, but I can *make* embarrassing stories of you in the present."

Rienah raised her own brow, "Come now Belick, you know I would have you flat on your bum before you could even come close to my husband."

Belick winced, remembering something, and then cupped a hand on the side of his mouth, as if trying to keep a secret message to Rienah from Nethaen.

"May I please have permission to teach your brute of a husband a lesson?"

Rienah laughed then, cupping her own hand in mock secrecy from Nethaen.

"Okay, but only once."

Belick slapped the table and roared in laughter, pointing at Nethaen.

"You see, even your wife sides with me! I told you one day you would get a return on all your little jokes, and now is the time! All we need now is..."

The smile faded from his face, and Syra didn't need a special connection to feel his heartache. Nethaen's smile also faltered, and the joking was over. Rienah looked at the group to explain.

"We lost a dear friend to us long ago. He is in almost every memory of ours, always the careful one. Always the student of truth." She sighed, smiling a little. "And he was always the best one to play jokes on."

A small chuckle followed from Belick and Nethaen, before silence again ensued.

Kallaren folded his arms, distrust evident on his face.

"And where did you say you were from again?"

Nethaen looked confused, looking up at Kallaren with raised eyebrows.

"We are from here. Why do you ask?"

"I have never seen anyone with yellow hair, so she must not be from Anaratha, and you *look* Anarathan, but seem all too accepting of certain things, and unsurprised by other things." Kallaren's eyes shifted to Syra, before flashing back to Nethaen.

Syra could feel her own cheeks warming, and she locked her eyes on her trembling hands, tensing as she waited for the scoff or insult to come.

What she didn't see was Nethaen's eyes harden to stone, all good nature gone, and his wife put a hand on his shoulder to hold down some of the anger building inside of him.

"To be clear, you are talking about the Jyre-blooded girl, am I correct?" he paused and looked toward Syra, who now wanted to drop into a hole.

His tone softened as he addressed Syra, and Rienah's face filled with compassion. "What is your name?"

No one answered, and Syra took a peek at those around her, realizing Nethaen was speaking to *her*, and panicking for a moment as she forgot her name.

"My name is Syra."

Kallaren rolled his eyes and tipped his chair back, eyeing the couple in front of him as if trying to get a read on them.

"So it is Syra you are talking about, correct?" Nethaen pressed.

Kallaren nodded slightly, uncomfortable now with Michale and Enith shooting daggers at him.

Nethaenial leaned forward, looking at him with such intensity Syra thought ice might actually shoot out of his eyes. His voice was soft, but held a power, captivating the room like a storytelling melody.

"There is no difference between you and her. She has been born exactly how she should be physically. As have you. With dignity, value, and honor. Those three things are to be given to every human alive-"

Kallaren scoffed and flung his hand in Syra's direction, "Her blood is closer to a twisted delviors than—"

In his condescending speech, Kallaren hadn't seen Rienah stride around the table and come up behind him, using one arm against his neck to pull him back, and her own weight to twist his body to the ground. He lay on his back with her knee firmly on his chest, his sword flung away as he gasped for the air that had been knocked out of him.

Her eyes were narrowed at him, and she spoke lowly, "You are more like a child needing to be taught a lesson on life than a man with wisdom. What you have been taught is a lie. You are no better than another. Wake up, Kallaren, and be a man."

Enith stood on the other side of the room, looking shocked, while Michale sat at her place darkly amused, and Ilytha watched with her mouth parted in astonishment.

Belick didn't even turn around to look, he just sat smiling, as did Nethaen, who muttered something to Belick as they both grinned. They obviously were used to this.

To Syra's surprise, Kallaren had taken on a dazed expression, shaken by Rienah's words. His anger changed to confusion, then hurt, and finally ended in what may have been misty eyes.

His only response was to whisper, "Fine."

Rienah searched his face for a moment longer before standing and helping him up. Everyone sat back at the table, tension still weighing the air, but it was Kallaren who spoke first.

Without looking up, he continued the conversation, "It would seem I have been taught wrong."

Nethaen sat quietly, studying Kallaren.

"We are all taught wrong. Either by the customs we are born into, or our inner man who urges us to be above the rest. Now," he glanced at Belick and then rested his eyes on Michale'thia, "Who are *you*, and what are you doing?"

Michale seemed to measure her own words now, not wanting to give away too much, yet sensing that she could trust the couple already.

"I am the daughter of King Jorren, and have been named the Heir of the Prophecies. Now my kingdom is about to do something terrible. We are journeying to try to both warn others and find information that can stop it."

Nethaenial and Rienah seemed to accept the vague explanation with a nod.

"So you made it through The Jyre Forest without giving in?"

Michale nodded, and Syra could tell the princess wanted to spill out her thoughts on it all but stopped herself. Nethaen whistled, a grin creeping onto his face as he leaned back in his chair.

Syra wondered what this couple must think of the Anarathan traditions. Would they side with Belick and see it as nonsense? Syra wasn't sure why, but she trusted their opinion and waited eagerly for it to come. To her surprise, Nethaen just nodded thoughtfully and clapped his hands on the table lightheartedly before he stood up.

"Well, thank you for being our guests here. I will let you continue your journey."

Michale's eyebrows drew together at this abrupt end to the conversation. Enith took lead, standing to shake his hand and thanking them for their hospitality.

Kallaren muttered a thank you and then shuffled out to ready the horses.

Syra stood in the corner of the room, not wanting to leave this small land of peace so hidden in the brush. Ilytha, however, made her way over to Rienah, and the two took up a corner of the room, discussing something with their heads together. Syra took it all in, hoping to breathe this lighter air for as many more minutes as she could, thankful when Belick came to stand beside her.

"This place is like my mountain. You will like it there."

Syra looked at him with a sad smile, knowing she could never leave Michale'thia. Even if it meant feeling her soul at rest.

Ilytha finished her conversation and seemed to float over to Enith and Michale, waiting for them to finish before she spoke.

"I am staying," she said.

Enith just lifted his brows in surprise and shrugged, not saying anything, but Michale brought her head back in confusion.

"What do you mean? Why would you stay here? We told you, you would have your own land and space in Anaratha."

Ilytha took Michale's hand in hers and spoke quickly, "You have been gracious, and I have a chance now at a new life. I want to learn how to live it. From Rienah. She said they would build me my own room here, and I could learn to fight from her."

Even from across the room, Syra could see the newfound fire in Ilytha's eyes. Something about Rienah had given her more than hope. It had given her a picture of the future.

Michale shrugged then too, smiling at Ilytha with warmth.

"You are free. If you choose this, I am happy for you."

Ilytha smiled slightly, holding her hands together at her chest and rushing over to give Syra a hug goodbye.

Belick moved to grasp Nethaen's arm, and Nethaen held Belick from the back of his head, bringing his forehead to his own.

"May we meet again."

"May we meet again, brother."

Syra could almost see water pooling in Belick's eyes, but he turned away before she could be sure.

Nethaen and Rienah filled their bags with fruit and fresh bread, and with that, they were off into the cold winter air. It was only a half day's ride now to Luik's small kingdom, and the group rode in ease, believing the worst to be over.

***

The sky began turning deep hues of blue and orange behind the coming clouds as the sun set on the horizon. The cool wind had settled into a gentle lull, wanting to rest its own weary soul for the night.

Syra's legs were more than sore this morning after she decided to try to ride most of the day yesterday in order to cut a few hours off of their journey. Today, her entire backside was aching. She could see Michale and Kallaren fidgeting on their horses as well, while Belick and Enith seemed comfortably still.

Memories of twisted creatures that once had been horses came to mind, and she squeezed her eyes shut to block the images out. All the blood...

Belick's hand on her back startled her back into reality. He squeezed her shoulder while looking out at the land.

"Stay with us, sister."

It was easy to forget that whatever connection they had went both ways, but she was thankful. It wasn't just alone her in her head anymore, and she was more than okay with that.

Enith's tense face scanned the countryside, watchful and careful. He almost looked... afraid.

Michale, on the other hand, was oblivious as she grunted and slid off her horses. She could sometimes be such an odd mixture of both catching everything and missing what was right before her.

Enith turned around, looking back and forth around the landscape, almost frantic.

"What are you doing? Get back on your horse, Michale, this isn't the time to slow down."

Michale sent a death stare his way, leading her horse at a fast walk to keep up with the group.

"I can barely feel my legs. I need to walk, Enith. If something happens, I'll just hop back on. It's not like I can't mount by myself."

Enith ignored her, studying the countryside again. Syra, not wanting to stir up more trouble, but desperate to move her legs, quietly slid off her horse too, maneuvering so she could walk beside Michale, who gave her a smile when she did.

"Do you know how it went for Luik, taking the kingdom from his father?" Syra asked, her heart hurting for the man.

Michale shook her head, pursing her lips, "All that I know is from Dagen. He said they removed his father, but there have been clan wars all over the kingdom now; everyone fighting for power. He said even the guards have taken sides. But Dagen was hopeful since Luik has been hosting leaders and making alliances. For now, he holds the throne and has the greatest following." She looked at Luik's small kingdom, growing in the distance and turned back to Syra.

"I wonder what it will be like. Luik's always made it sound so laid back and accepting... but my father had heard reports of violence that terrify me."

Syra had heard similar things about the Brends Kingdom. She could only hope at this point that they could get in and out as quickly as possible.

"Anyway," Michale nudged her friend, "I'm sure *you* will be excited to see him."

Syra's face heated, and she smiled as she looked away, pretending to study the landscape. Belick's ears had perked up and nudged his way into their bubble of conversation. The large warrior looked sternly at the women, eyeing them before crossing his arms across his chest, *still* riding the horse.

"And why would you be excited to see him?"

Syra looked up at him, her eyes widening at his disapproval.

Michale saved her from responding, grinning. "King Luik of the Brends. He is completely smitten with her."

Belick waited, his eyes comically wide and his body leaning impatiently. When Michale and Syra both didn't answer, he threw his hands up, nearly shouting.

"And is he a good man? Is he worthy of Syra Ngari?!" He thumped his chest, anger growing.

"He must first fight me, and I will measure his strength!"

Syra laughed at that thought. She had never had someone so overly protective of her, and she felt just like a normal girl with a normal father. Or brother. Whatever he was.

"I am fine with-" Syra started, but suddenly stopped mid-sentence.

The sun was completely gone now, and the sky was a dark blue, just light enough to see silhouettes. Something stirred within her. A warning. A panic. She could feel it far off but approaching quickly, something dark with a hollow soul.

A screeching howl filled the air from only a few miles away. Not the full howl of a wolf, or a hunting dog, but of a mangled, raging creature intent on a hunt. Syra shuddered. Delvior.

Enith turned around, eyes round, and jaw clenched as he screamed at the women.

"GET ON YOUR HORSES! MOVE!"

Michale jumped on her horse, and Syra ducked around the front of hers to climb on, her heart thundering in her chest. She had watched these creatures being created when she was very young, a memory long forgotten until now. Images of white hands passing over their fur, twisting and pulling, breaking bones and stabbing them with serum... Then, when her father was especially angry, he would chain her just inches from them for hours, leaving her terrified and sobbing alone, with the perverted wolves biting, salivating for just one piece of her.

"SYRAAA!" Michale's broken scream reached her from farther down the road, and Syra blinked as she came out of the memory, panting and sweating. She turned to look where her friend was pointing, only to see a delvior just hundreds of feet away, galloping over the land at incredible speeds.

Syra scrambled onto her horse, barely hitting the saddle before it took off. Belick and Enith rode toward her as quickly as they could, both with swords drawn, but they were too far. Kallaren urged Michale, and they galloped toward the distant Brends city.

Syra kept her eyes trained forward, holding on for dear life as she fled, hearing the thundering of paws and the hungry snarls coming closer and closer, as angry wind roared against her, making her escape even harder.

She could see Belick raise his arm, yelling for her to duck, and in a blur, she crouched down close to her horse as the spear whizzed past.

And then the hot, searing pain began.

Syra could vaguely register hitting the ground, rolling again and again before coming to a stop, her breath shallow.

She could hear shouts and snarls, but all of it was drowned by the searing pain making her vision blur. The side of her face was pressed against the ground, and it was as if the grass and roots and everything else around her had begun to wilt. She heard the gentle hum of the earth's heartbeat getting slower and darker… fading. Or was it hers?

She could hear screams and clangs above and tried to lift her head, but everything spun, and the smell of metal was too great. Too soon, the world faded away.

CHAPTER 19
LUIK

The man's bones stuck out at every joint in his body, and his skin sagged with a yellowish tint as he fidgeted his hands nervously. Luik had seen this a million times by now, and he had the problem at its roots, but that didn't make it easier.

Those traumatized by violence stopped working, unable to function as they used to. Then, they couldn't eat without money to pay for food. And finally, they succumbed to the false feeling of fullness in their stomachs the *jinti* gave, putting their aching minds to rest with the ecstasy it brought. But unfortunately, that ecstasy also made them temporarily mindless followers, unable to resist obeying commands. Which is why those who sold the drug often gave it out for free—at least in the beginning.

The man before him had murdered a guard while others snuck into a house and robbed the family of their jewels and violated the daughter. It was the cycle starting again. The family would likely fall into despair and eventually welcome in *jinti* with open arms. Bloody Springs, there was no way out. The outcome caused the root, and the root caused the outcome.

And was he to sentence this man who committed the crime to death because his wife had been raped and murdered before his eyes a half year ago, and now he holds fast to a drug that takes the memories away?

Bloody, bloody springs.

And yet, what of this family? Or the poor woman who could never regain her innocence?

Luik's fists were balled, and he ran an angry hand through his hair. He had to look away as he lifted his own hand, sending the man to his death.

He was already lost. At least he could bring justice to the family.

He waved off the rest of the people about to stand trial, too weary in spirit to continue. If only Dagen were still here.

He walked back through the throne room and toward his chambers, trying to stamp out thoughts of running away and leaving the bloody mess to someone else. He bent over his washtub and splashed water on his face, looking in the clouded mirror for a moment.

The truth is, he loved these people. *His* people. The Brends Kingdom didn't use to be like this. He had childhood memories of dancing in the street with the magicians, and the brightest, wildest parties where everyone and everything was celebrated. His kingdom was one of acceptance and love. But some of that acceptance had gone too far, giving freedom for things unspeakable to be done under his father's reign.

He clenched his jaw, trying to push away the bloodied knife from his memory, or his father's lifeless eyes and slack jaw as he fell to the ground …

Luik swallowed and shook his head, striding out of his room and toward the rum cellar. He did what he had to for the sake of his kingdom.

There was just too much to drown out these days.

He was just rounding the final corner when Fain came jogging down the hallway, catching up with him and matching his stride.

"Come to have a drink, did you?" Luik gave a half-hearted smile, not slowing his pace in the slightest.

Fain ignored him, pulling out a rolled-up parchment from his coat.

"They did it."

Luik stopped mid-step, freezing completely and looking down as he processed Fain's words.

"They…"

Fain grinned as he rocked on his heels, holding out the parchment to Luik.

"They all agreed to it. And not only that, but they have requested that tomorrow be named a national holiday. The Day of Peace."

Fain hurried on, explaining in more detail.

"Dagen's plan worked like clockwork. The Northern clan was willing to give up territory for more ground resources, and the Eastern has approved the trade of their vineyards and wood for the Southern region's right to hunt in their areas. Basically, none of the clan leaders will deal directly with their rival, but I looked *each one* in the eye and saw them all tired of the fighting. Most of them have lost family to this chaos your father brought, and they want a strong king again. As long as they can maintain regency over their regions, they will cease their wars with each other and aid in stopping the spread of *jinti.*"

Fain stepped in front of Luik and put his hands on his shoulders, looking him in the eye.

"Luik. You won. You are king, and your first act as king has been to bring peace."

The words sank in slowly, almost like a dream from afar coming closer and closer until it collided with reality.

Luik raised his fist in the air and sank to his knees, disbelief turning to joy. How quickly his life had become nothing but death and chaos. He had gotten less sleep in this past month than he ever had before, but now this. Peace! Now he could get a good night's rest.

Springs, he may even take a day off.

He stood, grinning wide.

"Well, tell them I approve of the holiday, on one condition—it starts now!" He threw an arm around Fain's neck, and they pranced down the steps, his escape rum turning to celebration wine.

***

The festivals went on well past evening and into the night, the whole kingdom rejoicing. The Day of Peace had commenced and would continue until midnight the next night.

Luik sat at the head of a great table, where his guards had been instructed to gather their families and bring another family to join at the king's palace. And oh, the feasting that was had. The maids had been given bags of gold coins to spend so flowers could be bought and given out freely to those on the street, and now they were strewn about, people danced, and musicians played at every street corner. Empty bellies were filled, wine cups were overflowing, and it was to be a night that would fill history books across Elharren.

Luik smiled at the children playing games with rocks on the steps to his throne and laughed when one wise toddler found a shirked pillow and nodded off on it, seeming to know his parents weren't about to leave any time soon.

Bloody Springs, he loved these people.

A soldier burst through the door then, running around the table and skidding to a halt before Luik, panting and clearly having run there from the city's far outer gate.

Luik's hair stood on edge, dreading word of warring again in the kingdom that would shatter their celebrations and hope for change.

"Out with it, man!"

The soldier pointed out the door, "They said they needed to see you," he sucked in more air, trying to regain control. "One of them is injured—but sir, they have a Jyre and... a Botani!"

Luik stood quickly, eying the man sharply, "Is the Jyre a woman."

"Well, I-"

"IS SHE A WOMAN."

"Yes! But she is injured awful bad, sir! The Botani is carrying her, and I can't tell if she is pale from blood loss or natural skin color!" The guard scratched his head, his deep brown eyes having never met a Jyres before.

But Luik also knew Syra was Alethian. Pale was bad.

"Bring them in, quickly, but through the back halls and to the rooms next to mine. GO!" He searched out another guard, "Get a doctor, now! The best in the kingdom!"

He jogged down the hall, reaching the bedrooms in seconds and paced restlessly, readying the bed. From what Dagen had written, this could only be Syra and the Botani warrior.

He heard the footsteps before he saw them, opening the door as Michale'thia and Enith came into view, followed by a cocky royal he vaguely remembered, and the Botani, his shirt bloodied and Syra limp in his arms.

"Come in. A doctor is coming." He got out of the way as they filed in, and the Botani warrior set Syra on the bed on her stomach. He could see her torn flesh through the ripped back of her shirt, deep holes causing his throat to constrict.

"What happened?" There were too many questions, but all else would have to wait. The cause of injury was just as important for healing as the medicine itself.

Everyone was silent, and it was Enith who spoke up, looking Luik in the eye with a grim expression.

"The delvior are back. We met one on the road."

Luik only nodded. He had gotten her letter and moved his outer farmers inside the gates.

"How was she the one attacked? Of all of you, why was *she* left—"

Enith lost his composure and raged back then, exhaustion and desperation seeping out.

"She stopped! I don't know why, but we all rode as fast as we can, and it wasn't until we looked back that we realized she was just staring at her horse!"

The doctor entered then, hesitation on seeing Syra, unsure of what to make of the scene before him, but shaking his head and hurrying over anyway.

He asked the same question and received the same answer, freezing for a moment to think, then ushering out anyone who didn't need to be there, and sending for another doctor to help.

"She has lost too much blood, and her wounds need stitching up as quickly as possible. Then, it is in the hands of fate. The twisted animal tore through too much muscle, and I'm afraid she will be bedridden for quite some time… at best."

Luik and Michale left the room in a tired daze, knowing they could do nothing but wait over the next few days.

Enith and Belick were getting their own smaller wounds stitched and cleaned. Afterward, they were set up in their own rooms where they would have space to rest and heal.

It was well past midnight, and Luik was having a hard time keeping his thoughts straight. Or was it being near Syra again? Seeing her in this state made him feel sick to his stomach.

He turned to Michale, wondering where the other stuffy royal had gone off to.

"There are more questions to come, Heir of the Prophecies." He softened, seeing how haggard her face looked. "But for now, let me show you to your room—"

"I want to stay with Syra. Please. I'll sleep on the floor if I must."

Luik let out a breath of relief, thankful someone of the *same* gender was volunteering to care for her so closely.

"I'll have the maids bring in a smaller bed for you, no need for the floor. Sleep long tomorrow, and then join me for breakfast."

She nodded, and they bid each other goodnight. Both were asleep within minutes of laying on their pillows.

***

Luik woke earlier than he had expected, deciding now was the time for a bath and a shave. With the new peace and all. Bloody... even half-dead, this woman made it impossible to think straight.

He left his rooms, nodding to the guards posted on every side, then pointing toward the room Syra and Michale were staying in, asking the silent question. The guards shook their heads, and Luik ran a hand through his hair, deciding between staying right there in front of the women's door or going to the dining hall to work while he waited for Michale to wake.

Opting for the less embarrassing option, Luik grabbed a stack of papers he needed to read through from his room and walked over to the dining hall.

He pulled out a chair, thanking a maid—was her name Gretchen?—for the kauf he had instituted into his morning routine since drinking it at Michale's on his last visit. In fact, his own farmers had begun growing some around the countryside. It would only be a matter of years before that aided in the growth of their economy.

The economy. Luik rested his head on the back of his chair. Last night one of the clan leaders' wives had taken him aside, pointing out the lack of feminine touch in the castle. He had first thought she was simply promoting herself, but instead, he saw a keen eye and apt understanding of money flow in her next suggestion.

He should marry. With a wife would come ladies in waiting. And with those ladies would come a fashion boom as women in the rest of the kingdom tried to imitate nobility. The fashion boom would bring competitiveness and creativity to the clothing market, which would give new drive to burned-out tailors, now too used to sewing the death sacks they put bodies in. It would also open up more jobs and provide a greater need for new and different clothing to be made down the line, which would again, create more jobs.

He looked around the room, plainly decorated in browns and blacks. It *was* rather ugly in here. Maybe Syra really could...

He shut his mouth and sat up straight, realizing where his mind was going. He shuffled some of his papers and began reading through the documents, crossing out paragraphs with disdain, and checking other lines with approval. Who knew being king meant *actually* using most of his schooling. He ought to save all these drafts for his children one day; if they were as moody and nonchalant about the throne as he was, they'd need a good reminder of why they would spend so many hours learning to read and write.

Footsteps sounded behind him, nearing at a quick pace. Luik stood to see Michale'thia heading toward him, a smile on her face.

"Sweet Springs," he muttered, thankful for a reason to stop and eager for any news. He stood to greet her.

"Is she well?"

"She is awake and weak, but the doctors are calling it a miracle. They said she had healed a month's worth in just one night!"

Luik stopped to look at Michale, suspicion rising. Syra had been nearly dead last night, her back *shredded* to pieces. He looked at her pointedly with furrowed brows.

"And you are just *so excited*"—he danced a jig and said the last words in mock imitation of a girl—"that she has healed so 'miraculously', yet you, the most nosy, inquisitive scholar I know, are not in a book trying to understand why?"

He folded his arms across his chest.

"What do you know?"

She looked away, sheepish for a moment, before setting her jaw and lifting her chin, the same determined look she used to give him when they were kids. He never did get around that look.

"It is not for me to tell. If you wish to know, you can go ask her, but I'll not be going around gossiping about my best friend."

Luik smiled. There was the annoying Anarathan in her.

Enith strode into the room, shadows under his eyes, and his face lined with worry. Before he could ask, Michale relayed the news to him, and he closed his eyes in a sigh. "Thank the Ancient Magic she is alright."

Knowing Enith, he blamed himself for this, and Luik could only imagine the fitful night that would have brought.

"Where are Belick and Kallaren?" Michale turned to her brother.

"Kallaren, I'm not sure, I assume still sleeping, and Belick was heading to Syra's room. I doubt he will be persuaded to leave, so we may want to bring him some food."

Luik swallowed down the jealousy that surged in his throat. What was the Botani doing in her room? He knew journeys and battles tended to tether people together but... the Botani had just better not get his feelings bloody confused.

Enith cleared his throat, grinning at him like a teasing schoolboy.

"Belick did some sort of ceremony bonding thing and adopted her as his sister. He is *quite* interested in meeting you, I hear." Luik felt his face heating even as his own nervous fear kicked in. That Botani was huge.

"Well, uh... Bloody Springs, Enith, shut up!" Luik coughed into his hand and cleared his throat, trying to get his face back to a normal color.

"Let's eat and talk then, I don't have all day to lollygag with you royal runaways." They took a seat at the large table, feeling smaller because of it.

Luik looked around. He supposed he should have a smaller table made for more intimate dining. A wife would probably have already thought of that.

He cursed his thoughts, straying on their own accord.

"Luik, we have news. And I'm afraid it is... horrifying."

Michale's voice jolted him to attention, and he looked up at the two seated beside him then, taking in Enith's dark look and clenched jaw and Michale's pursed lips.

He took a big gulp of his kauf, then set it down and looked back at Michale, readying himself for her to continue. What? Were they going to stop trade with them? That would devastate his kingdom. His brain began surging as he worked through ways to stay afloat if something like that were to happen.

"You know I passed my Testing Day," Michale eyed him, demanding his full attention.

He gave a curt nod, wanting to speed this up.

"Well, I am convinced the kingdom of Anaratha has gotten the prophecy wrong somehow. A misinterpretation, or missing prophecies altogether. Whatever it is, I am *not* the Heir. Or, there may not even be an Heir. I met a Loharan in the desert after my test, and she told me they have more information we need. But as I was preparing to leave..."

She trailed off, shutting her eyes and making Luik more concerned.

"My father called a meeting with his advisors. Enith was there. They..." She looked away from Luik, her words faltering again.

She continued after a shaky breath. "They believe the Ancient Magic wants the lands to be rid of all those of mixed descent, and that we should carry out a cleansing." She rushed on now, and he could see her anger growing. "Enith tried to stop them, but they are so convinced, Luik. If I stand against them, they will consider me sick and go around me anyway. Enith bought some time, we should have two months, but unless I can find ancient scrolls saying something different..."

Enith gave Luik a dark stare, picking up where Michale had left off.

"You need to be ready for war or annihilation."

***

Luik sat in his room, his head in his hands. It was funny how the world goes so quickly from dark to light, then light to dark.

Days turn to night, every time.

The kingdom of Anaratha had the greatest army in the lands. Their men were trained from just 12 years old. *His* army right now consisted of the few loyal soldiers he could pay to patrol the streets.

He hit his head with the palm of his hand.

Think, Luik!

There must be a way out of this. In two months they could have boats ready and get as many out as possible. There would at least be a small chance of finding more land out there.

He shook his head. They would never have enough food or resources saved up by that time. They would all die within a month.

There was nowhere in the land they could hide that many people, well over 100,000. Probably close to the size of the Anarathan army.

Luik's head was pounding, and he was struggling to think straight. A knock on his door made him groan. He couldn't take people right now.

The knocking turned to pounding, and he finally got up, throwing the door open with full intention of letting all his anger out on whoever was behind it, but to his surprise, he found himself looking up at the dark, over-muscular (in his opinion) Botani warrior.

The Botani looked at him silently, holding some kind of spear in his hand.

"Come."

And he began walking away. Luik's shoulders slumped, and he rubbed his eyes. Bloody Springs. What could he lose at this point?

He followed the Botani just to the room next door where Syra lay, sleeping on the bed, face discolored and bruised on one side, but the rest of her wounds hidden now beneath the covers.

He tore his eyes away and took a seat on a couch, waiting for the Botani to explain. If this was to be an interrogation over Syra, he was going to walk right back to his room.

But the Botani surprised him when he spoke. "What I am about to tell you has been kept secret for hundreds of years."

Luik sat up straighter, his attention held by the melodic hum of the Botani's voice.

He pulled out a map from his loose tunic and unrolled it over the desk, picking up a writing quill to draw a small circle on the mountains where his kingdom lay.

"This is what we have allowed the outside world to believe our kingdom is. Barely surviving. Choosing the hard life in the snow rather than ease on the land." He looked into Luik's eyes.

"But this is not the full truth."

The Botani drew another circle, including lands behind the Indigo Mountains and a piece of land along the beachfront.

"Our kingdom expands back. Down the cliff sides there are houses and villages carved into rocks, and then here, below them"—he pointed to the coast—"are more villages. We have estimated close to 400,000 people live there, and we have barely taken up half of the land available."

Luik sucked in a breath, heart racing as he looked at the Botani, then back down at the map.

"Once in a while, outsiders are drawn here for one reason or another. The elders say it is the Ancient Magic calling to them. We live with the Magic still pulsing through the land, and through some of our wise ones."

He drew a line from Luik's kingdom going west beyond the Loharan Desert, following the sea, and to the valley between two Botani mountains.

"This would bring you to our land unseen. It would be a few weeks' journey, but there is a river that runs from our mountains to here," He drew an X on the map three-fourths of the way through the desert. "And then the river turns east. You would need water for a week of the journey, but after that, you would be through the desert and could find it on the way."

Luik studied the map, wheels turning.

"And you would welcome us? Just like that?" He eyed the Botani, not wanting to let hope rise just yet.

The large man nodded, thumping his chest.

"We would not turn away those in need. Your people would be spread out among villages and would have to learn the Botani way," his eyes twitched, looking over at Syra, "but our people would share with you our joyful life. There is plenty of food, the mountain makes growing rich and easy, and villages take care of one another. You wouldn't be the first people we have brought in."

Luik sat back down, taking it all in. He would lose his kingdom to save it. Somehow, the thought of stepping down as king didn't bother him. If anything, it felt more like a deep relief than it did a letdown.

A knock sounded at the door, and he walked to open it. The Botani already had the map rolled up and out of sight.

A maid stood at the door, ducking in apology.

"Excuse me, sir, but I was told to tell you there are two visitors waiting in the throne room for you. They said it's urgent, and to bring Michale'thia and Enith."

Luik's eyes narrowed at the thought of outsiders being able to know his guests by name, and he marched toward the throne room warily.

He entered with half-closed eyes and took a lazy seat on his throne, eyeing the Alethian and… other, before him.

He dropped a leg over the side of his chair and gave a bored sigh.

"And you are?" he waved his hand toward the couple, studying the woman's armor and the man's tall form.

Before they could answer, the Botani strolled in too, walking straight toward the couple and grasping forearms with the man.

"Brother."

"Hello again, Belick."

"What news do you bring?" Belick stood, watching them intently, already worried by the sight of them.

The woman responded then, shaking her head.

"We came as soon as we could, Bro... Belick. Soon after you passed, an Anarathan army marched after you."

The man took over then, his hand going toward the hilt of his sword.

"Not just any army. There had to have been ten thousand in each grouping, and they've brought weaponry. Big weaponry. We snuck past and rode straight here. They looked to be a day out.

Luik jumped off his throne and made his way down to the group, no longer caring about appearances or anything else for that matter.

"What did you just say?"

The man looked him in the eye, a steadiness there that Luik couldn't bring himself to have in that moment.

"The Anarathan army is at your doorstep, and they mean to have blood."

***

CHAPTER 20
MICHALE'THIA

The Brend castle library was nothing more than piles of books everywhere, layers of dust collected over stacks, and a musty smell of mold in the air. Michale'thia had tried to hold her breath and dust off a few, hoping she would find *something* helpful here, but it was too chaotic. It would take a year to organize this place into something any scholar could navigate.

She dusted off her dress, coughing as she did and pushing the door open to the hallway. She would *certainly* be speaking to Luik about this.

The halls were bustling with servants, smiling and chatting amiably as they went about their business, still joyous from the celebrations the night before. Enith had told her of Luik's victory, and she could see the glow of peace still hanging over the city.

A sadness crept over her, one she had been trying to push back. She had a job to do. Now was not the time to feel.

And yet feel she did, deeply, for Luik's strife. To now have to bear arms and rally his people because *her* own people saw them as unworthy of life...

Michale breathed out slowly, opting to think on other things instead. Like Syra's progress. She smiled, closing the library door. It must be the Ancient Magic inside of her that was healing her, which she hadn't heard of It doing before, but was thankful nonetheless.

She passed a young mother carrying towels, her daughter carrying a stack and a toddler son holding a single towel tightly, his tongue out as he concentrated on hauling the cargo *and* not falling over. Michale smiled, enjoying the way families seemed to work in closer proximity here. She wasn't sure she had ever seen a child in the palace halls who wasn't a royal.

Reaching for the door to her and Syra's bedroom, Michale was startled when she heard someone calling her name urgently. Enith was running down the hall toward her. She groaned inwardly. Too many things these days were urgent.

He skidded to a stop, not waiting for her to speak, just taking her arm and hurrying her away from the bedrooms.

She wrenched her arm free of her brother's grasp, anger flaring at his rudeness.

"Enith, just because our lives are changing *does not* mean you ought to throw gentleness out-"

He rolled his eyes, his own anger skyrocketing, "Michale! Listen for once, and quit being the spoiled princess. There is an urgent meeting in Luik's War Room. We need to get there. NOW."

She glared at him, but took the rebuke, her mind flashing back to images of Syra's flesh being ripped apart.

She matched his quick pace, and they were at the War Room within minutes. Luik was already sitting at the head with steepled hands, Belick and Kallaren on one side and, to her dismay, Nethaen and Rienah on the other, leaving the end of the table to her and Enith.

They took a seat quietly, and Michale surveyed the mood in the room. Something had happened. Even the air seemed to crackle with anticipation.

"Right then," Luik sighed, seeming resigned and beaten by life. "Let's get to it. Anaratha is at my front door, ready for battle, as Nethaen and Rienah so kindly raced here all night to tell us." He nodded toward the pair and continued.

"If we had a month even, we would be able to take up Belick's offer to escape to their kingdom. But it would seem we have a day. This meeting is to find *any* way to stop this."

Michale sat in horror, trying to make sense of all that was going on. Nothing was lining up right. Anaratha's army was here? Belick offered to let the Brends move to his kingdom?

She froze, a detail from Luik's explanation coming to mind.

"Enith, how long would it have taken to prepare an army? We would need at least weeks, wouldn't we?" She could see the question had already occurred to him, and he shook his head.

"At best we could get that kind of movement in a month and a half. *Maybe* a month if they really had been stocked for that. But the army being here now would put this all in motion close to when Luik first left… " He trailed off, starting to see a connection.

Luik finished the thought, speaking softly.

"Someone knew about my father's decree."

Enith nodded, going on, "I'm not even sure it stops there. The fact that your father would even make such a decree was odd, and then for our kingdom to secretly, without me knowing, begin preparing troops..." He looked up at Luik, shaking his head.

"Someone is pulling strings in both of our kingdoms."

Michale saw Belick turn his head slightly, catching Nethaen's eyes, who gave a nod in agreement. She couldn't hold back her suspicion and was just about to ask when Kallaren spoke up, his eyes boring a hole through the table.

"Jyres."

He almost said it too quietly to be heard, but it still rang out across the room, connecting pieces and making sense of all that hadn't made sense before.

Michale's eyes widened.

"The man in the tavern had changed his hair... Why hadn't we thought of this sooner? If one had done it, how many more?"

Enith suddenly stood, glowering at Kallaren and nearly roaring out his next words.

"Kallaren, spit it out!" Enith wasn't going to wait another moment before attacking the man, who sat there, unfeeling and resigned to whatever happened next.

"I received a message from... my father." He muttered the words, and Michale could see something had changed in him.

"He sent a message... back in the Syllric trading city. I went to meet him when we first arrived, riding hard all night. I saw the army; they are ready. My father... they said the Jyres are purebloods in their own right and want redemption through carrying out the Ancient Magic's will in this." He looked up at Michale, eyes pleading.

"I swear I didn't know. My father asked me to keep an eye on you all, but I never thought they were gathering an army! I can't—I..." He clenched his jaw and continued quickly, looking around the table with a wild hope in his eyes.

Then he looked straight at Michale. "He also gave me a message. They said they will back down if you agree to come back and sit on the throne. He said the king and the queen have agreed that if you are not ruling, everything else is lost. If you come back, they would be willing to hold off and look further into this."

Michale's head spun. Too many things were not lining up. They were willing to destroy a kingdom if she said no? With her in it?

Had they gone completely mad, or was there something they were missing?

The room was quiet. So quiet, it seemed like they were frozen in time.

"Fine. Then there is only one option."

There was no argument. There was no other option. Those around the table settled into grim acceptance.

Luik nodded, standing up and pointing to a map, "This will give us time to travel around the back of the Loharan Desert and to the Indigo Mountains."

Belick nodded, turning his attention to Michale, "Syra cannot travel. She has made much progress, but to ride a horse would split everything open again, and she has lost too much blood already."

Michale breathed out slowly, willing away the tears that were springing to her eyes and nodding in acceptance.

"I will go with you. You won't be alone, Michale," Enith said gently. And she knew what a sacrifice that would be. He finally had the chance to be free of Anaratha, and to experience different people and cultures to their fullest, but for her sake, he would stay.

Luik turned to Nethaen and Rienah, "And you? Will you go back or stay?"

They looked at each other for a moment, and then Nethaen's eyes locked on Belick.

"I will stay. She will go. She has business in the foothills, and I have business here."

Luik accepted that and then turned to Kallaren, not giving him the option. "And you will go back to Anaratha."

Kallaren nodded, looking up at Michale and Enith again, "I can try to convince my father from the inside." Enith didn't let up on his seething glare, but Michale nodded absently, already working through who and how she could send someone to the Loharan Desert in her place.

"Meeting adjourned then." Luik stood and marched out of the room, flanked by Fain the moment he stepped out.

Belick stepped over and began talking with Nethaen quietly. Enith rounded the table to her, ignoring Kallaren, who had also come.

"You have until sundown today. They will be a few hours ride away by then. I'll go pack up." Kallaren kept his eyes down as he left the room.

"When you get back, take the throne," Enith told her. Michale nodded in agreement, troubled by the fact that a Jyre spy was already on the advisory council.

"It would seem a strong ruler is needed. And a new council." She arched a brow at him, giving him a half-smile.

He sighed and groaned, "I will be whatever you want, but when this is over, can you just give me some land in the country? I'll be a farmer. Get one of those cool hats." He motioned to his head, bringing out a laugh from Michale.

"Whatever you want, Enith. I can even arrange for you to have a wife waiting for you on that plot of land." She smiled as she walked away, not needing to look at him to see his cheeks heating.

***

Michale entered Syra's room, thankful to see her awake and drinking a broth. Her color was slowly returning, and she could see a liveliness to her eyes again.

Syra smiled at Michale and gave up on her broth, lying back on her pillow.

"I haven't seen you all day. You look worried." Her voice was still groggy, but she managed to get the words out.

Michale sat beside her, feeling her forehead for a moment before explaining all that had transpired.

Syra took it all in while staring at the ceiling, quiet tears streaming down her face.

"It would seem my people have come out of the woods more than we thought." She squeezed her eyes closed, a small sob escaping.

"Michale'thia, I am so sorry."

Michale held her friend's hand, confused, but not wanting to speak too soon.

"My people are destroying everything."

Michale sighed, knowing too deeply that was not the case.

"Syra, I am not sure your people did anything mine were not ready to do. It would seem your people lived inside the dark, but mine lived with the dark inside. I am not sure which is worse."

They sat in the quiet, laughing and crying. Michale hated admitting it, but Syra would only be in more danger in Anaratha right now. At least here, she would be with Belick and Luik, who both seemed ready to give their lives for her.

Michale replaced the few things she had taken out of her pack, knowing the time was drawing near to leave. A knock on the door brought in Belick and Nethaen, followed by Enith, who dropped his own full pack by the door.

She looked at them, tucking a stray curl behind her ear as she bent to tuck a water flask in her bag.

"Where is Kallaren?"

Enith shrugged, pointing his head in Belick and Nethaen's direction.

Nethaen gave a sly smile and spoke quietly, "I am still not sure I trust him. And I like to think I am a pretty good judge of people's character."

The inside joke brought an eye roll from Belick, who folded his arms, obviously bored with his friend's humor.

"That joke will be funnier in a moment. We came because there is something you need to know before you leave." Belick's strong voice caused Michale to pause in her preparations.

Nethaen smiled sadly, looking at Enith and Michale, "You may want to take a seat."

Michale sat down on Syra's bed and folded her hands while Enith folded his arms and waited, unimpressed. Belick and Nethaen looked over at each other one more time, and Belick rolled his eyes in exasperation, motioning forward with his arm.

"Well, go ahead, wordsmith."

Nethaen gave him a friendly smirk and took a small step forward.

"We haven't been… totally honest with our names. But the time has come." He looked each of them over one last time before his eyes rested on Syra and seemed to soften a little, like she already had a place in his heart.

"You remember after the Dark War, the Ancient Brothers disappeared, and prophecies began?"

They nodded.

"Well… they are back." He looked over to Belick, again. "*We* are back."

Suddenly it felt like the wind had been knocked out of Michale's chest as his words sunk in. They couldn't be... Could they? Thoughts began to whirl about her mind as she tried to recall any information she had read about the Brothers coming back, but nothing came up.

Enith chuckled, looking up at the ceiling while he shook his head, "Alright, well, thanks for the information. We will be on our way, and you two can keep being 'the Ancient Brothers.'"

He took a step to leave, but Belick stepped into his path.

"Wait, Enith. Let us show you, and then you will believe us."

Belick began looking around the room until he found a small crack in the stone. To the rest of the room, it was an empty crack, but Belick saw something there: the potential for life. He cupped his hands around the crack and smiled, a delighted look, like a father's joy on seeing his child walk for the first time. He began to mutter something in the ancient language, and Michale strained to hear but could only make out a few words. He wasn't chanting into the air; it was as if he was conversing with the land.

Then, she began to see green growing slowly from the crack, a small thin vine stretching out its arms. It was fragile, a newborn in a new world, but before Michale's eyes it grew, overtaking the wall slowly until its tendrils had reached every corner, and then from the vines there began to form small bulbs which first were a light green but changed to a deeper hue, their leaves a darker shade with tints of blue emerging at their tips. And then, as they opened, the wall began to sparkle with white flowers.

Michale heard a quiet gasp behind her, and she turned to find Syra with a hand over her mouth and tears in her eyes. Belick turned around and found her eyes immediately, a sharp look pinning her to the bed where she sat against several pillows.

Belick looked back over to Nethaen, whose eyebrows were raised.

Nethaen took a few steps toward Syra, gentle and calm in his every movement.

"Syra, have you seen these flowers before?"

Belick was still looking at her with intensity, waiting for an answer he already knew was coming.

"At your cabin. I... I could almost see them growing from the earth. They are a flower I created when I was just a child, to represent myself." Tears streamed down her cheeks now, and Belick's eyebrows furrowed.

"When you were a girl, what exactly did you imagine?"

Syra's brows lowered then, seeing a problem in her memory.

"I imagined a white wildflower, with wide petals that could be lifted up by the wind and taken far away. I never thought of the blue on the leaves until I visited your cabin."

Belick turned around and brought a hand over his face, but Nethaen just nodded kindly, giving her a reassuring smile.

"And Syra, would you agree with me when I guess your father is a king of the Jyre people?" Nethaen asked.

Syra looked down, nodding slightly.

"And would you say he is remarkably more evil than his people?"

She nodded again, shame evident on her face.

Nethaen moved over to the bed then and knelt down by Syra. Michale shifted out of the way, now even more confused and dreading where this all was going.

"Syra. I do believe you are my niece."

The weight of the words hit Syra as she began to put his questions and words together in her mind. Choked sobs began to rack her body as she shook her head, as if denying it would make it less true.

Michale turned sharply to look at Belick, calculating everything now, sure she couldn't deny it but also sure she couldn't believe it.

"You told us you had parents. Was that all a lie?"

Belick… or Broyane shook his head, saddened.

"No. They are my family. When I rose from the dirt the second time, I had little memory and no direction. They found me and made me their own child until I remembered again."

Michale softened, her anger dissipating. She turned to… Aleth? She sucked in a breath, realizing who she was talking to.

"And the woman with you?"

Aleth gave a wide grin, glancing over to Broyane.

"*That* really is Rienah." He took on a dreamy look, remembering the days of old.

"When I created peoples, I first created women, but like usual, the Ancient Magic had wisdom in its own tweaks to my creation. The first women were warriors, a council set up to bring balance to the brothers and keep us *good*." He laughed at a thought. "And they'd do it by force if need be."

He looked back at Michale and Syra, enjoying his own story.

"Rienah was the leader. The first woman ever created. And she was fierce. A sight to behold, like fire itself. No, even stronger than fire. When I first saw her, it was like everything I had ever created sang a devastating melody—the fall of my heart. We were the first love story."

Broyane waved off Aleth, still looking troubled.

"Yes, yes, the famous love story of history." He looked at Syra again, pacing the room.

"Your father is likely Jyren. And *you* seem to have inherited his power." Belick watched Syra, seeming to wait for something, a sign, anything.

But she just closed her eyes as tears streamed out. Michale moved over onto the bed beside her, realizing how heartbreaking this must be.

Her whisper came out broken and pained, and Michale could see her now fitting her father into his true name.

"It all makes sense now. When he would appear in my dreams, he would boast about the 'power' we could use together." She looked at Broyane with such heartache Michale'thia found tears swelling in her own eyes.

"He *made* me on purpose. He told me my mother was an unwilling Anarathan he had disposed of," her sob choked her throat at the memories.

"And now... that means he..." She lost all control then, her body racked with sobs as she held her face in her hands. Michale pulled her into her chest and held her there, grieving with her.

Michale had always wondered about her mother but never knew *this* was how she was conceived. The weight and burden she must have carried her entire life...but now *this*. To know your existence caused such pain to another... that you were a tool.

Syra's sobs racked her small frame. "I am the cause of my own mother's violation... why didn't she just kill me and save herself?"

Michale looked up to see Enith's hands clenched at his sides, angry over the injustice of the world, and Broyane had tears streaming down his face as well, a tenderness there where hardness had been.

His arm pulled her into his side, and his low voice rumbled.

"Because she knew you were worthy of life."

Enith's eyes widened then as he looked over to Aleth and Broyane, hope filling his face.

"So you both go and tell our people who you are, and take control. That's it, no war, no killing."

But they both shook their head, having already thought of this.

"What Broyane did is all he could do in a week. We are not who we used to be. Or at least, the land is not what it used to be. The Spring we all drank of had been used to keep this land alive, but it is almost empty now." Aleth hung his head in shame.

"We used up for war what was meant for creation."

Broyane nodded solemnly, carrying the same weight as Aleth.

"I thought maybe you were a spy. Apt in lying and manipulating like Jyren was. But Syra, make no mistake who you are: you are *not* a product of Jyren. You are a miracle *despite* Jyren. If Jyren had simply made you, you would truly be his child—evil, power-hungry. Instead, the Ancient Magic created beauty where there was darkness, and despite my brother's evil, you were born. You are more a child of the Ancient Magic than you are of Jyren."

Syra could only manage a smile through her fresh tears, but Michale could see her relax and breathe again.

There was a knock on the door, and Kallaren stuck his head in.

"It's time to go."

Michale looked at the Ancient Brothers before her, now even more thankful Syra was staying with them and said goodbye, hugging Syra again and again before she left.

The Ancient Brothers had returned. The Jyres were creating a dark army. And the world was running out of time.

Michale shook her head. Now was the time for strength.

Enith picked up her bag alongside his own, and made their way outside of the palace. Then they mounted their horses and rode off to the south, where the army awaited.

***

The sun had begun to lower behind them as they rode toward the army at a slow but steady pace, reluctant to be bound within their kingdom's borders again.

Kallaren rode behind them in silence, still stuck in his sullen shame, Michale'thia guessed. Enith pulled out his water flask and took a sip, eying the landscape before them. They weren't far now, and she could see smoke filling the sky from the army camps that crowded the foothills. She turned back to look at the sun, then frowned at the army before her.

"They are closer than where we thought they'd be." Enith voiced her own thoughts, a grim look on his face.

Michale nodded, turning to Kallaren, who just shrugged and shook his head, unable to give an answer for the people he had so slyly worked with against them.

Michale sighed. The more she thought of the entire situation, the more her anger grew. But this wasn't the end. They may have just wasted two weeks, but they would stop a massacre and find another way to the Loharan Desert.

Needing to get her mind off all the injustices, she forced a laugh out.

"When we get back, I fully plan on having some of the cook's sweet bread again. There's at least one good thing coming from this."

Enith gave a half-smile of his own, likely imagining his childhood years spent sneaking into the kitchen to swipe as many of those sweet rolls as he could.

"And I suppose you will be going home to Dagen, too." Enith waggled his eyebrows at her.

"He is probably still at his own estate for now. I'll be writing to him once we are back. I suppose *you* will have to do for now, since you will be ordered to rarely leave my side in the coming months."

Enith sobered then, giving her a sideways glance.

"Michale...are you *certain* your orders will be followed when we get back? If Father can do all this," he pointed toward the army encampment, "without your approval, it is hard to imagine what the future will hold now."

Michale had thought of this already, having had the last hour to mentally prepare herself for life to come. She tucked her hair behind her ear, staring at the dark clouds ahead. They would be stuck in a storm soon. She wondered if that meant they would camp here for the night.

"I know. They believe me to be a puppet at best. As a woman, too weak to fully understand the prophecy, and made out to be confused or sick if I disagree." She looked at her brother intently, lowering her voice so Kallaren couldn't hear anything but the wind.

"I will take back this kingdom. It is time they realize the Heir of their Prophecy is their new ruler."

She straightened her shoulders and kicked her horse into a faster trot then, knowing how she rode up to her kingdom would matter even more than what she said.

***

The wind whipped her face violently now as it seemed Michale and the storm met at the camp in perfect unison. Rain had just started its downpour as she stopped, close enough to be heard but still far enough away to be out of reach.

A trumpet sounded, and then another, declaring her arrival to soldiers pouring out of their tents for a glimpse of the Heir. A crowd beyond number had formed, and she could see her father and Lord Thilan pushing their way to the front.

Her father's voice bellowed, calling her name, but she raised a hand, cutting him off. This was *her* kingdom, and it was time her father stepped down.

Lightning began to flare in the sky, and thunder roared as Michale'thia sat still on her horse and let silence hang, the patter of rain the only sound among the quiet mass of soldiers.

With her voice as loud as she could make it without screaming, she called out to her people.

"You have waited for the Heir for hundreds of years. We have sacrificed the childhoods of our young royals, and scarred the minds of our older royals, to find the one perfect being, without fault, without blemish. I rode through the Dark Forest, and came out without imperfection!"

The soldiers began to cheer and yell, banging on shields and lifting swords high into the air. Michale surveyed them all, taking in her father's careful look and Lord Thilan's darkened expression.

When all quieted, she continued, the rain now pouring down over her.

"Now you have your Heir. Will you let me lead you, or shall you continue to be ordered about by men who FAILED their Testing Day?!" She was nearly screaming then, struggling to be heard above the storm.

She looked at her father and Lord Thilan, grabbing her brother's sword from his belt and pointing it toward the pair.

"King Digarrio, will you relinquish the crown to your daughter, the Heir? Staying on as council in the greatest times of joy and need?"

Her father looked at her with sad eyes, far from the anger she believed to be coming. He looked around at the still crowd, waiting for an answer.

She had forced him into a corner; they both knew that. For him to resist now would likely mean a riot of soldiers all targeting *him.* He could only say yes.

In one grand gesture, he lifted his crown off his head and thrust it into the sky, shouting back.

"All hail the Heir, Queen Michale'thia Aleth Thorn!"

And the stamping of feet, clanging of shields, and roars of men joined in the chorus of thunder.

***

Michale lost track of Enith as she was ushered into a large, warm tent laden with colorful rugs and candles. An eager soldier ran and brought her a heavy cloak lined with fur, likely one that had been sent by the maids for her return.

She took a seat at the table as Lord Thilan, her father, and several other men filed into the room, all taking seats around the table. She breathed, reminding herself that *she* was the queen, not a child about to be rebuked.

They settled, and she looked each of them in the eye, knowing the truth would need to come out sooner or later.

"Gentlemen, we have much to set behind us today."

They nodded in reply, seeming to be all but tamed now. She let out a breath of relief, thankful for what could be a more unified future.

Her father spoke next, looking more bare without his crown and his beard a bit longer than when they had left.

"What we are all wondering is, why did you leave? You are supposed to be leading this country, and it is only by your rule that we can be led into the Age of Perfection." She ground her teeth at his placating voice and sharpened her voice.

"If I am the Heir, then my actions would be perfect and unquestioned."

He didn't lower his eyes in embarrassment, instead, studying her while stroking his beard.

"That may be true, but you are young. You still have much to learn about ruling."

Michale smiled at that: the irony of her journey to learn more being cut off by the man accusing her of knowing too little.

"Yes, well that is why I left." She folded her hands on the table and took a breath.

"I have been studying the scrolls and have found a discrepancy in our translations. We do not have the full prophecies; we have been resting our hope on a sliver of the information we need to move forward. I intend to find the rest and align our kingdom with the Ancient Magic's true will."

Lord Thilan waved away her last sentence, squinting in confusion.

"What are you saying? We have not gotten translations *wrong*. Do you really think hundreds of years of study would not have found that out?"

Michale nodded, thankful he had brought up the point.

"I would think that even the study of many can be distorted by what we *hope* to be true. Anaratha only has one prophecy, but it would seem scholars have read that fact into the histories where history itself might prove different. Just as we may have done in this quest to 'cleanse Elharren of mix-bloods.'" She pierced every man around the table with a glare, preparing her heart for the disappointment she would soon bring.

Muttering began around the room as the councilmen looked back and forth between each other, her words sinking in as the subtle accusation they were. Lord Thilan and her father exchanged a look before turning their attention back to her.

Her father pleaded with her, ignoring Thilan as he got up, muttered something about needing a drink.

"You are still the exact person the prophecy describes, are you not?"

Michale shook her head, desperate to make them understand.

"That is just it—we *interpreted* the prophecies that way, but nowhere does it actually say an *outward* perfection is what marks a person as perfect, or that pure-blood is needed at all for that matter—"

The men around the table gasped and stuttered, outraged by such a notion, and Michale knew she had said too much too soon. She smoothed her dress while they quieted down again, then directed her gaze to her father, who seemed to be the most understanding at this moment.

"Perhaps I'm wrong. Perhaps not. We still have much to figure out."

Her father nodded thoughtfully, and Lord Thilan entered the room again, bringing her a small glass of wine and pouring some for the others. Lightning flashed outside, and she could feel the force of the wind again, battering the sides of the tent.

She took a sip of her wine, thankful the men were at least considering her proposal.

Her father looked at her sadly, hesitant in voicing his next question.

"Michale'thia, are you saying you do not believe the prophecy?"

She paused, knowing she was walking on perilous ground and already feeling a headache began to throb at the back of her skull.

She nodded, to the dismay of all the men around her. Michale had succeeded where no other royal had and brought more hope to the kingdom than any other in their history. And here she was, throwing it all away. So much for fighting from the shadows.

It was then she knew without a shadow of a doubt she could not continue this life. She couldn't lead her people into a false future or lead them in a sham of superiority over all others.

She looked back up at her father, feeling her headache growing with the ticking clock.

"I believe it is possible we have sought our own gain in our reading of this prophecy, instead of seeking the truth. And I aim to find what *is* true, and lead our kingdom in the fight to right our wrongs."

She took another sip of her wine, warming her body to the core. Instead of disappointment, or anger, a freedom of sorts welled up inside. It was as if everything tangled up within her unraveled, releasing every worry that had bound her soul.

Her father folded his hands, nodding to others around the table.

She smiled widely, her focus struggling against all the glorious dreams arising in her mind of apple trees on mountain tops. She stamped her thoughts down, needing to be taken seriously once again but losing in the fight against the ecstasy growing inside.

Her father stroked his beard, and leaned back, looking at her with such sympathy.

She grinned and closed her eyes, breathing in deeply the sweet air around her.

"Well then," he said, "we are thankful we have been told of... another way to bring our kingdom into the Age of Perfection. A sacrifice of one can fuel the joy of the many..." His words trailed off, and he was lost in thought for a moment.

"But first..." Thilan urged him on.

Michale struggled against the unbridled joy that seemed as though it would burst from her chest. She was free. The world was alive, and it was beautiful.

"Yes, yes. Michale'thia, you will still serve this kingdom, but you will first lead us in our greatest victory."

Everything began to swim then; even the colors of the world suddenly felt brighter, lighter, and her father's words sounded like the sweetest lullaby. Sweet honey dripping from every word.

"You will march out to the front lines and tell the men to attack."

Michale felt a painful stab in her gut as the words brought warning bells to every nerve in her body, physically hurting her all the down to her toes. She was so thirsty… water… she gulped down more wine, desperate for…

But the freedom she felt, like she could walk on clouds and fly if she wanted to…

"Go tell the soldiers to attack. Use their full force."

Michale'thia smiled at the idea; it smelled like warm sweet breads and those white flowers—

Syra.

Michale blinked, remembering something… some reason to say no— But just as quickly, the feeling left and, almost as if watching someone else, she walked outside, her cloak dragging on the ground, half off of one shoulder. Her eyes sparkling as the storm thundered overhead sweetly, proudly, even joyously.

Rain poured down now, dangerous in its wrath, but she didn't mind. The wind blew her hair free from its low bun, sending her curls flying behind her, tamed again by the soaking rain.

Soldiers gathered behind her, and she could hear her own heartbeat pounding in her ears, beating almost as if in another world now.

Thud.

Like she wasn't Michale'thia anymore.

Thud.

Everything began to register in short moments, the space in between the details filled only with warm, dark elation.

Thud.

The girl named Michale'thia took a sword from a soldier and walked to the hill overlooking the small Brends Kingdom.

Thud.

She raised the sword and screamed the terribly perfect word. Attack.

Thud.

Running. Lighting. Explosions.

Enith screamed somewhere to her left, held back by soldiers keeping him from her. She smiled.

Thud.

Catapults were let loose, felling walls in an instant. So many walls crushed to ruins.

Thud.

Fire, and all of its beauty, now devoured the kingdom, and she could hear the most wonderful screams…

Thud.

Galloping, galloping, galloping. More wine, and more beautiful, wonderful sleep.

Thud. Thud.

Home. She was home! Her home and her mother's eyes came into view, slits of a snake rather than a human.

Thud. Thud. Thud, thud. Thud, thud.

***

Michalethia's head stopped spinning, and she could feel an itch inside of her… like something she couldn't reach but *yearned* to be fed—the wine! She needed more wine.

Water splashed over her head, and her senses jolted awake. Where was she? She struggled against metal restraints holding her hands, waist, and legs, anger surging at whoever would dare to keep her down.

Her eyes widened as her body craved the wine once again, her hands shaking as she lay on her back, shivering from cold as much as from need.

"My daughter," her father's sad voice echoed in the dark cavern, turning her attention toward him.

He stood there, finely adorned with his crown flashing on his head once again, her mother at his side, with Lord Thilan and Thalem Ornto beside him.

"Today, you sacrifice for our entire kingdom."

She fought her restraints, fear rolling over her as memories began to flash before her eyes. The fire. The falling walls.

No. NO. They were dreams. They had to be dreams.

"What did you do to me?" she heaved, fury seething in her eyes.

Lord Thilan answered in a rage of his own, "We did what we had to. Just a small dose of *jinti,* and you played your part perfectly. Now, you will be the reason this kingdom reaches the Age of Perfection."

She yanked at her restraints, desperation mounting as her eyes swiveled between her father and Thilan.

This was a nightmare. A terrible nightmare. Ancient Magic, let this be a nightmare.

But even as she said it, the memories of Luik's kingdom falling in flames were too real.

Her fury deepened, and she could barely speak, screaming at the ceiling instead as her whole body shook. Syra. Luik. Belick. All gone beneath the weight of her sword.

"*I will never help you!*"

Her voice bit out, sobs welling up behind her rage as she fought manically against her restraints.

She expected her mother's haughty eyes or her father's chiding look, but instead, it was Thilan who walked to her side, beginning to replace her bindings with chains.

"Oh, but you will." He smiled at her endearingly, a dangerous spark in his eyes.

"Our Jyre friends had much to teach us on the subject, we have come to find out." He paused as he sat her up, standing her before them in chains.

"One Perfect Heir, sacrificed for the rest, will work just fine." He pulled her over to the large cage in the corner of the room, just big enough for a person to stand in, strings of various colors hanging from the bars, leading upward to a dark tunnel she couldn't see into.

"They even provided this, which will hook up to the bars, using the Magic of Jyren himself to create a chamber that will *force* every small unblemished, perfect, royal bit of Ancient Magic that still pulses through your veins into the kingdom's soil, fueling Anaratha into the Age of Perfection, where there will be no more tears and no more pain... except for yours, of course." He chuckled darkly, and she could see the cold, power-hungry gleam in his eye. Oh, how he'd fooled them.

She struggled now, panicking as he dragged her toward the cage. She screamed and begged, swinging her chains at his hand and jerking herself away in every desperate attempt to flee.

"This can't be real. It won't work! *Something* in the prophecies would have spoken of it." He grabbed her hair and yanked her head back then, smiling at her with menace.

The councilmen and her father looked away, but her mother looked on, her face blank as she watched with her chin raised in acceptance.

Michale continued to scream and struggle against Thilan, but he was a large man and stronger despite his age.

"What you haven't thought of, *princess,* while you spent so many hours studying the past, is what may be in the future. We have created new devices and found *our own* way to fulfill the prophecies."

Michale's mind swam. This couldn't be right. It couldn't possibly work.

Her parents began filing out of the dark cavern, and Thilan bent down to whisper in her ear one last thing before pushing her into the cage.

"You should have accepted my son's offer."

And with that, he shoved her in and slammed the door shut, moving to the wall to pull a lever. Michale looked up to plead with her parent's retreating forms, and instead caught the eye of Thalem, whose dark hair looked paler than normal, framing the dark smile on his lips.

It hit her all at once as flashes came back from their time in the Syllric trading post. His hair was dyed. The scholars were Jyres.

The clang of the lever was the only warning given before pain, unlike anything Michale had ever known, pulsed through her body, eating her bones and twisting her organs from the inside.

It gnawed at her from within, leaving no area untouched, nowhere to escape from this endless torment. She heard someone's screams, far away, echoing throughout the cavern, then realized they were her own flung back at her from the cold, wet walls. Searing agony took over her body, and time became nothing. Her throat bloodied quickly, and within hours she was frozen in silent torture. Lost in a dark cage under the dark kingdom.

Kingdom walls arched high and proud over the golden city. A bright light shone just above peaks in the distance, bringing life to the steam of the sweet breads baked every morning for the swarms of children who, too antsy to stay in bed, made it their joyful duty to pad out of the house long before anyone else woke and fill their baskets with fresh rolls and pastries for the day.

Their soft chattering of shy wonder woke the kingdom from its peaceful slumber, whereupon each would enjoy their families and relish their freely chosen way of contributing to the kingdom.

The school system incorporated tender care for the elderly, alongside rigorous study and innovative inventions, which propelled greater crops and a wistful ease of life for the kingdom's citizens.

As evening came to a close, older children were excused to the streets where lively discussions and dramatic exhibitions of theater, music, or painting ensued. The adults would gather together with family and friends, or tuck in as still love-struck couples, ready to laugh the night away. There was no kingdom in the land like this one, perfect in every way.

Today, as on every first day of the new year for what seemed like an eternity, was the day each citizen would shuffle down into the city's deepest caverns with trepidation and face the reason for their utopia. It was their yearly reminder of what their joy cost: the girl ceaselessly tortured in the cage.

Children younger than five were spared the tradition, but for all else, the law declared each must pass by and lay their eyes on the girl whose own treacherous life propelled their perfect lives on.

When they trudged in their eyes would meet a skeleton of a creature instead of a girl, held up only by chains, face contorted in eternal agony, hair matted from sweat and dirt, and eyes pleading for an end. For a moment, the younger ones would turn away and sob, thinking there must be another way, but soon after the realization of all they would lose if the girl were set free would settle in, and they would look away in shame before fleeing in both grief and relief.

Some would return, but only for a few moments. In the end, this was the price every citizen agreed to for the sake of their own beautiful lives. This condemned, rotting girl fueled their kingdom. She was their savior. Whether she wanted to be or not.

A man walked through the cavern, looking about the empty room carefully before walking up to the cage. The site inside was chilling, the girl's face contorted, hair a tangled mat, ribs showing through just strips of cloth left from her former clothes.

He clenched his fists and beckoned to someone at the door before turning back to the girl.

"Michale'thia," he whispered, not gaining a response.

"Michale'thia, it's Dagen. We are here to get you out."

To be continued...

THANK YOU

Can't wait for more? Follow me on Instagram for sneak peeks!

https://www.instagram.com/charity_brandsma/

Wow, what a wild ride. It's ok, you can cry and laugh and even hate me. This book brought all the feels.

Thank you so much for sticking with Michale, Syra, Luik, Belick, and Enith through this first part of their journey. There will be so much more to come! I hope that you as a reader were spurred on to think through the hard questions this novel brings up, while still enjoying the story that it was.

I can't wait for you to read book two! It is coming oh so soon, and I'm working day and night to get it into your hands. I love hearing your thoughts, so Email, DM, whatever you need- I'm here for you, friend.

Until next time,

Charity Nichole Brandsma

AKNOWLEDGMENTS

Thanks, mom, for teaching me a deep love for reading. You are still the best librarian the world could have.

Thank you, dad, for all our conversations over milkshakes about kingdoms and universes, it brought to life the creative in me.

And my dear, sweet, strong husband, thank you for working hard and providing me the opportunity to chase this crazy dream. Thanks for the hours watching our son, the hugs when I was exhausted, and the encouragement all along the way. You have my heart, forever and always.

Lastly, my little, wild boy. Thanks for always interrupting my writing to snuggle, bringing me back from the land of Elharren to my own greatest treasures. You'll never quite understand what your hugs mean to me.

Printed in Great Britain
by Amazon